'TIS STRANGE BUT TRUE

(Tales from a GP's surgery)

Derek Gray was born and educated in Aberdeen and graduated from Aberdeen University in 1963. He entered General Medical Practice and spent 38 years as a GP in the same practice.

The author was appointed Club Doctor to Aberdeen FC in 1989 and also worked as a Clinical Tutor at Aberdeen Medical School.

Derek is married to Allison and has two daughters.

'TIS STRANGE BUT TRUE

(Tales from a GP's surgery)

Dr Derek Gray

'TIS STRANGE BUT TRUE

(Tales from a GP's surgery)

Olympia Publishers
London

www.olympiapublishers.com
OLYMPIA PAPERBACK EDITION

A CIP catalogue record for this title is
available from the British Library.

ISBN: 978-1-84897-124-0

First Published in 2011

Olympia Publishers
60 Cannon Street
London
EC4N 6NP

Printed in Great Britain

Acknowledgments

To my wife, Allison, who has patiently listened (and laughed) to
repeated telling of these stories

The Opening Gambit

This must happen at so many consultations, when the doctor greets the patient.

"Good morning, how are you?"

Almost without fail the patient replies, "Very well, thank you."

The doctor then enquires, "How can I help you today?"

The patient then replies that he is feeling very unwell with many and various symptoms, not quite what he had stated at the first greeting.

Furry Missile From The Kitchen

The three-year-old was a lovely little girl although she was fevered and coughing badly, and mother had demanded a house call and resisted all attempts to bring the child to the surgery.

History having been taken I proceeded to examine the child and was kneeling down listening to her chest with my stethoscope.

Suddenly a furry object hurtled from the adjoining kitchen and bit me quite severely on the hand holding my stethoscope. I leapt to my feet and wrapped a handkerchief (clean) round my hand and requested that the dachshund be removed from the room.

Mother's reply to this request was quite staggering. "Doctor, do you realise that you are dripping blood on my carpet, please do not make any more mess!!"

Too Tired

The delightful, pretty, petite 18 year old came in to see me with a sore throat. After examination I treated this appropriately, but she remained in her seat in the consultation room.

I enquired as to how I could help, as she obviously had further problems to discuss, but she remained silent until, after further questioning she started silently weeping with large tears rolling down her cheeks.

At last she spoke. "Dr Gray, I've only been married six months but my husband does not love me any more!"

At this, my heart sank; visions of a long painful consultation came into view. "Whatever makes you think that?" I enquired.

"Well," after more tears and gulps, "after we make love three times every night, he falls asleep."

This then was when my experience of thirty years in practice came into use. Keeping a straight face was the first important requisite, and then gently explaining to her that 'three times a night' was not exactly the norm for any married couple. She looked at me in slight belief as if she did not believe that all married couples did not behave in this fashion.

Two weeks later, without revealing her identity, I told the story to our coffee room, with nurses, receptionists, other doctors and secretarial staff present.

It was wonderful to observe, shock, envy, relief or disbelief around the table.

Bitten By A Parrot

I had been many times to the flat on the 14th floor of the multi-storied block to visit the elderly lady, who was slowly dementing and very breathless due to heart failure.

On previous visits her parrot had always been in his cage in the corner of the room.

On this occasion my patient was up and sitting by the fire. She invited me to sit on the couch opposite her as we discussed her medication.

In the midst of explaining how to take her tablets, I was aware of the parrot sitting on the back of the couch, head cocked, piercing black eyes observing us but I thought nothing more until a few seconds later I experienced severe pain on my left ear where the bird has viciously bitten my ear lobe.

My reactions were swift and to the point, I swung my medical case and knocked him halfway across the room, at which my (breathless) patient, despite her infirmity sprang to her feet and rushed to the squawking bird, the parrot being her pride and joy.

Blood was pouring down my neck, the patient was weeping and distraught and the parrot was heading back to his cage in double quick time.

Later, my patient's daughter told me that the bird did not like men and would attack any man sitting on the couch. However, since that day he (parrot) is firmly locked in his cage whenever I visit, but I feel he gives me black looks from the sanctity of his cage.

Yes And No

Mr A was a successful businessman, who consulted me but infrequently. However, on this occasion he obviously had important problems to discuss.

After the usual greetings and pleasantries he lunged straight into his problem.

"Do I qualify for Viagra on the NHS?"

"No," I replied, as there are strict criteria for those able to obtain the drug without paying a private prescription charge.

"Do you have a problem?"

"Yes and no," he replied.

"What exactly do you mean, 'yes and no'?"

"Well, yes and no!"

I tried to clarify the situation but still he insisted 'yes and no'.

Just as I was becoming rather frustrated with his replies I asked, "Do you have a problem with erectile impotence?"

"Well yes and no," was his repeated reply, to which I asked for a fuller explanation and then he asked, "is this strictly confidential?" After reassuring him that everything was completely so, he stated, "I have problems with my wife, but not with my girlfriend!"

Caught In The Act

The house call came in at 8.15am and as it was within walking distance of the Practice and my consulting did not start till 9 o'clock I decided to pop round prior to starting surgery.

I rang the bell and as usual walked into the house and called 'doctor'. From behind a closed door I heard noises, so thinking that would be where the patient was I opened the door.

Quite oblivious to me however, were the naked couple making love on the rug in front of the fire. A gentle cough and a quiet "good morning" interrupted the activity and sheepishly they 'uncoupled'!

I was able to confirm that the patient's problem was not of a gynaecological or sexual nature.

Injecting The Wrong Patient

She was a very pleasant retired Matron from a hospital in what was then Rhodesia. Unfortunately, she developed cancer, which required regular treatment given by intramuscular injection.

As was her usual habit, she exposed an area of skin on the buttock and lay down on the couch.

I loaded the syringe and as was my habit in those days, I slapped the skin prior to giving the injection as I had found that patients did not feel the needle to the same degree.

Unfortunately I was too quick for my own good and managed to stick the needle right through the tips of my middle and ring fingers of the left hand and never even touched the patient's skin.

What of course made it worse was the degree of hilarity shown by my patient who no doubt related the incident far and wide to her friends and colleagues!

Not His Usual Self

The Church of Scotland Minister was the most charming polite gentleman who was a pleasure to meet. However, on a very few occasions he changed in a quite dramatic way.

He was a diabetic who usually was extremely well controlled with diet and injections of insulin but on occasions...

Unfortunately when he became hypoglycaemic i.e. low blood sugar, he changed character completely. His command of basic Anglo-Saxon words on these occasions was quite comprehensive and his ability to string complete sentences of four letter words was amazing.

Of course his wife was usually present when he was in this condition and understandably was quite devastated by his 'vocal performance'.

Treatment consisted of restoring his blood sugar to equilibrium and thereafter recovery to his normal self was rapid and dramatic.

However, one look towards his wife was sufficient to intimate to him that his behaviour and especially language had left a lot to be desired in the preceding few minutes and the poor man was quite devastated and embarrassed!

The Sermon

The Church was packed for the Communion Service and the Minister had just started his Sermon. I was seated at the end of a row when I was tapped on the shoulder by one of the Church Elders.

He whispered in my ear, "Could you help a lady who is unwell about four rows behind?"

"Certainly," I replied, although I did not have my medical bag with me.

I followed him down the aisle and discovered a lady having an epileptic seizure and unfortunately she was at the end of a pew, nearest the wall.

As can be imagined it was fairly difficult asking people to move and allow me access to her. The Minister kept preaching his sermon as I struggled to treat the lady in the very narrow space available and without any drugs to administer.

I was aware of many eyes focussing only partly on the Pulpit and mainly on the medical drama. Never has the time passed so slowly as I waited for the seizure to end and of course it was impossible to move her from her seat.

Finally she relaxed as the seizure ceased but outside could be heard the wail of an ambulance, some well-meaning person had dialled 999!

Now there were paramedics at the door of the church, a Minister preaching his sermon, and one hot and flustered doctor sitting with a lady in a post epileptic sleep.

Like A Yo-yo

He was a huge man who was employed as a Forestry worker. All of 6 foot 4 inches and weighing about 20 stones. His wife by comparison was 4 foot 11 inches tall and weighed about 7 stones.

One Saturday lunchtime there was an urgent house call because he was having an epileptic fit. Normally he was very strict taking his medication but on this occasion he had missed his breakfast dose.

When I arrived he was lying fully clothed on an armchair and having a Grand Mal seizure as it was called in those days. His tiny wife was vainly trying to restrain his convulsions and was being bounced up and down like a yo-yo at the end of his arm.

Obviously he had been fitting for some considerable time and was entering what was known as Status Epilpticus thus immediate treatment was necessary.

There was no chance of undressing him to give an injection of phenobarbitone so I simply used my largest needle and plunged it through several layers of clothing till I hit muscle.

Within a very few minutes he had stopped convulsing and drifted into sleep but there was chaos in the room and his poor wife was totally exhausted.

Mighty Mouse

Dod was well known at the Accident and Emergency Department and invariably he appeared by ambulance on a Sunday morning. He was a tiny man, not more than 5 foot 2 inches tall and weighing not more than 7 and a half stones. Dod enjoyed his little (?) tipple (rum) on a Saturday evening, and sometimes did not know when to cease drinking and retire home to bed quietly.

It was not only the alcohol which caused the trouble, it was the fact that Dod was a brittle (difficult to control) diabetic, and sometimes on a Sunday morning he forgot to take or took the wrong dose of insulin and inevitably he became 'hypo' and then became violent and hyperactive.

As can be imagined chaos ensued in the A & E department as we tried to treat his condition, and on many occasions there might be as many as 6 policemen trying to pin him down long enough for the necessary injection to be given.

His condition rapidly returned to normal with treatment but by this time the department looked as if a bomb had hit it and police and bodies were scattered all around.

The Lady Lawyer

The carving knife thudded into the wall just above the light switch. This was my introduction to a new patient who had just registered and had requested a house call.

Knowing nothing about the lady I gaily proceeded to her flat. The door was open so I entered and called 'good morning'. There was no reply so I opened one door but the room was empty, similarly with the next two doors, one being the bathroom.

Still there was no response to my call so I opened the next door. The room was in darkness so I felt for the light switch, and just as I switched on the light there was a flash of metal and a large carving knife missed my wrist by a whisker and embedded itself in the wall.

Hastily withdrawing, I then had the most bizarre 'conversation' with the patient along these lines.

"You are a messenger sent from the Devil. You are here to corrupt and ravish me! I am the true spirit of God the Almighty and will bring vengeance upon you and all of your kind. Enter at your peril!"

Realising that dialogue was fruitless I withdrew quickly but later returned with a Psychiatric social worker who thought when I phoned her that it was not necessary to admit her to hospital as I suggested.

"No," she said, "this lady can be managed at home."

She then tried to enter the room but on this occasion it was a small axe, which hit the wall. Sense prevailed, so as I wanted in the first place I returned with 'the gentlemen in white coats' who quickly transferred her to hospital.

The poor lady was a retired lawyer aged 82 and was virtually a hermit who lived in one room in a huge flat and virtually never strayed out from her home.

She was a severe schizophrenic and never left the Mental hospital, so I did not have the dubious pleasure of visiting her again.

Unusual Cricketing Injury

The scruffy ten-year-old entered Accident and Emergency clutching a grubby handkerchief to his bleeding head.

"How did this happen?" I asked.

"Playing cricket," he replied.

"Were you batting?" I asked.

"No." he replied.

"Fielding?"

"No."

"Keeping wicket then?"

The reply was again in the negative. "How then, did you end up with a split head?"

"Oh," he replied, "I was the umpire and gave my best friend out!"

Home Early

He was a professional man, tall, handsome with a full head of thick silver hair, senior partner, in a large law firm; his wife a charming very elegant lady did not work but was heavily involved in charity work. To all appearances an ideal couple with a happy secure marriage. I seldom saw either of them except for immunisations necessary for some exotic holiday location.

It was therefore with some surprise that I saw the lady sitting in the waiting room looking very unhappy, and not her usual self.

She entered the consulting room and sat down, hands wringing in her lap, and not having any eye contact. I knew this was going to be a difficult consultation.

After the usual greetings I asked how I could help, to be met with silence and a very tearful patient. It was obvious she was having a great struggle knowing exactly what to say. Eventually she told me.

"Last night I went to the cinema with a girlfriend. After a short time we realised the film was not for us, being violent, with dreadful language and gratuitous sex, so we decided to leave and return home for a drink."

"We entered the house and I called to my husband that we were home. He then appeared at the top of the stairs and welcomed us in his usual manner, but to my amazement he was in a long dress and high heels shoes. We both stared in astonishment at this vision which greeted us but worse was to follow."

"From now on I intend dressing as a woman and when we go out together I shall be as I am now. I have been dressing like this for many years in private but now I intend going public, 'coming out' as they say."

I felt quite at a loss how to react and my response, whatever I said, was going to be totally inadequate. My medical course had not prepared me for this scenario.

'Don't worry, it will pass' somehow did not quite fit the bill and there was a long, long silence as I racked my brains to give an adequate explanation, and course of action. Unfortunately there seemed no good and easy answer and my patient left feeling, I am sure, just as unhappy, as when she entered.

The Odd Couple

They were the oddest couple. She was 5 foot 10 inches and a veritable Amazon of a lady, who towered over a typical seven stone weakling who wore a long black coat reaching to his ankles and NHS wire rimmed spectacles. He was a university graduate in sociology although he was employed as a school janitor and had the most abrasive manner, which snarled out of his weak mouth below a straggly moustache. She, on the other hand, was a charming Swedish girl with long blonde hair and a beautiful smile. How they had ever got together amazed me but there they were sitting opposite me in my consulting room.

"How can I help you?" I enquired.

"We have a sexual problem," he stated and I immediately had visions of this little man having major problems coping with the tall elegant Swede given the reputation that the Scandinavians had in the free love atmosphere of that time.

"Could you elaborate further?" I asked.

"Well you've got to give her something to keep her going!" he said rather forcefully in his usual aggressive manner. "She can't manage more than five times before she becomes too tired and wants to stop!"

Just how wrong could I have been, he was the sexual athlete and she was the weak partner, a strange couple indeed.

Seasick

This was the first occasion I had to visit the attractive 25-year-old American patient at home, although she had consulted me in the surgery. Today she was suffering from severe vertigo and could not stand up and was experiencing constant nausea.

She had recently arrived from a three-year stay in Nigeria and Aberdeen was paradise compared with the heat, insects and humidity they had experienced.

Her husband was a senior executive in an oil company and they lived in a huge house with a beautiful garden and two Mercs in the driveway in the suburbs of Aberdeen.

She lay motionless in the centre of a huge circular bed, pale and wan. As usual I sat on the edge of the bed but it seemed extremely hard and while adjusting my position I suddenly found myself lying next to my scantily covered patient.

Hastily trying to retrieve the situation I discovered I was unable to sit up, as the 'bed' kept moving. Was I also suffering from vertigo I began to worry? No, there was no medical cause for my predicament; I had unfortunately fallen into a waterbed.

The warm liquid sloshed and gurgled as I struggled to get up and the more I tried the worse it was for my patient and her problem.

Finally, I made it to the edge and clambered out on to 'terra firma'. My poor patient was still in constant motion and my mishap certainly made her vertigo worse.

This was my first (and last) experience of a waterbed and on this occasion, my consultation was certainly 'all at sea'.

Etiquette

Although I had been senior partner in the practice for some years, the occasion when I was asked to visit a retired, very respected consultant, from the University Teaching Hospital where I had done my training, left me with a similar feeling which I had, prior to the grand weekly ward round, when I was his houseman all those years ago.

He had the reputation of not suffering fools gladly and also having a wonderful command of English, which could reduce any junior doctor to a quivering wreck in the wink of an eye.

Tentatively I rang the doorbell and his wife, a distinguished lady directed me upstairs.

"Good morning, Sir," I uttered on entering the bedroom.

"Good morning to you, Doctor," he replied. So far, so good!

"There is a chair for you to sit on. Do not sit on the bed! You will address me as Mr and I shall address you as Doctor during the consultation, you understand!" he barked looking me straight in the eye.

Numbly I nodded my agreement.

I hesitatingly started taking a history very carefully in the manner of a junior doctor and when I had finished he asked, "Do you wish to examine me?"

Carefully and doing everything exactly as I remembered from my days as his resident doctor I examined him thoroughly leaving nothing out.

"Now," he continued, "let us discuss the findings of your examination and the treatment you wish to prescribe."

Tentatively I explained my diagnosis and preferred treatment and very surprisingly he agreed with all my decisions. Happily I wrote out the prescription and gave it to him. "Doctor!" he said, "is the consultation at an end?"

"Yes," I replied.

"Then you may call me by my first name and I shall call you Derek. Now it is time to have a sherry."

With that, exactly on cue his wife appeared with a silver tray, a decanter of sherry and glasses.

"You did well, young man," he said, "from now on I will expect you to look after me!"

The subsequent consultations never had quite the anxiety as the first and I happily cared for him for many, many years.

The Bill

As I drove up the long avenue to the large elegant house surrounded with mature beech and oak trees in an extremely exclusive part of Aberdeen, I reflected on the reception I was going to get with my patient.

He was a private patient with whom I had had relatively little contact as previously he had been looked after by one of my partners who had recently retired.

His wife who by all accounts was a bit of a 'battleaxe' had made the demand for a house call, and I was warned to make it my last call of the day and set aside plenty of time for the consultation.

He did suffer from a heart condition and was slowly deteriorating and, having examined him and carried out an ECG I was able to change his medication to hopefully improve his condition.

His wife was hovering at all times in the background and I was aware of her presence, which did not lead to any degree of relaxation on my part. However, he dismissed her stating he wished to speak to the doctor alone and she withdrew not altogether in good grace.

"I wish to discuss my account with you," and at this my heart sank. My predecessor had rendered previous bills and this was my first encounter regarding private patient's accounts.

"Well, we are guided by the BMA in such matters," I stuttered, "and charge what they recommend."

"That is not good enough, I am disgusted by the amount you charge!"

I really did not know what to say next when he continued. "Doctor, when my plumber charges more for coming to the house than you do, there is something badly wrong. In future you will kindly add a naught to the end of your bill and I shall be much happier!"

With that he smiled and I breathed a sigh of relief.

"I presume this is your last call," to which I agreed, "then we shall have a drink. I take it you enjoy Macallan whisky?"

Thus started a long and very enjoyable association with someone who appreciated the value of his doctor.

Relief

Miss W was to put it mildly a cantankerous, bad tempered, extremely difficult lady. She was a retired teacher who I believe ruled with a rod of iron and no doubt a Lochgelly belt.

She joined our practice having been for many years with another GP who had retired and was no doubt delighted to pass on Miss W to another doctor, and unfortunately that doctor was I.

The very first day I met her, we got off on the wrong foot, as I rang the front door bell and it was ages before she appeared to open the door. She then berated me very forcefully for not going to the back door, because she did not ever open the front door to 'strangers'.

Consultations were carried out in the kitchen and she produced a list of symptoms, none of which could be found between the covers of any medical textbook, and, she demanded answers to each and all of them.

Investigations were out of the question as she did not believe in blood sampling and would only permit the scantiest of examinations. After all, I was a male and in her eyes, just a whippersnapper. (At this point I was about 45 and senior partner in the practice.)

Any prescription issued was treated with great caution and only after lengthy explanations as to necessity for the treatment, and possible side effects.

Escape was only usually possible after about 45 minutes and still she was not satisfied, as on several occasions she demanded a return visit to complain that I had not warned her of the rarest side effect mentioned in the drug information leaflet issued with the prescription.

After one particularly stormy consultation when she called my medical knowledge, my manners, my dress code and the length of my hair into question, I suggested that she consulted one of my partners, perhaps a lady doctor.

This idea was treated with anger, contempt and scorn. "You are my doctor and I wish only you to visit. Are you abrogating your responsibilities to me?"

Eventually I was able to share a little of the load by involving our district nurses who were treated at least a little better than I was.

One day many years later, after many very difficult consultations, the nurses reported that they could not enter her house. Accompanied by a police officer we proceeded to break in and found our patient dead behind the kitchen door.

I am ashamed to say I breathed a sigh of relief in the knowledge that I should not have to visit the old lady again, and this shame was compounded about 6 weeks later when I received a letter from her lawyer expressing her grateful thanks for my excellent medical care over the years and a bequest of £1000!

With the money, I bought a silver tea service and every time we use it, I feel a pang of guilt for Miss W.

A Beautiful Temporary Resident

It was a particularly busy Friday afternoon surgery when my secretary buzzed through to inform me about a guest in a hotel, which we attended who required an urgent house call. I asked my secretary to get some more details about the call and she buzzed back to say that the guest had an important function to attend later that afternoon and that she required a call immediately!

Rather sharply I replied that I would attend after I had finished consulting, but this did not satisfy the caller who demanded an immediate call as this was an important guest.

By this time I was a little annoyed and inquired who this guest was that she required an immediate call prior to going to a function.

"Oh," said the caller, "she is the current Miss World!"

Thus I had a slight dilemma, should I go immediately, should I finish my surgery or what?

I compromised by speedily finishing my consulting, and also promising that I would visit as soon as possible.

The Hotel Manager showed me to her suite and announced me. At this her chaperone left and I was thus alone with the most beautiful young lady dressed in a silk dressing gown.

History taken, I asked her to slip off sufficient clothing to let me examine her. My back was to her as I took my stethoscope from my bag, but on glancing up I had the unusual picture of my patient slipping off her gown reflected in the mirror opposite.

So now I have Miss World standing stark naked about 3 feet behind me waiting to be examined. It certainly was a prettier sight than most of my other patients that day.

Consultation over she asked if I would be kind enough to return the following day to give her a full check-up as she was feeling rather tired with all the travelling she had been doing.

I must say I was only too happy to oblige!

Dad Looking Over My Shoulder

The family were new to the practice, the call was urgent – an eighteen-month-old baby was having a convulsion and the family were panicking. I dashed to the house to be met by a distraught mother at the door.

In the living room was the child, in father's arms, having a major seizure.

Hurriedly I drew up some valium into a syringe and asked father to hold the child as firmly as possible while I attempted to inject the drug into a vein (no rectal preparation in those days).

Father was quite hopeless at this so I requested mother to hold the child and after a great deal of difficulty I succeeded, all the while, being aware, of father, looking over my shoulder and getting in the way.

The child relaxed and fell into a sleep and I examined him and diagnosed a febrile convulsion due to an ear infection and prescribed an appropriate antibiotic.

In a slightly more relaxed atmosphere I introduced myself to the parents. They did likewise and then I discovered the father was a new Consultant at the local children's hospital.

Perhaps if I had known that I might have been less relaxed and just as anxious as the parents.

Not This House

The phone rang at 3am and an agitated voice demanded a house call to an area of Aberdeen where we had virtually no patients. It was a miserable night with fog and pouring rain and I had a little difficulty finding the house as in that part of town the numbers were removed or broken or covered with expressive (usually rude) graffiti.

Eventually I found the house I was to attend and was a little surprised to find it in darkness, as usually there are lights and activity where a night call is requested.

However, I rang the doorbell and after an age the door opened revealing a giant of a man in a filthy singlet and rather stained pants. "Yes," he snarled.

"I'm Doctor Gray," I replied.

"So effing what?" was his charming reply and he slammed the door shut.

Tentatively I rang the bell again and when he opened the door again with a ferocious scowl I said, "I received a request to do a house call to this address."

"What name?" he demanded and I told him whom I was seeking.

"They've moved!" he shouted and slammed the door shut once again.

Drenched and suitably chastised by this little experience I returned home and settled down to sleep.

About two hours later, the phone rang again and a furious voice yelled down the line. "I asked for a house call three hours ago and no one has visited."

"Which address?" I enquired and was given the address of the house I had attended.

"I have been to that address," I told the angry father. There was silence at the end of the phone, then in a small voice he said, "Oh we've moved!"

I'm NHS

I parked my modest vehicle next to the gleaming white Rolls-Royce convertible outside the door of the hotel. This I knew belonged to the patient I was to visit next.

Certainly when I entered her suite of rooms she looked decidedly unwell, lying in bed, fevered, perspiring freely and coughing very badly. Definitely not the image she usually portrayed on stage or TV. She was due to appear as Peter Pan at the Theatre but I felt she had no chance of appearing that day.

"Good afternoon," I said, and her reply surprised me somewhat.

Without so much as "good afternoon" she immediately stated in what could only be called a very aggressive manner: "I'm NHS patient!"

This aspect had not at that point crossed my mind but I confirmed to her that that was fine by me.

I examined her and prescribed some medication for the obvious 'flu like illness she was suffering from and warned her she must remain in bed till I saw her for review the following day.

"Doctor," she croaked, "I must and will be on stage this evening, and I intend performing no matter what you say."

Perform she did and despite her earlier behaviour I had to admire her and the old adage 'the show must go on.'

A Fry

Mr C was deaf as a doorpost but a lovely man despite this. He attended the surgery with his faithful mongrel dog that sat outside the front door patiently waiting for his master and greeting every patient with a gentle 'woof' and a vigorously wagging tail.

Unfortunately Mr C's main problem was his bowels and he felt it necessary to discuss this in great detail. Like so many deaf people he shouted rather loudly and as a result most of the other patients received a blow-by-blow account of the trials and tribulations of his alimentary tract despite our background music to try and mask the content of the consultation.

He always carried a pocketful of sweets, which he dispensed to the receptionists and any children in the waiting room, and inevitably I received some for my daughters when they were small and latterly for my grandchildren.

He and his son ran a fish business and always without fail at the end of the consultation he handed me a package wrapped in newspaper and containing the freshest fish you could imagine.

"There you are doctor, there's a fry for you," and for many years I did not have to buy any fish from a fishmonger.

Eccentric Brilliancy

Perhaps every practice has one, but this lady was different from any other, I have met. She was in her 70s and had lived alone for many many years. A graduate of Oxbridge with an honours degree she had been, I believe, an outstanding teacher firstly in a rural Welsh village where Welsh was the first language of many of the pupils. To communicate better she taught herself Welsh in a matter of weeks and was thus able to speak to her pupils.

This was only one of the nine languages she spoke, having self taught Icelandic (in order to understand the folklore better), Gaelic and Russian. The others she spoke fluently were French, German, Spanish, Italian and of course English.

Coupled to this she was also a brilliant pianist, and could dabble on the violin and on many occasions she would break off from a medical consultation and demonstrate her virtuosity on the keyboard playing anything from Beethoven or Handel to popular songs.

She was also very talented artistically and had wonderful drawings and paintings of still life, especially fungi and flowers.

She had, however, had a sad life. The eldest of four children her mother took to bed, after the birth of the fourth and expected my patient to act as mother and housekeeper to the other children. Despite this and with no encouragement from her parents she studied late at night and achieved wonderful Higher examination results and obtained a place in one of the leading Oxbridge colleges where her talents were nurtured and developed. In her last year at University she was 'crossed in love' by her female companion and suffered a severe nervous breakdown which was badly handled by a male doctor who diagnosed over active sex glands as a cause of her problem! This cross she bore for the rest of her life and, unfortunately, she felt compelled to relate the whole of her history on virtually every occasion she consulted a doctor.

I am afraid to say that latterly having heard the story so often I attempted to devise ways of curtailing the consultation or arranging for the surgery to phone me after 30 minutes and intimate my need at another call. However, as she was one of these intelligent beings that needed little sleep and whenever she asked for a night call (and these were relatively common) due to some crisis or catastrophe there was no easy escape and one was obliged to listen for the umpteenth time to the saga of this poor woman's traumatic life.

A Charming Gentleman

His voice had, what can only be described as, the most wonderful 'growl' of any film star. He had requested an appointment because of a rash and as he was appearing in a matinee performance at 'His Majesty's Theatre' in a play I fitted him in prior to afternoon surgery.

With his rugged good looks and charming manner, the receptionists were soon acting like swooning teenagers over a pop star but he was far more dashing, rakish and debonair and most of the patients in the waiting room were delighted and surprised to see such a well-known figure sitting waiting for his appointment with myself.

When I called him, he immediately exclaimed, "Thank you, Dr Gray so much for being so kind as to see me so promptly."

The diagnosis was straightforward so he departed with many thanks and again charmed the ladies by his wonderful style and delightful manners.

Early In The Morning

Morning consulting started at 8.30 and I usually arrived at the surgery about 8.15. This, however changed, due to the antics of one patient.

Arriving at my usual time, one morning, just as I was locking my car, I was approached by a patient who, when he consulted me, inevitably took 30 to 40 minutes for his consultation and even then he complained that he had many many more problems to discuss.

"Can I speak to you Doctor?" he said and I (mistakenly) agreed. He launched into a long long diatribe about his ongoing and longstanding medical (and other) problems.

Holding a consultation on the pavement outside the Surgery is hardly ideal but he was determined to tell me all his history and I quickly realised that to invite him into the surgery would mean a long consultation fitted into an already overbooked morning.

Patiently I listened to him and gave what advice I thought necessary and he appeared quite happy with the outcome. However, that was a big error on my part. The very next morning, there he was again, and the whole episode was re-enacted.

I asked him to make an appointment in the usual manner but he complained that I was too busy in surgery to listen adequately to him, which annoyed me somewhat as I always gave him as much time as I thought I could spare and certainly longer than the normal 10 minute slot.

When he was there on the third morning I was rather brusque with him and told him I could not give him time as I was due to start my morning surgery.

The next day I decided to arrive a little earlier and thankfully I avoided meeting him. However, one of my partners reported that he was sitting in his car outside and had obviously noticed that I had arrived earlier than usual.

The inevitable happened; the next day, there he was, waiting for me having decided that he too, would make an earlier start to his day, and much against my will I was again accosted before I could enter the building.

Mistakenly on my part, I decided to arrive even earlier but he became wise to that move and was always there.

Why did I not refuse to speak to him you may ask? It was almost impossible to avoid him. He was a huge man and blocked any attempt to proceed. But eventually I told him enough was enough and that he must stop this nonsense, as I would only see him inside the surgery.

What happened next, thankfully, never happened with any other patient. He drove to my home and parked outside waiting for me and tried to bribe me with a box of fish (he was an ex-fish merchant and still had many contacts in the Fish Market). As expected, I was furious and exploded at his behaviour. He did apologise and promised to end his 'lying in wait' tactics and for several weeks peace ensued. Somehow, I knew this would not last and I had several extremely difficult consultations with him. He did have major anxiety and stress due to the failure of his transport business and the break-up of his marriage several years earlier but which had quite marked delayed effects. He and his son battled through many rows and arguments and unfortunately his son is following in father's footsteps and cannot cope with life.

The saga had a sad ending as one day the police reported to me that he (father) was found floating in the boating pond at a park in Aberdeen having taken a massive overdose of tablets. An unhappy ending for an unhappy man.

Which Name?

My senior partner was on holiday and I as junior assistant was covering his consulting hours. Normally if I had any problems then one of the other partners would advise and assist me, as in the main, I did not know his patients as they regularly consulting him exclusively. It was therefore important to have read the case notes prior to each patient. However, late one Friday afternoon I was the only GP doing surgery.

Halfway through the clinic a very distinguished gentleman in a beautifully cut tweed suit with an easy relaxed manner but obviously used to taking control came into my consulting room.

"Good evening," I welcomed him, "please have a seat. I am afraid I do not have your case notes to hand, please let me see if my receptionist can find them."

I called the front desk and requested that the staff draw the notes for this patient but after a few minutes they admitted that they were not to be found.

I then checked with the patient that I had his correct name and mentioned that name on my surgery list. He confirmed that that was indeed correct but it might be under another surname and gave me another name.

I looked at him quizzically and queried that it might be either the first surname he had given me or alternatively the second.

"Yes," he agreed 'Mr' to the first or 'Duke of' to the second. Thus my distinguished patient was indeed a Duke of the realm although he usually preferred to be plain Mr when he visited the surgery!

Hand In Hand

In my professional career there was a certain type of person that I never felt totally comfortable with. The afternoon surgery was proceeding quite smoothly with little out of the ordinary, when my next patient, an attractive young lady, beautifully dressed, entered my room.

The consultation seemed quite normal – she had discovered a lump in the genital area she was concerned about. As usual, in such cases I arranged for my nurse to attend as a chaperone but my patient vehemently refused.

"I do not wish any nurse to be present."

This left me with a dilemma as I was unhappy about examining her on my own and told her so.

"I will deal with this," and she left the consulting room. Bemused, I sat at my desk and a few moments later the door was flung open and in marched what could only be described as the most 'butch' woman I have ever encountered with short greying hair and an unsmiling face, followed meekly by my patient. This evidently was her companion and 'friend' and obviously the 'male' and dominant partner.

"Well, get on with it, I believe you wish to examine my friend," were the first and aggressive words she uttered, "we haven't got all day!"

Carrying out an intimate examination with such a domineering woman right at my side was not easy and I was glad when the pair left the surgery hand in hand. Definitely not my type of female!

The NHS As It Should Be

At 9.45am my phone rang; this was a patient asking for my help regarding his wife. While in the shower she had found a lump.

"Come down immediately" I instructed, and at 9.55am I was confirmed her findings.

Realising her condition was not life threatening, but potentially serious and requiring surgery, I phoned a consultant friend and he saw and examined her at 10.15am. Her operation was carried out that afternoon.

Thus, it was 30 minutes from first phone call to seeing consultant, and 6 hours to completion of operation.

Sometimes, just sometimes, the NHS works as it should.

A Stag Party Gift

She was a rather unhappy young lady who sat down in my consulting room. Her complaint was a sore throat but there was not much to find on examination and I advised paracetamol and hot drinks. She accepted that advice then hesitated, obviously embarrassed before asking, "Do you always have to have sex in the same position?"

"Of course not," I replied, "whatever is acceptable to you and your husband in the privacy of your own home is fine!"

Still she looked unhappy and I asked her why she had asked me that question. The story was quite interesting.

She and her husband had only been married two weeks and at her husband's stag party one of his friends had given him the book 'The joys of sex'. He apparently had started at page one and seemed intent on trying every position illustrated.

My patient had scanned further through the book and certainly did not fancy what was demonstrated!

I suggested that she take charge and made the decisions, and at that she brightened up considerably and as far as I am aware there have been no further problems.

The Student

'Her beauty was such as to cause a Bishop to kick a hole in a stained glass window.'

This was the quotation apparently given to this student in her final year magazine.

She arrived one Monday morning to start her four week, final year attachment, in General Practice, and what a beautiful girl she was. Blonde, slim, large blue eyes and a figure that could have graced the cover of Vogue, elegantly dressed in a dark suit with short skirt fashionable at the time.

She was to be my shadow in practice and learn all she could in the next four weeks. Introducing her to my partners brought smiles and sighs and muttered comments like "lucky so and so" etc., but of course to me she was just another student requiring all my teaching attention!

During consulting I felt that most of my male patients had eyes only for her and that I was superfluous to their needs. Some female patients on the other hand seemed a little envious!

After surgery, we proceeded to my home where I introduced her to my wife prior to having coffee. Then it was house calls for the rest of the morning. She certainly brightened up my day and also those of many of my patients, especially the older gentlemen.

Later in the day I learned that my wife had had several phone calls along the lines of "Oh, I saw your husband today!" After several calls it twigged what these 'friends' were saying and my wife's reply thereafter was, "And did you notice the beautiful blonde with him?" This question usually left the caller with a difficult reply!

Artistic Licence

A typical artist she was temperamental, talented but eccentric. Her artistic ability was without question and testament to her talents hung in many lounges of the north-east of Scotland.

Coping with illness however, revealed a different picture. The extroversion was replaced by introversion, the joie de vivre by pathos. Even the slightest ailment was worthy of Shakespearean drama with Tchaikovsky's 'dying swan' enacted several times almost worthy of an Oscar.

I acted almost like a theatre critic as I watched the scene unfold and then realised I was a principle player and had an important role to perform.

However, even in illness, she had to be admired and house calls were always entertaining.

Recognition

The attractive air hostess had a wonderful (all over) suntan, which I observed, that dreary, dismal February day, as I examined her at the hotel where the aircrew of British Airways (or, BOAC as they were called in those days) stayed.

She had become ill on the flight north to Aberdeen and I was asked to see her, as the hotel was one, which our practice covered.

After the consultation was ended I asked her where she got such a suntan at that time of year. She had been in Kenya at a certain hotel where the roof top terrace was secluded and allowed nude sunbathing and all the girls took advantage of this!

She told me she loved Kenya in the winter, South of France in the spring, Barbados in the summer and New England in the autumn. Enviously, I remarked, that my chances of travel like that, was remote, especially being junior partner in the practice at that time, and General Practice was not very well paid.

Approximately a month later I was selected to referee the Welsh versus French under 19 international in Chalon-sur-Saône in France. It was a splendid match played in glorious sunshine and after the game I was presented with six bottles of excellent Burgundy wine.

I was last in line leaving the airport buildings at Heathrow and as it was pouring rain (after all, we were back in UK) I was running across the tarmac when surprise, surprise I dropped the carton containing the wine. Desperately trying to gather up the bottles watched of course by the aircrew at the top of the boarding steps I heard a voice calling, "Come along Dr Gray don't keep us waiting!"

Flustered I collected the bottles; surprisingly none were broken, and climbed into the plane and found my seat. When the hostess appeared to help I asked, "How did you know my name?"

She replied, "Do you not remember me from that hotel bedroom?" And then, much to the amusement of those round about, said, "Perhaps you did not recognise me with my clothes on!!"

After The Ceilidh

He was a senior tax inspector in Aberdeen and he appeared at the Saturday morning surgery, which is supposed to be for emergencies only. He was just 39 years old and he complained that while dancing the Eightsome reel at a ceilidh the previous evening he had become breathless and so wanted to be 'checked out'.

Examination was unhelpful but I was a little suspicious and carried out an ECG, which revealed some heart strain. Again being suspicious, I arranged for him to see a cardiologist that afternoon! (It helps to have private medical cover.)

The result was that he had cardiac bypass surgery three days later from which he made an excellent recovery.

He was, to give him his due, extremely grateful for my part in treating a potentially serious condition and promised that he would deal personally with my tax return to ensure that I did not pay unnecessary income tax. This obviously pleased me considerably for none of us like paying any tax and I looked forward to the end of the tax year.

However, as Robert Burns said 'the best laid schemes o' mice an' men gang aft a-gley'. My patient was transferred to head office in East Kilbride a few weeks later!

Disappearing Keys

I found Stanley a fascinating character. He was a music teacher of note and had a large number of pupils under his care. Visiting him was always entertaining as he would inevitably demonstrate his ability on the piano and perform a musical ditty.

Stanley enjoyed the good things in life and being a bachelor he drank only fine wines especially claret and vintage port, and unfortunately paid the (medical) penalty!

On the occasion of this call he was unable to move due to gout. He was seated at his piano with his foot resting on a stool, the offending joint red and throbbing like a beacon.

I entered the room and closed the door behind me perhaps a little forcibly and then witnessed a remarkable sight. The vibration of the door closing was sufficient to cause severe pain in his gouty toe and he literally levitated from the chair – a most remarkable sight.

However, even more surprising, he told me that the uric acid in the sweat of his fingertips was dissolving the ivory keys of his piano.

Hinge And Bracket

The stage name of the well-known theatre performers, two males who dressed in drag and who were prominent during the 1970s and 80s fitted completely the description of a pair of elderly sisters who I dealt with in the practice. They were like the stage actors tall and thin and even their accents were similar.

Theirs was the classic love-hate relationship. On the surface they apparently cared dearly for each other but under the surface!!! One was unmarried and her sister was a widow and I imagine her husband, who I never met, he being dead before they joined our practice, would have had a fairly hard time dealing with the pair of them.

They lived together in what could only be called a chaotic house. It was cluttered with furniture from both their previous homes, neither being willing to discard anything. Antique pieces were strewn around but never dusted, housework being rather below their dignity and a poor cleaning lady used to do her best, but they refused to pay her for more than 2 hours a week, and even that, was too expensive, and she really did not achieve enough according to her employers.

Like the house, the pair of them looked reasonable on the surface, but perhaps their underwear could have been cleaner and the Glasgow expression of 'fur coat and nae…' springs to mind!

Consultations were long and tiresome, the house was stuffy (one did not open windows, it might let in germs!) and they were constantly outdoing each other in their symptoms and the apparent seriousness of their illnesses. The symptoms were usually of the variety, extreme fatigue, constant dizziness, not able to lift my head off the pillow and of course they never slept at night, 'not a wink of sleep in forty years'!'

Classic expressions such as "Well, I am not able to look after her as I am an ill lady myself" and "I have a sore back, extreme tiredness, stress and anxiety etc". Thus, I was put under pressure to admit the patient to hospital even though this was totally unnecessary and then the veiled threats were uttered.

"What if something goes wrong? What if your diagnosis is incorrect? My neighbour thinks she should be in hospital, etc." I resisted any pressure and promised to visit the next day or fairly soon thereafter. However, one day I unexpectedly called back about two hours later and discovered both ladies who had been at death's door just a few hours earlier sitting up enjoying a drink and a half-empty bottle of brandy on the table!

"Just for medicinal purposes, Doctor," said the elder sister in a slurred voice and, of course, I believed her implicitly!

Below The Bed

She was the sweetest old lady who usually saw one of my partners but on one occasion, because he was busy, he asked me to call and take some blood tests as she had been rather under the weather for some time.

I called around 10 in the morning and was shown in by her daughter who lived nearby and visited every day. She ushered me into the dining room and closed the door. "I am a little worried about mother," she said, "her memory is slipping and she is not nearly so alert as she used to be!"

While her daughter was talking I noticed a bottle of Tio Pepe, that very dry sherry only drunk by a small minority of people and I should have been alerted at that time.

Upstairs in the bedroom lay my patient looking tired and weary. "As I think you know I am here to take some blood tests." She agreed and I prepared to take the sample of blood. I inserted the needle into the vein and gently drew off blood. I stretched across the bed for a gauze square and in doing so kicked over a china object below the bed. Thinking the worst and that I had knocked over a china chamber pot I glanced down, and to my surprise I saw a 40 oz bottle of Bells whisky.

As the needle was still in her vein I drew off a little more blood and arranged for the laboratory to check a blood alcohol level.

The result of the test revealed nothing too serious except a blood alcohol level at 10am, which was four times over the legal limit for driving!

The 58 Steps

No, not another novel by John Buchan; it was the number of steps I climbed on innumerable occasions to visit one of four elderly patients. They consisted of an old couple, both in their nineties and their daughter and son-in-law mere striplings aged 68 and 72.

Interestingly, it was not the parents who caused most of the calls, but the son-in-law, who was to say the least, very sorry for himself whenever he became ill. To be fair he did suffer from chronic bronchitis due to heavy smoking earlier in life, and each winter he had frequent exacerbations, which necessitated repeated house calls.

He had been an insurance door-to-door salesman and was very precise in all his actions, pernickety in fact and liable to drive everyone especially his wife crazy.

They all lived in three rooms at the very top of a tenement block and obviously were often on top of each other.

On the occasions that I had to visit him he always demanded to be seen by himself without anyone else present. I did not think too much of this and always complied with his request. Later, however, I discovered that he would not undress in front of his wife unless it was in the dark and I suppose I was privileged (!) to see him without some of his clothes on while I was examining his chest.

Of course the inevitable happened. He developed a bowel problem with the passage of blood and even he could not ignore this. He was on a cleft stick. He worried, quite understandably about this symptom, but this would require a very intimate examination! What should he do?

As chance would have it, I was off the day he asked for a house call, and one of my female partners visited. Well horrors upon horrors, a female doctor dealing with this complaint. The poor man just had about apoplexy and totally refused to allow himself to be examined. Next day I had to pick up the pieces and reassure him that I myself would visit and I suggested over the phone that he remained in bed to allow me to examine him.

So there I was again climbing these 58 steps to see my shy patient. Thankfully it was not too serious but it did require a visit to hospital, and after that experience he did not seem quite so shy and diffident and actually allowed a female student to visit and examine him and I secretly feel he enjoyed the experience!

The Budgie

She was an ex-midwife from the more remote areas of Aberdeenshire and had worked in houses with no running water, no sanitation, poor lighting and in the middle of snowstorms when she fought her way to her patients and delivered their babies.

A colossus of a woman she must have acted both as a tower of strength to the mother and a fearsome tyrant to the father. Her reputation was legendary and she was well known and well respected figure in the district.

Now retired and aged well into her 80s she was for the first time in her life experiencing illness. For one who had enjoyed the rudest of health all her working days this came as a massive blow and she found great difficulty in coming to terms with it.

She eventually developed heart failure and was virtually unable to leave her flat and her greatest pleasure was her budgie called Freddie. He was allowed out of his cage and would happily fly all around the room and then settle either on your shoulder or the top of your head and of course occasionally he left 'a calling card'!

He was a wonderful speaker and had a fairly wide vocabulary and it was easy to see how my patient was so attached to him.

One glorious Saturday afternoon when I was sitting in the garden I received a call to this patient. On visiting her it was quite obvious that she had suffered a fairly severe heart attack so I arranged for her admission to hospital. So far so good but then the trouble started. "I am not going into hospital unless Freddie comes with me!"

Of course, this was impossible, so she refused to leave her flat. In desperation, I phoned some of her friends but no one was willing to look after Freddie. By this time, I had other calls to make but I could not leave her at home, but she would not leave home and no one would look after Freddie. The ambulance men had arrived and were waiting to take her into hospital when I told them the sorry tale.

"No problem," said one of the ambulance men, "I will take Freddie home with me." So my patient and Freddie left together in the ambulance. Thus, after taking approximately 2 minutes to arrange hospital admission it took me about 2 hours to arrange budgie care!

First Impressions

"How dare you send this young doctor to me!" was the opening line on the telephone to one of the partners when I called at a couple whom I was going to get to know very well over the ensuing years.

"I was expecting you, not this whippersnapper," she barked as I still stood at the front door, then slammed down the phone.

"Oh well I suppose you had better come in and see my husband," she said, still in a very indignant tone of voice.

This then was my introduction to a very brusque lady and her rather meek husband. "I do not think there is much wrong with him but he says he has a sore chest."

I examined the gentleman who was a little breathless and had a slight cough. She stood observing me with arms crossed across a fairly ample bosom and an unsmiling face. "I told you there was nothing wrong!" she exclaimed.

"I am sorry to disagree, but your husband has pneumonia and pleurisy and I am about to admit him to hospital."

10 days later, I revisited and discovered that he had had a very stormy time in hospital and was really quite unwell. His wife, to her credit, was apologetic and contrite and we later became firm friends and often joked about our first meeting.

The Kiss

I am sure this introduction to general practice was not what my final year student imagined.

9am, Monday morning, my first patient entered the consulting room. She was an elderly widow and before she actually said "good morning" she put her arms around me and gave me a big kiss and then said "thank you."

The expression on the student's face was one to behold, surprise, shock and amazement were only three of the words that could describe it.

"Thank you so much for what you did for me, I shall always be grateful to you!" and with that she then said "good day" and left the room.

My student was of course more than intrigued at this consultation. There were no symptoms, no history taking, no examination and no treatment, merely a kiss and goodbye.

I explained the background – my patient had noisy, nasty and aggressive neighbours who made her life very difficult. My input was to phone a lawyer friend and ask him to lean heavily on the neighbours to modify their behaviour. He must have leant very heavily on them as forthwith they changed from 'neighbours from hell' to 'neighbours from heaven' and obviously my patient was eternally grateful and so she came to see me and thanked me with a kiss!

Not The Phone Again

I hate being interrupted by the phone when I am consulting. My staff know only to buzz me through for a special reason or for a medical colleague. That morning I had a medical student sitting in with me.

Everything was proceeding well, I was up to time, and the cases were interesting until one patient known to be 'difficult' entered. His complaint was weird and complicated, his manner aggressive and demanding and the consultation was not going well. Then the phone rang and my receptionist asked if I would take a call.

"No," I replied, "ask them to phone back at the end of surgery." The response to this was that the call was from Saudi Arabia where one of my patients there was ill.

Against my will I took the call and discovered that it was a public holiday in Saudi and doctors were not available till the next day. As to be expected the call was difficult, as it appeared the child might have meningitis so giving advice took some time.

My patient in the surgery was glowering and gradually getting more and more annoyed but I ended the call and returned my attention to his problems. However, not more than 5 minutes later the phone rang again and this time it was a patient on holiday in Australia asking about her medication, as the tablets she had been prescribed there were of a different make and colour.

By this time my patient in the surgery was about apoplectic and as I attempted to placate him the phone rang a third time. I picked up the receiver and almost snarled down the line, "Yes, what is it now?"

"Sorry, Dr Gray but the patient in Saudi wants to know if they should fly home to see you?"

At this the patient in the surgery stormed out of the room and vowed never to consult with me again – a sentiment I was not too unhappy to agree with.

Meanwhile my student was open mouthed in amazement. Did all GPs have patients phoning from all over the world for advice?

I left her to ponder that question.

The Anniversary

A very downcast young man sat opposite me. Pale and a little dishevelled he looked as if he had not slept for a week.

"I cannot sleep," he complained, "I cannot concentrate on my studies."

I asked if he had suffered from this before and he confirmed it had occurred several times in the past.

"Do you have any idea what causes it?" I asked.

"Oh yes, I know the cause!" At this, he burst into tears and was quite distressed. "This is the anniversary of my father's death and every year at this time I feel low."

"Your father must have died quite young," I suggested, as he was only 23 years old.

"Yes" he replied, "he was only 45." And then the bombshell! "He was murdered by my mother and sister and they buried him in the garden! They were both sent to prison for a long time."

A Surprise

Tall, elegant, stylish and charming although now getting on in years she posed the picture of a bygone era where she would have been a society icon. She seldom consulted and her records were wafer thin and she had no history of note.

She had consulted me on a few occasions over the years but all for relatively minor illnesses.

Her home was as elegant as herself with beautiful china and pictures adorning the walls and tables. Her manner was genteel and polite and meeting her was always a special pleasure.

One evening there was a late call for her as her neighbour had found her quite unwell and a little confused. I visited and found her lying in bed in lace edged sheets and wearing a bed jacket and looking very ill. However, what was most surprising was the fact that her expensive and very authentic looking wig was on a wooden peg at the foot of the bed and that she was bald as a coot.

Adonis?

Tall, broad shouldered with a superb physique, he was a sportsman of note and known and admired for his achievements at both local and national level. His wife was the most striking lady, tall, blonde and lithe and an excellent sportswoman in her own right albeit in a different sport, her great love being show jumping.

It was therefore a pleasant surprise when they consulted me together since their marriage about one year previously, a glittering social affair that had been headlines in the press.

I immediately thought they had good news to tell me, and I brightly went down the line of thinking she was pregnant and wanted confirmation.

"How are you?" I asked, "you are both looking very well!"

Silence ensued and they looked at one another with unhappy faces. Oh dear, I thought, this is not what I expected and waited for their response. Then followed a prolonged and tense silence, as it was obvious neither wished to be the first to speak. I waited and eventually said, "I am here to help if I can, please tell me your problem."

Stammering quite markedly he began. "We are having a little problem with our sex life!" At this he stopped and looked helplessly at his wife, who patently was unwilling to contribute to the conversation.

After another long pause he said in a quiet voice. "We are not managing very well!"

"Not managing very well?" snorted his wife, "we haven't managed at all!"

At this, I said in my most professional manner, "Am I right in assuming that the marriage has not been consummated?"

"That's correct," he admitted tearfully, "and it's all my fault."

So even the apparently most ideal couple have problems, but luckily with some guidance and advice the problem was overcome.

A Little Too Much Alcohol

While acting as a Medical Officer for a shipping firm, I received a Call one Monday morning to visit a ship in the harbour, to attend to a sick seaman. There did not seen to be any great urgency, but I arrived on board after a short time and was shown to his cabin.

He was lying on his back in the semi-darkness and there was a pervading stench of vomit mixed with stale alcohol and I had a feeling this was not a straightforward case.

When I took his pulse his skin was cold and no pulse was present. Further examination revealed no heartbeat and fixed dilated pupils. This man was dead!

It transpired that he had last been seen on the previous Friday and not since, and on searching his cabin we discovered 2 empty vodka bottles and 71 empty cans of Tuborg lager!

He had gone to bed probably semi-conscious and then vomited and inhaled the vomit and had been dead for some time. I called an ambulance and then we had the most dreadful problem getting him up top, because of rigor mortis, which prevented easy carrying round corners, and up narrow stairs. There was one ominous 'crack' and I feared that a bone had broken, but eventually we succeeded and placed him in the ambulance.

Later it transpired that his alcohol level was 6 times above the legal limit!

Generosity

"Drinks all round," he called in the crowded pub. Everyone enjoyed the drink except his family, as this was completely out of character and he had been acting a little strangely recently. He was normally the meanest individual you could meet.

When the same scenario was repeated a few days later the family decided to consult me.

Thus the presenting symptom was 'generosity' surely fairly unusual in an otherwise seemingly normal healthy middle-aged man.

I examined him carefully much against his wishes. "Doc. I am fine, I am in good health and there is nothing wrong."

Interestingly there was very little to find on examination apart from mild blurring of the optic discs. There was no obvious mental or psychological abnormality but because of the strange nature of the 'complaint' I decided to refer him to a specialist. Investigations in those days were not so sophisticated and eventually he came to an exploratory operation.

What was discovered surprised us all. There was a benign brain tumour the size of a grapefruit from which he made a full recovery.

Never again did he buy drink for a crowded pub!

The View

The countryside was at its best when I was Locum Tenens for the local GP. After hospital practice it was a cultural shock to have ample time to speak to the patients, plus the added bonus that house calls were few and far between and the consulting was fairly gentle.

The weather was glorious and I was enjoying the experience. I had completed the morning calls, all two of them, and was having a peaceful cup of coffee after lunch sitting in the sun.

The phone rang and I was asked to call on a temporary resident who was staying with her parents, and whose father just happened to be the titled local laird. It was stressed there was no great urgency, but, as the call was at the far end of the practice I set off at a leisurely pace enjoying the pleasant journey.

The house sat on a hillside overlooking the river valley, and I met the patient who was pregnant for the first time. Thankfully it was not too serious, and a simple prescription was all that was necessary.

I accompanied my patient from the bedroom and she invited me to have afternoon tea with her parents.

I sat on the terrace and enjoyed tea with the family. "What a wonderful view you have from here," I said.

"Exactly what Her Majesty said yesterday!" was the reply.

Keep Taking The Tablets

In his full regalia, uniform immaculate, buttons gleaming and hat peak polished, he sat in the waiting room, dressed for his imminent meeting with Her Majesty, surrounded by mothers and toddlers because it was Baby Clinic day.

He was there at my request after his secretary had phoned to say "The boss is not well again".

I had treated him before for the same complaint but either he had not been taking the tablets or he was not following my instructions.

The receptionists were certain that all the patients sat up straighter, the children became better behaved when he entered. I called him for consultation and everyone in the waiting room seemed to relax and breathe a sigh of relief.

As suspected he had not been taking the tablets prescribed and I duly rebuked him and gave him strict instructions for his future treatment.

He left my room rather sheepishly as I told him to make an appointment for one month's time.

It gave me a strange sensation to tick him off but on this occasion it was definitely necessary; even though he was a very senior police officer.

Keeping Quiet When Necessary

It was obvious that the receptionist was struggling with the patient on the other end of the phone. She was trying in vain to speak but was clearly receiving a hard time.

I indicated that she should hand over the phone; I then listened to a torrent of abuse and invective. I remained quiet until he paused for breath then I said, "You are now speaking to Dr Grey."

There was silence and then came a very different tone of voice – polite and effusive. I interrupted and deliberately raised my voice, "I have listened to your disgusting language and abuse, you and your family will henceforth find another medical practice."

Observation of the patients in the waiting room was remarkable – shock, surprise and apprehension wire very evident.

Perhaps some patients had listened and learned!

I've Been There

In days gone by many consultants were personalities, either brilliant or eccentric (or both). Before the advent of political correctness, patients sometimes had a 'rough ride' during hospital consultations.

An extremely obese gentleman attended the medical outpatient clinic. He weighed at least 25 stones. His GP had referred him because of breathlessness and difficulty climbing stairs!

I took his history and examined him, and waited to present my case to the Consultant.

"What have you found?" I was asked.

"Very little apart from his weight," I ventured.

The Consultant agreed. "You, my good man, are obese, in fact grossly obese. You are at least 12 stones overweight. If you lose weight you will be in much better health. If not, you will die!"

The patient claimed that he ate very little. He claimed to survive on salads and boiled eggs but still the weight would not come off!

"Nonsense," said the Consultant, "you must be eating much more."

The patient strongly denied this.

At this he was told very forcibly. "That is absolute rubbish, you never saw a fat man come out of Belsen!"

"I was in Belsen!" was the reply, followed by complete silence and an almost palpable tension.

The Tattoo

Tiny but dressed in black leathers carrying a huge crash helmet she arrived at 8.30am for a pre-employment medical for an oil company. She sat down and after the usual greetings I asked, "What sort of bike do you ride?" expecting an answer such as a 125 moped.

"An 850 Suzuki!" was the reply and my mind boggled at the thought of this petite little female even being able to support such a massive machine.

"Top speed of 160 miles per hour," she told me, "but I have not been above 110!"

I took the standard history we took for pre-employment medicals and then asked her to undress sufficiently for my examination. I detected a slight reticence at that point but she undressed quickly and sat on the couch.

Having taken her blood pressure I proceeded to listen to her heart and observed a tattoo of a butterfly on the upper surface of each breast. I said nothing but continued with the examination.

At this point she exclaimed, "Are you surprised at my tattoos?"

"Well a little," I said, "although many young ladies have these nowadays."

She explained that having gone up to University aged 16, on the first Saturday of term, she had gone out with a crowd of students and they all proceeded to get drunk. Thereafter the entire group had decided to get tattoos and she had gone along with that idea.

I accepted that many students had a similar experience and some had regretted it later.

I then asked her to lie flat on the couch so as to examine her abdomen and perceived a further tattoo just below the umbilicus with an arrow pointing downwards and the words "It's here!"

I had no answer to that!

The Cat

Reasons for patients demanding house calls are many and varied. Usually it is because of genuine illness or a concern about taking a patient out of the house and exposing them to 'fresh air', which would cause deterioration in their condition!

Occasionally it is used as an excuse if a surgery consultation cannot be obtained and occasionally as a threat that should the doctor not visit immediately then complaints would start flowing about lack of care, etc.

Mrs M was a lovely patient in an Old People's Home. She seldom complained and calls to her were rare. Thus when a request was made for her I wondered what the reason was as the Matron of the home refused to give any details.

I looked forward to seeing her, as she was always cheerful and entertaining. A stern faced matron met me at the door of the Home and demanded that I come to her office

"You must do something about your patient, she is causing a lot a of trouble!"

I expressed surprise at this, as she seemed the easiest going old lady I knew. "What exactly is the matter?"

"It's that cat," I was told and this made me even more mystified as I thought personal pets were forbidden.

It then transpired that the cat belonging to the home had taken up virtual residence in her bedroom and slept on her bed, and it defied all attempts to remove it from the room.

"It will cause serious illness to your patient, and must be removed!" This then was the reason for the house call.

I took great delight in telling the pole faced Matron that I did not think the cat would cause any disease at all and that my patient got great delight from the cat's presence and, even more importantly, my patient was aged 99 and perhaps the pleasure of the cat outweighed any shortening of my patient's life, and that I would definitely not recommend removal of the cat.

Said In The Silence

I had just had my second hip replacement and was at a Sunday lunch time drinks party. I was discussing the operation with a lady and explaining that I had donated my marrow for research use in blood disorders.

Obviously I had to have my blood tested for various diseases prior to being used and during one of those strange moments when there is complete silence in a crowded room I was saying, "I have just had my fifth AIDS test!"

There was a palpable in drawing of breath and I got the feeling that everyone was standing just that little more distant from me than to be expected.

Help

I still remember the very first patient I examined as a medical student. We had left the 'Drain' (Anatomy Dissecting Room) and after a week or so of introductory clinical tuition we were each allocated a patient to clerk and examine.

My patient's name was Margaret and she was about my age. She weighed about 15 stones and was being investigated for chest pains.

As taught I took a history, slowly and tediously, as I was very green and inexperienced. Eventually it was completed and I requested and was granted permission to examine her. By this time I realised that Margaret had quite a good sense of humour.

I collected screens to place round the bed, as in those days there were no curtains on rails round each bed. These screens about 6 feet high, were in place, and I was taking my stethoscope from my briefcase at the foot of the bed when, to my dismay, the patient suddenly cried, "Help! Help!"

Deeply emphasised and not knowing what to do, I raised my hands above my head and thus visible above the screens, and called, "I'm not near her!"

Thankfully a nurse was nearby and she came to investigate. By this time Margaret was contorted with laughter and explained to the nurse that she was just having fun at my expense! That patient I have never forgotten.

Only A Game

I have not often been threatened during my medical career, but it happened in unusual circumstances.

While I was Club Doctor at Aberdeen Football Club we were playing in Germany against a team from Berlin in the UEFA cup. It was quite an unpleasant game with the German players 'diving' after minimal contact and in effect trying to 'con' the referee and get Aberdeen players booked. They succeeded to a degree and one AFC player had been shown the yellow card for a fairly innocuous challenge. A German player threw himself dramatically to the ground after a tackle and groaned and writhed as if he was seriously hurt.

He was booked for diving and at this decision another German player head butted an Aberdeen defender quite spontaneously without any provocation, and was correctly shown the red card and dismissed from the field.

I was attending the injured Aberdeen player who had sustained a broken nose when another German player approached and waving his fist at the player who was lying on the ground and called him a cheat.

I looked up from attending the injury and the same player then threatened me and it appeared as if I might be attacked as he screamed at me that I should not be treating a cheat.

I responded as calmly as I could (although not calm inwardly), "Kind German gentleman, please go away." I think he understood basic Anglo-Saxon vocabulary!

The Slap

She was a very uppity Californian lady who entered my consulting room. "I am here for my hay fever shot, and I do not like injections."

I commiserated with her and explained that I was not over fond of them myself and invited her to lie up on the couch and expose sufficient area of skin for me to inject.

I filled the syringe and, as I always did, I slapped her buttock prior to inserting the needle and then quickly carried out the injection.

She turned her head and glared at me with the most furious expression, "When, you have finished slapping my bottom, could we get on and give the injection!"

I stood back from the couch. "I have given you your injection and you did not feel it because of the slap I administered."

With that, she smiled and said, "Doctor, you may slap my bottom any time!"

(I am not certain if the General Medical council would have been particularly happy with that sentiment.)

The Fountain

It was three o'clock in the morning, and still the operating theatre was frantically active, with case after case requiring surgery. We, as final year medical students, were roped in, and either, clerked the new patients, or assisted in theatre, and it was one of those occasions when there seemed no respite or time to sit down and draw breath.

I had just examined an elderly gentleman admitted with abdominal pain, which radiated through to his back. Even more worrying however, was a pulsatile mass felt in the abdomen.

Hurriedly I summoned the consultant surgeon and set up intravenous drips in both arms and he was rushed through to the theatre. With all haste he was anaesthetised and the operation started.

The abdomen was opened and there for all to see was a huge pulsating mass due to an aneurysm in the aorta. This was a real emergency!

None of the students had even seen anything like this before and our eyes never left the beating mass, which seemed to enlarge as we watched.

Suddenly with no warning, the artery burst and a fountain of blood rose from the open wound and sprayed everyone, and of course the poor patient expired immediately.

Do You Know?

The pretty blonde Texan lady had just arrived from Houston with her husband who was an oil executive. It was her first visit to Aberdeen indeed her first time in the UK. She was expecting her first baby in about 5 months time and was obviously thrilled about it.

We met at a farewell party given by an American family prior to their transfer to Alaska after five years in Aberdeen.

While we conversed it transpired that her closest friend back in US had been in Aberdeen while her husband worked here. She asked if I was familiar with Aberdeen and I confirmed I was.

Did I know a certain gynaecologist who her friend had advised her to consult regarding her pregnancy and did I know where his 'office' was? I was able to tell her exactly where she could find him, as I knew him extremely well.

Then she asked if I knew a certain Family Doctor who looked after her friend's family while they were in Aberdeen and she gave me his name.

"Yes," I said, "I know him very well, you are speaking to him!"

One Lone Supporter

When a flu epidemic hit Aberdeen we were very very busy. One phone call made things really hectic. A boy's seminary with 150 boarders on the outskirts of the city requested a house call for some 47 boys who were ill.

Accompanied by another partner we visited, and with the excellent help of the Nuns, we examined all 47 boys, plus one or two of the staff.

The pupils each had a very basic little 'cell' with bed, table and chair, wardrobe and very little else. On the walls in each cell, posters of their favourite football team were pinned. For obvious reasons, Celtic football club was by far the most popular; there were however, 3 or 4 St. Mirren fans and one lone Aberdeen FC supporter.

Inevitably the epidemic affected virtually every boy, Priest and Nun in the school and for about 10 days we visited regularly.

About 2 weeks later Aberdeen beat Celtic 3-2 at Pittodrie Stadium. At that school there was certainly one very happy boy.

A Large Lady!

Standing on top of a box holding a retractor to keep open an abdominal wound in a rather large lady who was being operated on, was not a particularly interesting way of spending a morning.

She was so obese that it required 4 students to assist the 2 porters to transfer her from the trolley to the operating table! Once on the table she overflowed each edge by a huge amount as an apron of adipose tissue hung towards the floor.

The sound emitted when the first incision was made was like a knife splitting open a ripe melon and I will never forget also the 'splodge' as the abdomen fell open revealing inches and inches of fat. So there I was, up to my elbow, holding a retractor to keep open a wound I could not even see. Her bulk was so great that even with the operating table at its lowest level we all had to stand on boxes to peer over the whale like mass.

One had to admire the clinician who managed to diagnose gallstones through vast layers of tissue as this lady weighed an amazing 33 stones!

Early Beatles

'She loves you, yeh, yeh,yeh' rang out through the ward. This was the favourite piece of music of a six year old – he played it constantly on his new record player. No one minded – it was the latest record of The Beatles who had just hit the charts.

The six year old was a little blond blue-eyed boy who had been diagnosed with leukaemia. In the early 60s, treatment was very imprecise and one of the side effects was total baldness, so Billy had lost all his blond curls.

One day the music stopped! No longer did we hear The Beatles booming through the ward. Billy had lost his most important battle - the ward was a sad place – how we missed 'She loves you yeh, yeh, yeh yeh...!!!!'

More Than It Seemed

"I've cut my hand," stated the young lady as she entered Accident and Emergency with her hand wrapped in a blood stained towel.

"How did it happen?" I asked as I sat her down, as she seemed rather pale and shocked.

"I was cutting the grass with the motor mower, we do have rather a large garden in Banchory," a village 18 miles west of Aberdeen. "Unfortunately a large stick caught in the blades and jammed them, and I tried to pull it clear but the mower was still running and caught my fingers!"

By this time she was definitely looking very faint so I lay her down on the couch, called for a nurse, and started to unwrap the towel from her hand.

What greeted me was a bloody mess of parts of fingers severed and at least two fingers cut off completely. This was a job for the specialist surgeons and I quickly wrapped a dressing round her hand.

"It's not too bad a cut is it?" she asked.

Thinking of her future with a dreadfully mutilated hand was not nice to contemplate so I carefully said, "We will not really know till the surgeons have examined you." At that point, she fainted and spared me the task of breaking the bad news to her, as we transferred her to the surgical ward immediately.

The Planets

The tiny 4 year old had been admitted from Orkney to the Mother and Child Unit in the Children's Hospital. His problem was that he would not eat, apparently subsisting on a diet of Wheetabix and Ribena, and was well below the normal height and weight for his age.

Examination had revealed no obvious cause for his size and at the ward round a decision was to be made regarding which investigations should be carried out.

He was a serious little boy who did not mix readily with the other children in the ward and preferred to be by himself and read his own books.

Discussion was taking place between his mother and the consultant concerning exactly what to do next and I sat on his bed and asked him what he was reading. His reply astonished me. "I am reading about astronomy!" he replied.

Trying to show no surprise, I asked, "And what have you learned today?"

"Well" he said, "I now know that Pluto is further away from the Earth than Venus and that it takes 248 years to orbit the Sun!"

At this point the Consultant having heard our conversation, asked him. "Why do you not eat?"

His reply was superb. "I have more important things to do with my time than eat!"

It later transpired that his IQ was greater than 160!

Another Aberdeen

"Where are you off to this time?" I asked the tiny, bird like lady when she came to consult me.

"Aberdeen," she replied. "I am trying to visit all 8 in USA!"

The only time I saw her, was for immunisations, prior, to yet another trip to visit one of the 28 Aberdeen's scattered throughout the world.

She had been in the Army for most of her working life and had managed to visit many foreign countries. During these trips she had come across one or two Aberdeen's in what originally were British Colonies and she had decided to try and visit all the towns and cites named Aberdeen.

She was an incredibly active person and worked in various voluntary organisations such as WRVS, etc, between planning her next trip. She looked after her elder sister who had several medical problems but she coped beautifully with all these little hazards with aplomb and never seemed fazed or upset.

As mentioned, she was a tiny lady, and it seemed impossible that she would cope with the stresses and strains of foreign travel, but cope she did, returning home triumphantly and desperate to plan her next trip.

Unfortunately, her sister was admitted to an Old People's Home with dementia and this curtailed her travel for a time.

She has, however, a visit arranged to South Africa and no doubt by the next time I see her she will have ticked off another 'Aberdeen box'.

A Bottle Of whisky

The distinctive smell of metal polish was evident when I entered Miss C's tiny flat. Today was silver cleaning day as she was a lady with a strict routine.

Now in her 80s she had been a maid in a huge estate in Aberdeenshire and she told wonderful stories of life 'above and below stairs'. The laird she worked for had looked after his staff very well and she remembered the Christmas parties, the picnics in the hills and the 'below stairs' special outing when they were treated and served by the family.

She was virtually house bound because of arthritis but she still kept her flat clean and shining. Her speciality was jam and marmalade making and inevitably I left with a pot of her latest batch.

So she sat at a small table covered with newspaper and polished her silver lovingly. "But," as she told me, "it does not shine like the old days. Then, I used whisky and I just had to fill a bottle from the cask and use it to make everything gleam."

Surely an expected use of Scotland's favourite tipple!

The Glorious Twelfth

It was August and the 'Glorious Twelfth'. The weather was beautiful for the first day of grouse shooting and the practice was very quiet. I was reading the garden when the phone rang. An agitated voice asked, "Can the doctor come immediately, someone has been shot!"

The address given was that of one of the largest estates owned by a multimillionaire industrialist from England in residence for the summer. Was it he who was injured?

I hastily grabbed my bag, and drove rapidly to the house, mentally thinking of the possible problems of a serious gunshot injury many miles from a major hospital, should the police be involved?

When I arrived there were 3 or 4 Range Rovers in the driveway, several dogs, and gentlemen holding glasses of whisky, and the spoils of a successful shoot visible.

I parked and approached one group and asked where the patient was. I was met by blank stares and denial of any knowledge of any accident.

I rang the front door bell and was greeted by a maid who led me through to a huge kitchen with a polished flagstone floor. Sitting in a chair was a gamekeeper with a blood stained bandaged foot resting on a stool.

This then was my patient. I removed the dressing to inspect the wound. What I found was a single puncture wound, which had obviously torn a small artery.

It was a simply task to remove the solitary lead bullet, clean and dress his foot.

Not quite the scenario I had anticipated when the call came in!

Faded Elegance

The clothes did not fit the accent or the demeanour, being old and worn although originally good quality. It was my initial meeting with a lady who had joined out practice on the recommendation of an old patient who had recently met her several years previously while abroad.

The accent was loud, typical English upper class and attracted attention as she approached reception to announce her arrival.

"I have an appointment with Dr Gray at 2.30. I presume I shall be taken on time." She took her seat and haughtily looked around with some disdain.

When called she swept into my consulting room and introduced herself.

"I do not like to be kept waiting! If my appointment is for a certain time, that is when I expect to be taken!"

This is going to be interesting I thought and invited her to sit down. "How can I help you?"

"There is nothing wrong with me. I have just come to make myself known to you, so you will be able to deal with me promptly and correctly in the future."

I glanced at her address – a council flat – did not seem to fit the picture. She was, however, unwilling to tell me much about her background apart from the fact she had previously lived in London.

Her story emerged a few weeks later when the friend, who had introduced her to the practice, consulted me.

She and her husband had been in India for many years where her husband had been in emerald mining during the days of the Raj. They had lived a fabulous lifestyle as so many ex-pats in India did in those days. Unfortunately, when British influence there ended they lost most of their emerald wealth and had returned to Britain.

Her husband had died 2 or 3 years previously and money had become tight so she had decided to come to Aberdeen where her son was a police constable. She was unwilling or unable to alter her lifestyle and she still wished to give the appearance of living as previously in India.

She had a few baubles, such as crystal, china and jewellery but the clothes, shoes and furniture were absent and she did not endear herself to anyone by her attitude.

She received no help from her son who was an unpleasant person and tried to bully those like myself to treat his mother as someone special and different.

Unfortunately, this was a picture of a faded elegance and she was a miserable and unhappy lady.

The Wobble

It was a very pale and shaken and shocked young man who entered my room. I had known him for many years since he was a child and his parents had been patients long before I joined the practice.

He sat down and looked at the floor visibly shaking. He was big, about 6 feet 2 inches and very well built. He did not consult very frequently, but that day he looked a worried man.

As usual, when he visited, he was wearing his motorcycle leathers but on this occasion he was not carrying his crash helmet. Eventually he looked up and there was a distinct air of anxiety on his face.

"What is worrying you?" I asked.

An interesting story unfolded. "I was going to Inverness on my motorbike and when I reached the long straight outside Elgin I decided to push up my speed. I had reached 150 miles per hour when I started to wobble. As you know (at this time I did not know) if you wobble at that speed almost certainly you will crash and it is usually 'curtains' as it is virtually impossible to correct."

'Well,' I thought, 'you are here, so you have survived!'

He continued. "By some miracle I managed to stay on the bike and slow down and eventually came to a halt. I was so scared after what had happened that I about turned and drove all the way back to Aberdeen at no more than 30 miles per hour. I went straight to the company where I bought the bike and sold it and I have decided never to ride a motorbike again in my life!"

I had never seen a fit young healthy man so shaken that I gave him a mild tranquiliser and suggested he went home and thanked his lucky stars that he was still alive and in one piece.

When I next saw him, some weeks later, while visiting his mother, he proudly pointed out his new car, a not so sedate Peugeot 306.

A Changed Man

His suit was 30 years old and the cut had recently returned to fashion. Turn-ups, relegated from suits many years previously but now again acceptable, broad lapels and an unusual brown tweed material completed the ensemble for this slightly retiring and reticent patient.

He was a well-known figure in local business, but I met him in rather unfortunate circumstances. His daughter was in London with her younger daughter and his son-in-law had not answered his wife's phone call and she asked her father to visit to ascertain if anything was wrong.

Wrong it certainly was, and I received what could only be called a panic phone call.

It was about 11 o'clock when I arrived at the son-in-law's house and parked my car beside the silver Rolls Royce. I was met at the door by a worried looking gentleman dressed as mentioned above. His manner was anxious and uncontrolled.

"I have found my son-in-law behind the kitchen door but he seems unconscious and I cannot open the door. He is not responding to my calls."

His son-in-law was a large man and was well and truly wedged behind the door. However, with great difficulty we managed to force the door open sufficiently for me to squeeze through.

There, lying prostrate on the floor with a broken cup lying beside him was my patient, coffee splashed across his paisley pattern dressing-gown, and toast and marmalade a little further away.

"Is he alright?" I was asked.

"Well no," I replied.

"What seems to be the matter? Can I speak to him, I must know."

I hesitated for a moment or two but he demanded to know what was going on.

"Well, actually he is dead."

At that point there was a crash on the other side of the door and I realised I had a second patient to deal with.

Squeezing back through the door I found him lying on the carpet, pale and unconscious but breathing normally and obviously had simply fainted.

He revived but seemed totally incapable of rational thought. He requested that I call his daughter and tell her the bad news, as he could not bring himself to do it.

I complied with his wishes and then phoned the undertaker and organised the paperwork necessary.

This was a captain of industry; a self-made millionaire who commanded several huge companies and was I believe, ruthless in business, with a rapier mind and wonderful acumen in financial matters. At this time, however, he was incapable of making any decisions and I was amazed by the effect that a sudden death had caused.

A Husband's Bombshell

She always did give the impression that she was somehow superior and had an inclination to 'look down her nose' at all and everyone.

Why she had this belief was difficult to determine. She was a secretary in a small legal office, not apparently particularly well off, although she and her husband owned some property including for some strange reason quite a few lock-up garages.

Over the years, I became aware that occasionally there was a smell of alcohol in her breath. There was the classic denial response on probing her alcohol intake, with her. She continued to act in a rather high handed manner even on occasions to be rather rude to doctors and reception staff in particular. Consultations were sometimes quite unpleasant and I did not look forward to meeting her.

Then one day there was a sea change and it emerged that her husband had been grossly mismanaging the 'property portfolio'. Rent had not been collected on their more valuable flats and the cause was quite interesting.

Her husband it transpired, admitted that he was sexually AC/DC. He had allowed his flats to be occupied by his friends in return for mutual favours, and possibly a threat of blackmail and exposure. No money changed hands so the income to the household fell dramatically as he spent more time in their company than looking after the business.

He then confessed his sexual proclivity to his wife and understandably she was shattered and distraught. She consulted me and realised there was no easy or magical solution to the problem. She moved out of the family home and attempted to repair her life. She stopped drinking and became a far nicer person. I breathed a sigh of relief and hoped everything would settle down for the best.

After a few months, she reappeared and the deterioration was incredible. I found out on closer questioning that he had managed to persuade her, when she was under the influence of alcohol, to transfer all the title deeds of their properties into his name. She was destitute and had to depend on her husband for any financial support. By some miracle she retained her job but, unfortunately she spent most of her salary on drink. Things inevitably went from bad to worse and on one particularly bad day I checked her liver function tests suspecting she had alcohol induced cirrhosis. This was confirmed and because she did not heed medical advice, she slowly deteriorated and finally liver failure ensued and she died a broken and very unhappy lady.

Up to date her husband has not appeared in the surgery and was not at home when we contacted him after his wife's death. Whether guilt or relief is the cause, I cannot be sure.

An Early Case Of Road Rage?

Parking in every hospital is difficult and the Maternity Hospital was worse than most. The hospital authorities saw for to reserve bays for the on-call staff.

This worked well until one weekend when on the Saturday afternoon one space was occupied by a man visiting his wife and he stayed for the entire visiting period of three hours.

A polite notice was left on his windscreen asking him to desist from parking in that space.

He was observed from the Doctors' lounge, which overlooked the parking bays, approaching his car, reading the note, tearing it into little pieces and driving off with a smirk on his face.

The next afternoon, the same gentleman appeared and parked in the bay reserved for the duty paediatrician who was out on a call, and disappeared into the hospital.

Petty behaviour it might be, but blocking him in and leaving him to stew for an hour after visiting had finished, and watching him change from mild annoyance to blind fury was most enjoyable.

One of my colleagues approached him and enquired if he was the new duty paediatrician and offered to introduce him to the other medical staff.

This kind offer was refused but he never parked there again.

An Expensive Change Of Clothing

Early in my General Practice career many years ago, I was called one morning to a patient in his mid fifties with chest pain.

He lived with his wife in a very neat and tidy council house with an immaculate garden. He had previously served for many years in the Army as a Warrant Officer and now was a driver for the corporation transport of the city.

His uniform was always immaculate and his shoes gleamed just as if he were still on parade.

I examined him but, in those days, we did not have a portable ECG machine and my diagnosis purely on clinical grounds was of a myocardial infarction (heart attack).

Unfortunately, he did not have a phone so I went to his neighbours to phone the hospital and admit him and also call an ambulance to take him there.

I had just finished my phone call when his wife came running through to say he had collapsed.

On returning to his house, I found him lying halfway up the stairs lying face down against the wall. He was pale and sweaty and quite dead.

His wife explained that he wanted to change into clean pyjamas prior to being admitted to hospital and obviously the effort of climbing the stairs had precipitated a further heart attack, which had sadly proved fatal.

Thereafter whenever I diagnosed a heart attack, I strictly forbade any patient to move until the ambulance arrived. A salutary lesson but one I have never forgotten.

An Unfortunate Meeting

I have seldom seen a patient quite so agitated, and it took some little time to extract the story.

He had been at a conference in Warwick and a lady had approached him and asked if he remembered her. She was quite a few years younger than him but he vaguely recollected seeing her as a student from tutorial sessions at University where he had been a part-time lecturer.

They sat together at dinner and then had a few drinks in the bar. When he had decided it was time for bed she had looked him straight in the eye and said, "Your bedroom or mine?"

When he hesitated she said, "You're married, I'm married, I won't say anything, you won't say anything!"

He had hesitated again then relented and proceeded to spend probably a very pleasant night together.

And the cause of the panic and anxiety? His lady consort's husband had somehow found out about the liaison and was intent on causing as much trouble as possible. He had threatened to phone his wife, his senior partner and goodness knows who else. His erstwhile companion had telephoned that morning and warned him about these possible developments.

Result stress.

Anno Domini

I seldom cite age as the cause of a patient's problem. However, occasionally the aging process plays a part in the symptoms and signs of the condition.

A fairly fit lady consulted me with pains in the neck and arms, and I suspected she might have Cervical Spondylosis. I arranged for an X-ray to be taken of her cervical spine and asked her to make an appointment to see me one week after the X-ray.

She duly appeared and I discussed the X-ray findings with her.

"I can confirm that you have cervical spondylosis, and this would fit your signs and symptoms."

She accepted this fact but demanded to know the cause.

"Wear and tear," I replied.

"But why?" she queried, "I am fit and healthy."

I agreed but advised her that 'anno domini' played a part in her problem.

"I have never been so insulted in my life!" she stormed. "When you get to my age you will not enjoy a doctor telling you that the cause of the problem is old age. Please remember that!"

I looked her straight in the eye and smiled. "I appreciate what you are saying, but I am five years older than you!"

Are You A Doctor?

Beware of the title 'doctor'.

When I was relatively young i.e. I had been qualified about 8 years, I was on holiday with my family at a hotel in Kent.

Late one afternoon a child aged about 6 had fallen off a swing and although not badly injured, the parents were undecided whether to take the child to the Accident department at the local hospital which was some miles away.

On the hotel register there were three doctors registered, and the hotel manager requested one 'doctor' to examine the child. He turned out to be a doctor in theology and could not help.

The second 'doctor' was a PhD in physics, so belatedly I was asked if I could help. I gladly examined the child and reassured the parents there was nothing to worry about. I then sought out the hotel manager to ask why he chose the other 'doctors' first.

Rather sheepishly, he told me "they looked more like proper doctors than you!"

After that, I seldom registered as a 'doctor'.

Can I Help You, Doctor

It is not too often that I end up buying the groceries but on this occasion, I was entrusted to buy the weekly 'large shop'.

I visited Marks and Spencer's and proceeded with my trolley round the food hall. I quite enjoyed myself and perhaps chose rather more from the shelves than was strictly necessary.

Trolley fully laden, I stood in line at the checkout till it was my turn and then placed my purchases on the moving belt. The store was very busy and quite a queue had built up behind me as I loaded by groceries back into the trolley.

Then the moment of truth arrived. I discovered that I did not have a single penny on me. I had no chequebook, no store credit card, not a single bean. With great embarrassment, I admitted to the assistant that I had no money to pay for the goods. By this time the customers behind me in the queue were taking a great interest in my discomfort and I was becoming more and more flustered.

Suddenly a voice beside me enquired, "Doctor, do you have a problem?"

I looked up and here was one of the manageress's who just happened to be a patient whom I had seen professionally only the previous day. I rapidly explained my predicament and she kindly signed the till receipt and wheeled the trolley into a side room and informed me that I could collect the food when I returned with the necessary money.

I thanked her profoundly and left the shop. As luck would have it, I met a very good friend at the door of the store and he kindly lent me the necessary cash.

I returned to the checkout and paid the bill. My patient was extremely surprised to see me return so quickly but happy to have been of help.

It was an embarrassing experience I do not want to repeat.

'Doc'

Being club doctor to a Premier League football team is interesting, stimulating and gives endless opportunity to watch games.

Although I attend all first team matches, many reserve and youth fixtures also, many players I am sure do not actually know my name; to them I am simply the 'Doc'.

Their problems are many and varied from purely medical to social and family troubles and of course I am expected to deal with them all.

The medical problems are mainly straightforward, usually respiratory or soft tissue infections or injuries sustained at training or while playing. Of course there are rarer but expected infection due to fit virile young men at whose muscular bodies, girls, young and not so young throw themselves with inevitable results.

Some simply bypass me and attend GUM (genito-urinary medicine) clinic and I know nothing about it unless they volunteer the information.

Others, however, are waiting to see me on a Monday morning because of their activities during the weekend and this varies from panic to quiet acceptance. So, history taken, swabs sent to the lab., reassurance given (to some degree) then patience till the results came through.

Others occasionally find themselves in trouble by getting involved in 'forbidden fruit' and the problem here is usually anxiety that the partner of the young lady may find out about the liaison. Players like so many patients have very little patience and want treatment and cure almost immediately. They, however, pale into insignificance compared with football management and directors of football.

Their demands are always the same. "We need a medical examination done now!" Not in 2 hours or 4 hours time but now. "In fact why did you not do it yesterday?"

This, despite the fact that the transfer negotiations to sign the player may have been going on for days or even weeks. Also comes the warning: "This is confidential, tell no one!"

I got so fed up being given this advice I told one manager, "I deal with more confidential information in one day in medical practice than you deal with in a lifetime so kindly omit this gratuitous advice!"

Since that time it has never been mentioned. A small victory for the medical team, plus, if I fail a player on medical grounds, and this does happen, then they really cannot afford to ignore my advice.

Double Trouble

They were a strange couple. He was an Accountant and I believe very competent. She was a wife who spent her time shopping and going out each evening by herself to the local hotel where she sat at the end of the bar waiting for company!

He also had a psychiatric history, being subject to fits of depression, requiring drug therapy. He also had a liking for too much of Scotland's amber nectar.

Despite these apparently very different ways of living, they got on relatively well, and had two daughters who seemed to cope with this strange family lifestyle.

I received the call at 3 a.m., the story being that he had fallen asleep in front of the fire and could not be roused.

When I arrived he was sprawled out on an armchair, an almost empty whisky bottle on the floor, and his wife who had consumed a fair amount of alcohol herself, shaking and shouting at him.

The room was like an oven and smelling strongly of alcohol and bizarrely the family dog was lying on his stomach.

I checked first his pulse and then his breathing and both were absent. This man was dead! Further examination revealed an empty bottle of antidepressant capsules under the chair; he had taken about 30 with disastrous results!

Unfortunately, there was a sad sequel to this tragedy – about a year later, his wife was sexually assaulted and murdered by a man she had met at the pub, so the two girls lost both their parents in unusual circumstances within a very short time.

How Things Have Changed

The delightful Infant Teacher, whom I had known since birth, entered my consulting room with her two little children.

Her daughter was aged five and she was the patient. Her brother was 18 months old, and a proper 'little boy'.

Mum sat down on one chair and her daughter sat beside her. Her son proceeded to climb on to my knee and I produced some paper and a pencil for him to scribble on.

"Tell Doctor Derek (as I was known to countless children in the practice) what's wrong."

"I have sore ears and a sore throat," was the reply.

Examination was slightly hampered by the presence of one little boy sitting on my knee, but I managed to check her ears and throat and also listen to her chest.

With some difficulty I was able to punch out a prescription on my computer and hand it to the little girl; I always gave the prescription to the patient, especially a child.

Then came a comment that surprised me somewhat.

"I am not allowed to sit children on my knee during teaching," she said. "I run the risk of being labelled a paedophile."

What a sorry state our society is in when a teacher or (perhaps soon) doctors cannot sit a child on their knee. Such change is not a welcome one since I started in practice.

I may say the mum wished the old practices were still prevalent. She remembers being taught reading sitting on her Infant teacher's knee and it certainly benefited her.

Just A Little Prick

He was a big man from a big state in a big country. Recently arrived from across the 'pond' to work in the North Sea oil industry as a Petroleum Engineer.

He had an appointment for a pre-employment medical examination as required by his company, a subsidiary of a large multi-national with big interests in offshore drilling.

I took his history and asked him to undress for the physical part of the examination. He had a magnificent physique with a 'six-pack' belly and huge pectorals. He weighed 22 stones and then came the first problem. He was completely off my height scale. I had to stand on a chair to measure his height; 6 foot 10 inches. It transpired he played quarterback for a well-known American University football team.

The next part of the examination was to withdraw blood for various tests, so I asked him to lie down on the couch, but he preferred to remain seated.

I applied the tourniquet to his upper arm and inserted the needle into a very prominent vein with no problem, meanwhile chatting to him about this and that as I watched the tube fill with blood.

Suddenly I realised that I was having to bend down further and further to keep the needle in his arm and, glancing at his face I realised why. He had passed out completely and was slowly slipping off the chair. There was no way I could support his weight so with a final clatter he landed on the floor.

I decided to continue taking the blood tests and when I had finished I attended to him. By this time he was coming round and exclaimed, "What happened?"

"You fainted when I inserted the needle," I told him.

He was quite mortified and pleaded with me not to tell the company of his 'weakness'. I faithfully promised I would keep this quiet so that he did not lose face.

'Lie Still' You Charming Little Boy!

"Oh my poor darling," wailed the mother as she shepherded her 6 year old into A&E at the Children's Hospital.

The poor darling was, to say the least, difficult and uncooperative as the nurses attempted to clean the laceration on his chin.

He resisted all appeals to lie quietly and let the nurses do their job. In fact, he was downright nasty. He kicked, scratched, bit and screamed an ear shattering, piercing screech, which cut right through to one's brain.

After persevering for a few minutes and getting nowhere, I asked his ineffectual mother to take a seat outside the treatment room, explaining that sometimes children were calmer without their parents being present.

Very reluctantly she departed, casting anxious backward glances to her noisy young offspring.

Unfortunately, that did not do the trick and he continued to be anything but helpful. Indeed, if anything, his behaviour deteriorated. He bit, punched and kicked the nurses so in desperation I requested the two nurses to leave by another exit.

So it was him and I, eyeball to eyeball and no witness present.

I leant over him on the couch and quite softly whispered in his ear, "I wish you to lie quite still, desist from your appalling behaviour or I will rearrange the position of your front teeth."

My language was not quite Oxford English but perhaps a little more towards basic Anglo-Saxon, but he got the message, lay still and I inserted the necessary sutures in his chin.

If looks could kill, I would have dropped dead the moment I returned him to his mother, and especially when I informed her there was no problem in treating him.

No Friends

He really was quite distressed as he sat before me, a glorious suntan indicating a recent sojourn in the sun.

He was a teacher of mathematics at a local comprehensive school, mid thirties, unmarried and a fairly frequent attendee at the surgery for often quite trivial complaints.

He sat there wringing his hands, looking quite agitated, with almost a pleading look in his eyes. On this occasion I thought perhaps he had a more pressing medical problem.

He told me he had recently returned from vacation in Morocco, and it had been the most miserable holiday he had ever been on. The hotel had been excellent, the weather delightful, but this had not compensated for the misery he felt.

"I failed to make a single friend when I was away. I met lots of nice boys, but none of them would make any commitment to meet me regularly."

He had lain on the beach, swam, read, joined in the water activities, had drinks in the evening, but that was all. Nobody would come with him for a quiet nightcap on their own, after the first two nights.

But why, I wondered, although the reason was beginning to form in my mind, and I probed a little deeper. It was obvious it was only the male guests he was interested in, especially the younger members of the sex.

After much heart searching on his part, he finally admitted he was having erectile impotence, and had failed in his liaisons on the first two nights. His problem had spread round the group and no one wanted to be his partner. The holiday was a disaster of monumental proportions in his eyes.

It was my first consultation with an impotent homosexual. I fully expected him to request some Viagra before his next holiday.

Behaviour Unbecoming

Why is it that certain people act, as Gilbert and Sullivan said, 'above their station'? Interestingly it is often minor politicians, the nuveau riche, or those who think they are somebody important, who fall into that category.

In one such instance a gentleman (?) who never seemed to be out of the local press, complaining about the actions of the local town Council, or the Opposition Political Parties. He never had or gave a creditable or alternative solution to the problem himself, but boy did he complain.

I think it is fair to say that he was not the most popular person, as he seemed rather more concerned with his personal circumstances and image and was well known for 'looking after number one'!

Casualty Departments, as everyone knows, are never quiet, and, at any time of the day or night, they are filled with the drug addicts, the drunks, and those who could not be bothered to go to their own GP; and, scattered amongst these groups were genuine emergency cases.

One evening it was particularly busy, due to a multiple car crash caused, curiously, by a schizophrenic who had not been taking his medication, and who proceeded to drive down the wrong side of a duel carriageway. Amazingly, he was not seriously hurt himself.

The Waiting Room was packed and the waiting time was vastly in excess of the stupid 4 hour ruling demanded by the government of the day, none of whom I am sure had ever worked in a busy A&E Department.

During this period our local politician, looking remarkably healthy strode to the head of the queue and demanded in a loud hectoring voice, to be seen immediately.

The harassed receptionist very reasonably asked him to take a seat (none available) and wait his turn. This response of course, did not please, and he again demanded in an ever louder voice to be seen at once.

A hush had descended over the waiting room as he continued his ranting, using language which was hardly suitable to a person of his position.

"Do you know who I am?" he shouted.

Quick as a flash, the receptionist picked up the tannoy and announced, "Could the visiting Psychiatrist (who was attending the schizophrenic patient), please come to the front desk as she had a patient there who did not know who he was."

As the message boomed throughout the department, there was gales of laughter from the waiting room crowd, and several not too polite comments could be heard.

"F*** you!" he shouted at the receptionist who charmingly replied. "You have to wait in line for that too!"

It was a very red-faced gentleman who fought his way to the exit that day.

Doctor or Mister?

Sometimes is it a definite mistake to use the title 'doctor' when travelling. It can occasionally work in your favour as one of my friends treated a patient mid-Atlantic on a flight to New York and received upgrades on his next 2 to 3 flights.

Another friend carried out CRP (cardio-pulmonary resuscitation, or as it is better known mouth to mouth) and saved a patient's life. He received a bottle of champagne for his efforts. He had prevented the flight from having to make a costly and time-consuming emergency landing, with all the additional delays etc, but his effort was almost dismissed as nothing extraordinary, with not even a letter of thanks. Needless to say he has never used that airline again and neither have many of his friends who heard the story.

Two of my senior colleagues were travelling on the Aberdeen to London overnight sleeper train. One was awoken by the guard requesting his assistance as a lady had gone into labour. As he was a physician and his friend a radiologist, neither had delivered a baby since their student days many years previously.

He woke his colleague to provide moral support and together they assessed the lady in question, who was clearly in the advanced stages of labour. Forget all the nonsense about it being like riding a bike and never forgetting; this was for them a medical nightmare.

The patient had had two previous children, so at least one of the party had some recent experience of the procedure.

My two colleagues sweated and strained and finally, and probably with very little help from them, the lady produced a healthy boy. She was so delighted she named the baby after the two doctors.

They had only time to wash and shave before the train arrived at Euston Station, that being the night sleeper destination in those days. They disembarked from the train both mentally and physically exhausted, when, who should they encounter leaving the same train, but one of their colleagues, a Consultant Obstetrician in Aberdeen, who had booked his berth using Mr and not Dr!

He had enjoyed a pleasant uninterrupted sleep, his morning cup of tea with two Rich-tea biscuits, and was quite unsympathetic to the two shattered and erstwhile midwives.

Not Quite The Whole Truth

Whenever a couple consult together I can be sure that it is either a very personal problem of a very embarrassing one.

One such couple appeared, he looking nervous and she on the verge of tears. I knew this was going to be a difficult consultation. I only had his medical records as he had made the appointment.

"Well, tell the doctor," she said, tears beginning to flow down both cheeks.

He said nothing but stared at his feet and would not make eye contact.

"Go on!" she cried in what was now a furious high-pitched voice. "It's all your fault."

I waited and said nothing; this was not a family I had ever met before, so silence appeared the best approach.

After what seemed like an eternity he confessed, "I have been phoning a 'Chat line' number and my wife has found out."

"That's not all," she stormed, "there's far more to tell!"

The story slowly emerged. He had had an affair about 5 years previously and his wife had, perhaps rather surprisingly forgiven him, and apparently everything had been fine for a year or two.

Then she discovered he had been chatting regularly, although as it emerged later, she was unaware of the frequency to a lady on a Chat line.

However worse was to follow. He apparently was not a good sleeper and preferred to go to bed after his wife. She one evening found him watching 'porn' DVDs late at night and it was apparent that this had been a regular nightly occurrence.

A crisis had arisen at this particular time so I signed her off work and prescribed some mild sedation and arranged to see her in one week's time.

On the appointed day, she did not appear but her husband did. She refused to leave the house, answer the phone or do any housework and depended on the support of her girlfriends to get over this 'nightmare' as she called it.

Closer questioning of her husband gave some insight into the problem. Since the birth of their daughter 11 years previously there had been no sexual relations. She claimed she had been physically and mentally damaged by the birth. Sex was out of the question!

A day or two later I received an aggressive phone call demanding that I visit her, then arrange for a specialist to 'sort out' her husband, as he was the sole cause of her problem. In fact I should have dealt with him on the first consultation. Really I was not doing my job properly!

Keeping outwardly calm but inwardly seething I asked about the lack of sex for 11 years. I was told very forcibly that was none of my business and had nothing to do with the current problem!

Then I dropped the bombshell. "I have carefully read your medical notes. How did you manage to become pregnant then and have a termination 5 years ago? Is there anything you wish to discuss more fully?"

There was a pause, and then the phone was slammed down. I have not heard from her since that date.

Phone Him!

Unfortunately, some doctors of the 'old school' behaved like gods in their wards and in their dealings with patients and staff especially junior doctors.

One such was a consultant surgeon whose brilliant operating skills allowed him to behave in what would otherwise be an unacceptable manner.

He started operating at 8am promptly and on this particular day he seemed in a more unpleasant mood than usual.

His house officer, only a few months qualified, but one of the best students in his year and a very capable doctor, was the brunt of most of the blame that morning. Everything that was not just as the consultant desired or demanded was blamed on the poor houseman even though many of the complaints had nothing whatsoever to do with him.

Finally, around 10.30am having silently soaked up all the remarks said to him he finally had had enough.

"Doctor," said in that derogatory way which he a 'Mr' being a surgeon and superior in his own eyes, "I have a ten year old son at home who assists better than you."

At this the houseman stepped back from the operating table, peeled off his gloves, threw them on the floor and said, "Phone him!" and walked out of the theatre.

You could have heard a pin drop, no one said a word, everyone froze, but nothing was said either then or later. Almost as if it had never happened.

Scottish Surgeons Are Capable

They were a very pleasant couple from Toronto. She in her late 30s, with no children and she did not work; he a Chemical Engineer who was developing his own geological surveying company in the relatively new North Sea oil fields.

They became patients of mine but their attendances were fairly spasmodic till one day she developed classical signs of gallstones. She had severe pain with radiation through to the back, and I quickly treated this and made her more comfortable. I arranged for her to see a Consultant Surgeon and he confirmed the diagnosis of biliary colic secondary to gallstones and he recommended cholecystectomy, i.e. removal of the gall bladder.

They accepted the diagnosis and then amazed me by stating they would return to Toronto for the operation.

I explained that the surgeon I had chosen was excellent in his field and that I did not feel that returning to Canada was necessary. With, I may say, a little reluctance, they took my advice and had the operation performed in Aberdeen.

The procedure was a great success and the tiny incision scar surprised and astounded them. This particular surgeon was a pioneer in Laparoscopy surgery, which of course today, is commonplace, but in those early days was quite rare.

I think having discussed the matter with friends; they expected a huge scar, lots of pain and a prolonged recovery time. Instead she had minimal discomfort, rapid recovery and a tiny scar which was almost invisible.

The net outcome was I was asked to act as medical officer for his company, and enjoyed financial reward for many years thereafter.

Mentally I thanked the surgeon who had made all this possible and later in my professional career I told him so.

Tabletop Surgery

When I recollect some of the procedures I carried out when I entered General Practice 35 years ago it would make today's young doctors blanche with disbelief.

Carrying out minor surgery without apparently sterile conditions or instruments, or the assistance of a colleague or nurse would amaze them. But it happened and not infrequently.

An elderly patient suffering from lung cancer with secondary spread is a case in point. He was a rather stoic, stubborn gentleman from Buchan farming stock. He never complained and made light of his illness until one day he became acutely breathless and his breathing became laboured and difficult.

I examined him and diagnosed a pleural effusion, i.e. fluid in the sac which surrounds the lungs. This was a complication of his cancer.

I explained the condition to him and advised him he must be admitted to hospital for treatment; that met with complete refusal.

"I'm nae gaun to hospital," and he meant it. "I'm gaun tae die at hame!"

No persuasion would change his mind and then he asked, "Can you nae tak the fluid away?"

Having been in hospital practice until 3 or 4 years earlier, I knew I could drain the fluid, but at home? However, seeing how distressed he was, I decided to at least drain off some of the effusion to ease his breathing. I arranged to return later with all the necessary equipment.

I discussed the case with one of the partners and he advised me to go ahead. So, after some thought and a little apprehension I drained 2 pints from my patient's chest. He experienced immediate relief to his breathing and was quite delighted with the result.

I was very relieved and hoped I would not have to repeat the procedure. In fact, I did the same about 2 weeks later when the fluid reaccumulated, but from then on he deteriorated quickly and passed away 10 days later.

He died at home, which he wanted and was mercifully spared a long lingering demise.

When I tell this story to young doctors they are amazed and also horrified and cannot believe I would have been so foolhardy. On the other hand perhaps today, a patient's home is safer from MRSA than any hospital.

Two And A Half

Occasionally there occurs a consultation which is difficult for unfortunately all the wrong reasons.

One afternoon the wife of a colleague came in and sat down with what I can only call a deeply distressed look. I knew her and her husband well but had seldom seen her unless it was with one of the children who were unwell.

After the usual pleasantries I inquired how I could help. She really was quite reticent to speak and I assumed that it was a slightly unusual problem she was presenting.

She looked at me with tears welling up in her eyes and an almost pleading look in her face.

As gently as I could I asked her to explain how I could help her, and eventually the story emerged.

It appeared her husband did not have much sexual interest, and almost totally neglected that side of the marriage. He would rather stay up late reading or writing and seldom came to bed at the same time as his wife.

"At our age," she said, "we should be having sex two and a half times a week, but we are lucky if it is two and a half in three months let alone every week."

That, I could understand would cause her frustration, but I was not prepared for what came next.

She had met a married man and he had shown all the kindness, consideration and attention that she was not receiving at home. Eventually of course, one thing led to another and she enjoyed their sexual liaison, which she was missing at home. They had managed to keep this very discreet and no one was aware of the relationship, especially her husband.

Why was she consulting me? Unfortunately, she developed genital herpes from a 'cold sore' which he had, and she presented the classical signs of 'kissing ulcers' of this condition.

Now there was one huge problem. She might pass this on to her husband on one of the rare occasions they had sex and all hell would break loose. This was a moral and ethical dilemma of major proportions. I could and did treat the herpes infection very vigorously but it almost always recurred and then the fun (or otherwise) would start.

Unfortunately, that was one problem she had to deal with herself.

Just Fill The Bottle!

It goes without saying that we are playing either at the furthest away location possible or it was an evening game away from home.

The players were out warming up under the watchful eye of the management, the kit man was checking the shirts necessary for the forthcoming game, the physios were taking a well-earned rest after a short but hectic spell of rubs, strappings and stretching.

There came a knock at the door and an official of the Scottish Premier League informed me that we were subject to a drugs test.

Saying nothing to the players on their return to the dressing room, the final team talk and exhortations were given and the game started.

At half-time after ensuring that no one required my attention I proceeded to the home team treatment room, doubling up as the Drug testing station, where out of a bag I drew 2 opposition player's numbers followed by 2 reserves. The home team doctor did likewise for our team.

15 minutes from the end of the game I was informed who the players were and that they would be directed to the 'Testing station' immediately after the end of the game.

A bottle was provided for the necessary specimen and the form filling, in triplicate of course, started. Any drug, prescribed or otherwise, over the counter preparations, food supplements had to be recorded. Dosage, frequency and duration of medication taken were noted.

The volume required is only 100mls which seems a relatively small amount but not after a hectic game when lots of perspiration is lost, even more so if the weather is warm.

Form filling complete we await the successful production of the necessary volume of urine. Drinks are produced, taps are run to try and stimulate the brain centre, but, often to no avail. A dribble here, a soupcon there edging towards the magic 100mls. More drinks are taken in an effort to increase flow.

This may be counterproductive as the specimen provided maybe too dilute with a specific gravity below a critical level and the whole process restarts.

Very occasionally the team bus has to leave and then arrangements made for transporting the players back home. 1 hour passes, 2 hours pass, 3 hours pass and still no specimen is available.

Just when everyone is getting a little fraught the player manages to produce the necessary amount in abundance and the bottles are filled and the complicated rigmarole of chain of custody of sealing the bottles starts.

Finally into the car provided to get the players home. En route there are multiple stops at service stations, behind bushes or when desperate out in the open at the roadside as the late effect of a vast ingestion of fluid manifests itself.

For all the trouble in taking and checking specimens, as far as I am aware there is no drug problems at present in Scottish Premier League Players.

A Question Of Wills

"I need him to play!" Not a request, but a statement! Only someone with total power and control could say this so forcibly as the manager.

The manager, yes a football club manager. He, who, can control his players waking time, eating, drinking, training, use of mobile phones, dress code and sleeping patterns. He, who can make or break a player's career. If they do not perform to his satisfaction they can be relegated to train with the youth team, be a substitute on the bench at some godforsaken minor club's pitch in the front of three men and a dog!

Now he tries to control the medical team and especially you as club doctor. The statement is made, the instruction is clear, he will brook no contra-arguments, "I need him to play!"

Now the battle commences. I know the player is only 80-90% fit and may well breakdown after either a few minutes or an hour. Medical sense makes clear, 'he should not play'.

Unfortunately, if he does start the game and has to come off after a short time, this is definitely the fault of the medical staff. If he manages to complete the whole game, or even better score the winning goal, then the manager is vindicated. 'I told you so," etc, etc!

Likewise, if he does not play and the team gets beaten then again the fault is the doctor's. If, he had played we would definitely have won. 'You have cost the club money, prestige, a place in Europe', it the equivalent of losing a general election.

Life is not easy, and the financial reward is miniscule compared to players (albeit inflated) wages.

Why do we do it? I suppose we love 'the beautiful game'.

Our Continental Cousins In Soccer

It seemed inevitable that they all appeared tanned, muscular and walked with the ease and swagger of an athlete.

Their dress, however, varied markedly. Those from Eastern Europe and especially from the former Russian dominated countries wore suits of inferior quality, which somehow never seemed to fit. This however, may change as the wealth of the new rich oligarchs take over some unfancied football club and pour in unlimited money and buy the best players available.

The western European countries in contrast had beautifully cut, well fitted, discreet club suits, which if nothing else appeared to give them superior attitude as they descended from the team coach.

There seemed to be an army of ancillary staff carrying, pulling or transporting huge bags with kits, water, stretchers, medical paraphernalia and nets with practice balls.

The Manager led the way exuding confidence and command as he strode into the stadium. He was leading a team which would conquer all, seemed to be his message. We are here to give you a footballing lesson, defeat was not an option.

Despite the mountain of kit carried, they always seemed to require some additional item; ice or on one occasion an additional fridge to store their bottled water.

They emerged from their dressing room for the warm up and proceeded to undertake a strict regime of exercises and running not usually seen in Scottish grounds.

Kick-off time approached and the tension increased palpably. The referee knocked on both dressing room doors and the players emerged. Somehow our opponents seemed even larger and more muscular as they lined up like gladiators entering the arena prepared for battle.

Come the hour, cometh the man as the contest began. Perhaps despite their appearance they were not supermen, but simply eleven footballers who could be vanquished.

Unfortunately, during the game we observed the not so nice side of foreign football. Shirt tugging, obstruction and just slightly late tackles, followed by the look of innocence and the quasi-apologetic gestures seen so commonly. Perhaps the more apparent antic was the dramatic fall when tackled, rolling over theatrically due to the 'pain'.

Where in Scotland the physio attends the injured player on the pitch, it seemed that a veritable posse of medical attendants were necessary. Two ran on the pitch and another hovered on the touchline ready to spring into action to ensure the player was able to continue.

There must be something special about the medical attention received as within a minute or two, the critically injured player was up and running without any apparent pain or disability. Truly impressive treatment or perhaps truly impressive acting! Do they attend Drama school as part of their training or is it inbred to such a degree that all players are past masters at acting dead or dying?

Whatever the cause it is not an edifying sight and smacks of cheating and deceit. However, it is something British players have to live with and learn to adapt to. Part of the steep learning curve of European football.

Without A Pause

What is it about an affected accent which is so false that it causes the teeth to clench so tightly it almost hurts?

The pitch, the intonation are such that it demands the audience, usually captive, to listen to a continuous diatribe which, on the surface, sounds good, but on analysis reveals little of substance.

It is, however, uttered with such apparent authority and a wonderful ability to continue without a break, despite the interruption of the listener. Careful use of breathing allows no break in the torrent of words, and, when there is some difficulty in maintaining the flow, then the use of 'eh', 'ah' or 'uh' in a prolonged fashion gives the speaker a chance to gather more energy to continue the ongoing assault on the eardrums of those who are within hearing range.

Unfortunately, there is a strident nature to the voice, the desired effect being to break through any other speech.

It has been observed that there is a remarkable ability to continue the tirade for 10-15 minutes, by which time any wish on behalf of the listener to contribute to the conversation will have been well and truly extinguished. No one except the strongest character could force their view to be heard. Even then the speaker continues without a break, not apparently listening to anything else being said.

Lastly, as mentioned above, the actual factual content of the words uttered is minimal and the expression 'talks a good talk' springs to mind. Rather like a politician who never answers the question posed, but simply gives the reply that he wishes, which of course is often totally irrelevant to what is being discussed.

You're Making A Mistake!

The discovery of oil in the North Sea in the 1970's led inevitably to an influx of American expertise from the Texas oilfields.

Many of our cousins from across the pond were pleasantly surprised by the warmth and welcome they received. Aberdeen was a totally new experience for many of them as they had not expected such a flourishing and wealthy economy as they found in the Granite City.

The visitors settled in quickly and integrated well with the local community. The restaurants and pubs did exceptionally well off the expense accounts, which were lavish in those early days.

One of the main attractions was of course the huge range of Scotch whiskies available. Malts and brands unheard of in the US became very popular and considerable quantities were consumed daily.

The taxi firms had a steady flow of passengers to convey home after a few 'libations' of the amber nectar.

Of course, there were always a few who risked driving when over the limit and there were inevitably loss of licences and fines imposed when the drivers were caught.

One of my patients, a larger than life senior oil engineer from Houston started work at 6am but compensated for his early start by having a 'Happy Hour' stop at his favourite hostelry on his way home at 6pm.

Often he took a taxi home but on occasions he used his own car. He was a bon viveur and sometimes had more than a modicum of refreshment. He quickly gained a reputation as someone who enjoyed life and especially at formal oil functions he sometimes required assistance to ensure his safe return home.

Around Christmas time there was the usual flurry of police activity for drink driving and one evening my patient, a little the worse for wear, was observed climbing into the front offside seat, to join his wife who was already seated in his car.

A few minutes later he was stopped by the police and after admitting he had been drinking he was breathalysed and this proving positive he was charged with drink driving.

He repeatedly stated to the police, "You are making a mistake," but they refused to listen and eventually the case came to court. He pleaded 'not guilty' and protested his innocence but the prosecution correctly maintained he was over the limit and pressed for a guilty conviction.

Defence counsel asked the police only one question. "Will you confirm on which side of the car the steering wheel was placed?"

Yes, this was a left hand drive car and his wife was the (sober) driver!

You Know Nothing!

She had that ability to appear very pleasant but was in actual fact a difficult, objectionable and quite dangerous, nasty, unmarried lady.

She had been a District Nurse in Glasgow and had been retired for many years but still thought she had the knowledge and even worse the conceit to question every test or treatment suggested by a doctor. In her eyes, doctors were inferior in every way, most especially intellectually. She knew better and who was a doctor to try to advise what was best for her!

Unfortunately, she suffered from rectal bleeding and required investigation. While in hospital she was found to have high blood pressure and started on treatment. This was the start of a battle royal. She was convinced she did not need treatment and even if she did, what had been prescribed, was wrong. Every single consultation started with a 'discussion' (!) about blood pressure and the treatments used 50 years ago (which were practically none), when she was queen of the Gorbals.

Every single anti-hypertensive drug caused side effects, and no one had ever suffered the side effects she suffered. Even worse, it was the doctor's fault for (a) having prescribed the drug and (b) having the audacity not to listen to her advice. She knew best (about everything) and she issued veiled threats about negligence and any other possible complaint against her GP (me).

She always appeared with a faint smile on her face and an almost meek look but gosh was she dangerous and unpleasant. Luckily for me she developed a gynaecological complaint and consulted one of my lady partners. I mean, a male doctor dealing with a female problem, that would be almost sacrilege. I did not know anything at best and a woman's problem was definitely out with my knowledge and remit.

Perhaps one of her worst features was to openly criticise doctors both to patients and other doctors and she was not above exaggerating the complaint.

Eventually she was referred to Medical out-patients and the whole cycle of blame, criticism and annoyance started again, but this time directed against the consultant and his junior staff. Indeed, the consultant evoked the 'shared care' concept and referred her back to us as soon as he could.

Luckily for me I managed to upset her in some unknown way and suffered from having my competence and ability slated to all and sundry. I was very glad she moved on, but I had to feel sorry for my partner who had to face this unpleasant lady approximately every two months.

Not A Good Start To The Day

It was my habit to arrive at the surgery around 7.45 each morning. I found it was less hassle in the traffic (avoiding the school rush and competing with mums in their 4X4's) and it allowed me to catch up with paperwork without the interruption of the phone.

One Monday morning I arrived at my usual time, opened the front door, picked up a letter on the floor addressed to myself, turned off the burglar alarm, and proceeded to my room. I opened up my computer and then, remembering the letter opened it and read the following message:

Please find me before my family.

The signature revealed a patient I had seen about a week ago and had referred her to hospital because of a suspicious breast lump.

The address was only 50 yards from the surgery in a block of superior flats across the road.

I decided to visit immediately and entered the building using the 'service button'. When I arrived at her flat, the door was closed but not locked. I rang the bell and opened the door, calling out 'doctor' as I usually did. There was no reply. I opened the bedroom door, then the living room and found both empty.

I next opened the bathroom and this revealed a sight I would not want to see again. My patient was lying dead in the bath, lying on the floor beside the bath was a shotgun, and on the wall and ceiling were the remains of her brains.

There was blood everywhere running down the walls and into the bath and obviously the back of her head was blown off. She had placed the shotgun in her mouth and pulled the trigger.

I retreated to the living room and there found a letter addressed to myself. She had seen the consultant who had confirmed cancer of the breast. It appeared her mother had had a dreadful death from the same condition and she could not face going through the same miserable end as her mother.

When I reviewed her records I noted I had been very positive that the outcome was good as she had found the lump early. There had been no delay in seeing the specialist but obviously this had proved too much for her.

I found this a salutary lesson thereafter, in spending time with patients who had 'red flag' symptoms. Despite the fact her mother had died 30 years ago the memory obviously was crystal clear in her memory.

Flying Saucers

They must have seemed like 'neighbours from hell'. On the surface they appeared a normal couple, but together and alone they fought like cats and dogs both verbally and in her case physically.

Their rows were frequent and noisy and the shouting could be heard from a long way off and the poor neighbours were demented by their behaviour.

I knew the couple well from the time they lived quite close to the surgery. They were forced to leave that area because of the trouble they caused, but, unfortunately from my point of view they remained within the practice boundary.

She had a long history of back pain, which she claimed was caused by her years of auxiliary nursing. Extensive investigation had failed to reveal any cause for the pain, but she took to her bed frequently, for days at a time, and demanded that her husband, who suffered from high blood pressure and angina, looked after her hand and foot.

She made his life impossible with her constant moaning and complaining. Whatever he did it did not please. She complained about his apparent lack of care of her. She claimed she required regular pain killing tablets and frequent back massage during the night, so the poor man got virtually no sleep.

If he did not comply, she shouted louder and louder and her language deteriorated with the frequent use of four letter words. If this did not succeed then she became physically violent, throwing objects and occasionally punching and slapping her husband.

Sometimes a house call was demanded by a worried or often angry neighbour, although, I was never clear, what a doctor was meant to do.

On arrival, however, everything appeared quiet and peaceful and she denied any problems. I did, however, see the results of flying dishes and bruises on her husband, and in private he admitted that his life was miserable, but for some reason he would not leave her.

I eventually referred her to a Psychiatrist and although she acted perfectly normally at the consultation, she was diagnosed as having a personality disorder. This was impossible to treat so she continued to shout, punch and slap and throw any available chine dish.

The whole story ended in a rather peculiar way. One day her

husband when going for the morning paper simply did not return home. He disappeared and no one knew where he had gone and to this day there has been no sign or sight of him. Probably he is living quietly and peacefully, thankful to be away from his warring wife.

The Know-all (or self styled expert)

The 'just listen to me' voice gives the clue. He and only he can explain the nuances and finer details of play. Even the simplest rule or activity requires elaborate explanation and usually given in the manner as from an adult to a five year old child.

The listeners' eyes may glaze over but the know-all drones on and on relentlessly. No detail is spared, the show must go on. Monotonously and ad nauseam the voice persists. The same point is repeated and repeated until the audience within earshot feel like screaming. The most mundane fact is worthy of an in depth analysis and explanation.

All this would be helpful, even entertaining, except for the small detail that many of the opinions given, with such authority, are not accurate. In such a case there is no point in correction, the 'expert' is unshakeable in his beliefs, otherwise he would not be the self-styled fount of all knowledge.

The Foreign Transfer

It must be difficult. Coming from a different ethos, a different climate, speaking a different tongue. English is a difficult enough language when spoken in classical Oxford mode, but when it is further mangled by a variety of accents and dialects, coupled with the liberal use of four lettered words as nouns, adjectives, verbs and even adverbs, makes understanding even more unintelligible.

The food is strange, with much more carbohydrate than protein and green vegetables. Much less use of olive oil and not a structured diet for sportsmen as he was used to.

Training is a minor disaster. Where is the custom-built training ground and academy with indoor pitch for bad weather and fully equipped gymnasium. A public park is not quite the same; the grass is bumpy, the wind bitter, the rain incessant.

Why did he come? He could be back home playing albeit for the reserve team in warm sunshine, smooth pitches and fellow players who speak the same language.

However, on the following Saturday he is on the bench against a team he has read of in the sports papers back home; one who frequently play in European cup competitions. For once the sun is shining and the game thrilling and from end to end.

Suddenly the manager beckons him and indicates he is going on as a substitute. The game is finely balanced at 1-1, as he touches hands with the substituted player and eagerly enters the combat field. After a few minutes he realises the game is much faster than back home. The physical challenges are tougher but the players do not roll about as if mortally injured after the merest tackle as some of his previous opponents did.

In the last minute as he drove forward from midfield the ball rebounded kindly for him from a defender's head, and without hesitation he hit it on the volley and it flew like an Exocet missile into the top corner.

Mobbed by his delighted team mates and feted by the manager and the TV pundits after the game, life has suddenly improved and perhaps this cold, strange city he had arrived in, really did have a warm heart.

The Footwear Tells It All

Even on holiday our medical training still functions albeit sometimes at a reduced level. We of course spend our lives observing patients.

Surely one of the most revealing features of a holiday-maker is the footwear.

New white trainers on middle to older aged man look stupid, unnatural and plainly embarrassing. The pristine condition, the pure white colour often with metallic 'flashes' looks so out of place, and obviously is not what is usually worn on his feet.

The fact that they are new means that they are hard and not moulded to the foot; inevitably they are accompanied by inappropriate dark or even worse safari type trousers with multiple pockets, which might look good in Chobe National Park or on the Okavanga Delta, but definitely out of place in a European hotel albeit off the coast of Africa.

Socks and sandals unfortunately conjure up pictures of the Englishman on holiday. Shorts usually baggy and resembling army surplus, which had seen better days. Or, even worse, short, too tight with a floral or garish pattern, which looked so uncomfortable as they cut into those tender parts of the anatomy.

Returning however, to the sandals; multiple straps, thick soles and so inelegant as to draw ones eyes to them instinctively. These are often worn by the serious walkers. They have soles which resemble the heavy duty tyres on a Chelsea tractor. They are designed for walking over rough terrain and the usual accoutrement is a walking pole. These individuals are lean and fit, and do not waste time on chilling out or relaxation. He is here for exercise, purpose and achievement; many boxes have to be ticked by the end of the holiday.

Then we have the polished brogue brigade. Despite the temperature being in the high 20s, the sun beating down remorselessly all day, the heavy usually brown pair is worn every day, rain or shine, for work or pleasure. Nothing will shake his belief that even in the height of summer this is not the correct foot apparel to adopt. Admittedly, worn with three-quarter stockings and smart khaki shorts they look wonderful. But not, if accompanied by shorts bought from Asda or Matalan with short socks pulled up or even worse folded over like a schoolgirl; not a pretty sight.

Lastly we have the experienced old hands. The battered comfortable footwear with sensible accessories marks the seasoned traveller.

Totally Unexpected

I believe she had not really wanted to be a doctor but she had been pressurised by her family in England to study medicine. She had come to Aberdeen Medical School and graduated two or three years ahead of me.

Her first resident post in a General Medical ward was remarkable for a rather unusual reason.

In those days before the advent of phlebotomists, the resident house doctor started early each morning by taking all the blood samples ordered by the consultants from the patients. It was the policy to start at one end of the long Nightingale wards and progress from patient to patient taking specimens as required. Virtually all patients had this done at some time during their stay in hospital.

The doctor was passing from bed to bed and chatting to each as she pricked their arm for the blood. Suddenly there was a commotion further down the ward and a window was flung open and a male patient jumped out.

Unfortunately, the ward was on the 4th floor and although he landed on grass, he fractured both legs. He had been so nervous about having a needle stuck in his arm that he had panicked and jumped out of the nearest window.

Obviously, this shook the young Resident and she decided there and then to terminate her residency. She did, however, find a job in a laboratory in the Medical School where she had no contact with patients.

Even this, however, caused her grief and heartbreak but she met and married a University lecturer and proceeded to have two children. She coped quite well when she had one child to look after, but the weeks after her second delivery was marred by severe puerperal depression. I treated her but she was so severely affected that I referred her to a Consultant Psychiatrist for his opinion.

He decided she should be admitted and took her into his ward for intensive treatment including Electro convulsive therapy. When this was explained to her she apparently agreed this was the best course of action. Everything was planned for the next morning and she went to bed as usual.

Unfortunately during the night she cut the femoral artery in her groin with a razor blade from her toilet bag and bled to death in bed unnoticed by anyone. A very sad ending for a very sad lady.

Those Little Red Spots

She was slim and elegant and beautifully dressed, with discreet expensive jewellery and a simple understated manner.

I had known her socially for some years but was rather surprised when her husband phoned and requested I see her for a private consultation. She apparently had been seen by her own GP and her husband was not too happy with the conclusion reached.

I hesitated somewhat before reluctantly agreeing. Evidently he had spoken to their GP who had advised them to get another opinion if they wished, and hence the phone call.

I arranged an appointment and she appeared on time looking as attractive as ever.

Her complaint was one of those vague but potentially difficult symptoms, namely tiredness. I took an extremely careful history then proceeded to a detailed examination. I really could not find anything very significant apart from some red spots on her abdomen.

Then came a minor bombshell. She did not want any blood tests taken and insisted that only if I had found something abnormal in my history and examination might she have consented.

Was she hiding something I wondered, and carefully reviewed my findings. I checked the red spots again this time very minutely and asked specifically about her alcohol intake. She bristled a little and played down any suggestion of excess.

I told her I did not quite believe her, as the Spider Naevi, as these spots were correctly called, were indicative of liver problems. After a long long interval she agreed she was drinking, secretively, to excess.

I had confirmed what her GP had found but neither she nor her husband wanted that diagnosis.

The Wrong Side Of The Tracks

Having medical records passed on from practice to practice can often have interesting spin-offs.

A lady consulted me about six weeks after joining our list. She was dressed in a rather ostentatious way, with 'heavy' gold jewellery hung on each wrist and round her neck.

Her accent was a little variable and seemed to slip in and out of control and was rather artificial but verging on the posh side with occasional lapses. Judging by her voice she seemed to hail from several different social classes simultaneously. Her general demeanour was of an apparently superior being with an extremely haughty manner.

She looked down her long nose at me when I asked what seemed to be wrong and that was a big mistake.

"That surely is for you to determine, if, you are any good at your job."

I inwardly smiled and said nothing. I was not so green or inexperienced to rise to the bait. She then complained of a rash which was extremely itchy and she had a very important dinner party coming up with wealthy clients of her husband.

I examined her and found the classical signs of scabies. I told her the diagnosis and was met by a torrent of abuse. She told me very forcibly that persons in her (upper) social class did not get such infections. She implied that her family were so superior that she would never be in a position to contract such a disgusting and dirty disease.

When I pointed out that scabies is no respecter of class or creed she bristled and informed me that I obviously knew nothing of the disease patterns in her type of family, because they were just short of aristocracy!

I had been glancing at her medical records during this tirade and mentioned that the area where she grew up was well outside our practice boundaries but that I was happy to look after her now she was in the neighbourhood.

I did not have to mention that where she was raised was definitely 'the wrong side of the tracks' and had a dreadful reputation for violence and deprivation. Nor quite the background she claimed to have, although I acknowledge she might have been the exception but somehow I think not.

The Wrong Colour

Inseparable twins and lively happy spinsters, they were popular with everyone and willingly fetched groceries for the older neighbours and looked after babies for young mothers. They were committed to their church and were active members in many groups.

Both were tiny ladies who always had broad smiles and laughed and joked continuously. They were both reasonably fit although high blood pressure ran in the family and a check had to be kept on their blood pressures.

Many gifts of sweets I received for my daughters when they were young and always at Christmas, there was a little gift to us all.

One day, however, I visited them dressed in a dark grey suit and after hurried discussion between the pair I was told, "Doctor, we don't like you in that colour of suit. You look much better in fawn or light colours!"

It was the first time I had been asked to dress in specific colours to visit a patient!

Unfortunately, there was a sad sequence. One twin suffered a massive stroke and was unconscious for a year. Her sister visited her every single day until she died.

The Water Carrier

No, not the well-known Constellation Aquarius, but everyone from very young schoolchildren to middle aged adults, although seldom the elderly.

Are they so concerned with dehydration that fluid replenishment is required every few minutes? Did they miss their second cup of tea or coffee at breakfast?

Clutching their plastic bottle full of, often, foreign 'mineral water' or carrying it tucked into a designer pouch in their bag, belt or briefcase they set forth, readily prepared for the day's activities, certain in the knowledge that their fluid balance will fulfil their metabolic needs.

Perhaps it is the health aspect that concerns them? The apparently beneficial effects of water on the skin, renal system or circulation? Unfortunately the plus points of this endeavour are often negated by the bag or polystyrene box of highly saturated fat, too much salt or other unmentionable E numbers or additives in the fast food takeaway.

The water is taken during train or bus travel, walking along the pavement, during lectures, at work, at school, indeed, at any time convenient to the drinker.

It is tempting to believe this is a fad, stimulated by the media and lavishly copied simply because it is in vogue. Did we in the past suffer from some dreadful preventable illnesses because we did not adhere to the present trend? Somehow, I think not and perhaps we saved ourselves a vast amount of money by drinking tap water instead of Perrier, Evian or Malvern or some expensive distillate which has trickled over volcanic ash for the last thousand years.

It is difficult somehow not to be a cynic or a disbeliever.

The Ward

26 patients scattered among several 4 bedded wards, very occasional 2 bedded and several single rooms usually reserved for the patients in the day or two after operation.

I was admitted to a 4 bedded unit with 2 or the other 3 beds occupied by post-op patients, in both cases knee replacements. They were friendly, talkative but I did not let on what I did till a Staff Nurse exclaimed 'Oh Doctor' and the secret was out. Quite pleasantly they probed their own histories and also mine. I was asked advice for many and varied medical problems and I foresaw a long and slightly awkward spell in hospital. Luckily a combination of my Consultant and my conversations being overheard led to a move into a single room and boy was I glad.

Like so many men I have a dread of the 'bedpan'. Ever since my student days when a maverick physician spent hours discussing the merits, demerits and general interest of their contents. Plus, there was the privacy, the personal en suite and just being on one's own.

The varieties of personnel showed a broad section of social class and mix, severe illness and mild illness, patients who coped and those who did not.

Of course, I should have been used to the above ménage during my years in medical practice, but suddenly I was part of that conglomerate making up a hospital ward.

Meal times were illuminating. Orders had been placed with the catering staff previously, who to be fair were nice, friendly and understanding. The plated meals were served around the table of 8, but no one waited till all were served; it was like pigs at a trough, or dogs at a dish. They attacked the food with the only weapons available, viz. knives and forks. Salt and occasionally pepper was loaded on to the food prior to tasting and some dishes must have tasted rather strangely of excess condiments.

Such niceties as not speaking with your mouth full, replacing the cutlery on the plate between mouthfuls, and the very common pen grip of the implements were standard.

Admittedly, when patients are in recovery phase, deep and thoughtful conversation come low on their priorities. However, the banal, pointless statements uttered, sometimes beggars belief. The pronouncements of the Daily Record, the Star, the Sunday Sport (now that's an interesting journalistic publication) are gospel; nothing can possibly contradict the banner headlines screaming out lurid details of C rated 'celebrities' latest sexual adventures. To realise that this earth shattering expose can be discussed for about 30 minutes puts the more important news, such as the financial crisis in Senior Citizens, MRSA outbreaks in hospital, concern about the disappearance of the ice cap into almost intellectual stratosphere.

All this makes mealtime conversation almost impossible apart from discussing the weather.

The Witness

The recorded delivery letter came tumbling through the letter box. 'You are required...'

Not what I wanted then or indeed at any time. A citation to appear at the Sheriff Court in connection with a medical examination I had done on a third party after he was involved in a road traffic accident.

I only dimly remembered the case as it was over 2 years since I had completed the examination.

I extracted the report from my computer and re-read my findings. Vaguely I remembered the gentleman in question. My first impression was of someone who seemed to exaggerate his ongoing symptoms. He had been unable to resume his employment for rather longer than I would have expected, but he was able to return to his leisure activities of golf, swimming and working out in the gym, and also managed to sit in a plane for the not inconsiderable flight time to Indonesia.

The physical findings were a trifle inconsistent and I made use of distraction techniques. These are a series of alternative examination methods which should give identical results to normal examination findings. Unfortunately in his case there were quite widespread discrepancies and thankfully I had noted these in my report.

At the end of the consultation he had limped out of the consulting room and exited the Surgery front door, unaware I was observing him, and his limp magically disappeared as he climbed into his car, parked of course in a disabled bay, and driven off.

Not surprisingly his solicitor wrote a critical letter disputing some facts in my report, but I stuck to my guns and did not alter anything. I reiterated that I always repeated the history given to me to the patient and confirmed that this was accurate.

As the day of the trial grew nearer I hoped and prayed that the case would be settled out of court, but no such luck. I arranged for a Locum Tenens for my days off the Practice; cancelled my teaching sessions at the University Medical School and spent hours learning all the possible complications of his accident. I surmised which difficult questions about his ongoing symptoms might be put to me by some smart court lawyer wishing to demonstrate his superior knowledge over the medical witness.

At the appointed hour I presented myself at the appropriate court. I sat and sat until quite by accident a patient, also a lawyer enquired which case I was waiting for. I explained and he disappeared into the court. A few minutes later he reappeared and advised me my case had been settled out of court 3 days previously!

I took great delight in writing a scathing letter to the Pursuer's Solicitors and enclosing a substantial bill for my 30 minutes non-appearance in court.

The Voice

Apart from the obvious advantages of a single room, one great benefit is that it is not necessary to meet other patients at meal times.

Without ever having set eyes on the gentleman, I have already built up a profile of someone, who, I do not think I would enjoy meeting.

The said person is, at present, only a voice, but even an intangible connection has bad connotations. The tone is strident, the accent coarse, the emphasis forceful. He overlords the rest of the dining and sitting rooms, and his, is the dominant voice emanating.

The booming voice sets out his opinion on no matter which subject is being discussed, although 'discussion' is rather a loose word in his company, as any free transfer of ideas is strictly frowned upon unless it coincides completely with his lofty pronouncement.

Judging by the lack of other voices expressing any opinion, he has obviously browbeaten his companions into accepting his vision of the matter in question.

If I continue to improve, and I am able to take my meals at the communal dining room table, and, he is still an inpatient in the ward, then we may become debating adversaries in the future.

Having time to think tactics if this should occur, I think a total blanket of silence from myself may be my chosen option. It is easier not to express any opinion than to get myself upset by someone who is obviously an ignorant self-opinionated man.

The Specimen

It is part of a doctor's life to collect 'specimens'. These may be of varied types and produced in an incredible variety of containers.

Specimens of urine with the most dreadful smell and colour from almost black, through cloudy, smoky, orange or crystal clear. They appear in perfume bottles, milk bottles, lemonade bottles, and whisky bottles both miniature and normal size and many more.

These are the easy ones; what about the sputum, the faeces or the vaginal discharges. I guarantee nothing would put a smoker off continuing to puff cigarettes than to examine the products the mucus of a smoker with an infection.

Even worse for those who 'take the risk' sexually whilst abroad in Thailand, Majorca or even UK, especially when 'under the influence', and end up sleeping with someone unknown, is to observe the genital inflammation and discharge of some of these ladies. I am sure this would put them off casual sex for ever.

Specimens from dysentery or other diarrhoeal illnesses may have the foulest smell and appearance and I certainly had one Consultant who, as part of his teaching of medical students, conducted a 'bedpan' round and groups of students would observe, smell and poke the products of various patients' bowel movements first thing in the morning. Enough to put anyone off their breakfast or lunch.

Everyone thinks being a GP is glamorous but certain aspects of the examination of 'specimens' would change their vision totally.

The Sharp End Of The Needle

It is a huge shock to the system when as a member of the medical profession you find yourself at the 'sharp end of the needle'. I found myself in such a position when I required a total hip replacement for osteoarthritis.

I underwent the examinations, the X-rays without any problems and then the letter arrived for the date of my admission.

One week prior to this date I attended the preadmission assessment. Along with other patients who were to be admitted for operation, we had our medical history taken, examination by a junior doctor, bloods and ECG's performed by a nurse, then X-rays if required. The OT and physiotherapist explained their role and finally the pharmacist noted which drugs we were taking. It was all well orchestrated and completed in 2-3 hours. Thus everything was set up for admission the following week.

I duly presented myself to the ward at the appointed hour and was allocated a bed, and the admission process in the ward slipped into gear. There seemed to be so much duplication and paperwork that I wondered how any nursing was done.

An arrow was drawn on the correct leg requiring operation, and some young doctors demonstrated their hidden talent for artistic impression.

The anaesthetist explained what would happen the next day, and ensured that I had no allergies, and tried to allay my anxieties.

Early the next morning I shaved and showered, donned my theatre gown (a real passion killer), and lay on top of my bed awaiting transfer to theatre.

The operating theatre staff and a nurse took me along long draughty corridors to the theatre, the staff checking my identity, (several times), the assistant anaesthetist inserted a rather large needle, quite painfully into the back of my hand and within seconds I was in the Land of Nod. I knew nothing until I came to in the recovery room, several hours later.

The first thing I noticed was the profusion of needles and intravenous tubes in various veins and arteries. Clear fluid flowed into one drip, intravenous analgesia into another and others left unused presumably for drugs or suchlike.

Coupled with all this was the pain of the operated leg, and an inability to keep awake. I drifted in and out of sleep as nurses regularly checked my pulse, temperature and blood pressure. It seemed that I just managed to fall asleep when they returned to check me again.

Some hours later came the first crisis, I needed the loo. I rang my buzzer and in due course a nurse appeared, and on learning of my need proffered a 'bottle' made of reinforced cardboard, and told me to use that.

Now there is something about lying in a bed and trying to use this receptacle. I had a total mental block between my brain and my urinary system. There was absolutely no way I could 'perform'. I tried to force the issue but the more I tried the worse it got. I was getting perilously close to having a catheter inserted and this was the last thing I wanted.

I pleaded to be allowed out of bed to try and succeed. This was met by shock and horror. It being only 6 hours since my operation and this was completely forbidden, no, no, no. I pleaded even more and finally the staff nurse relented.

So here was I standing on my good leg, balancing on a Zimmer frame, one nurse holding my drip, another directing my private part towards the wretched bottle. However, after a few moments, success; everything flowed freely and I almost filled the bottle, or so it seemed, and the relief was great.

I was sworn to secrecy by the nursing staff. This episode never happened. If I revealed all, there would be hell to pay. Their life, and mine, would be a misery. So, it is only now, some years later I have revealed my secret. Many thanks nurses, you rescued me in time.

The Shakes

I suppose as in so many cases in medicine retrospective hindsight is a wonderful thing. This was a couple I did not know well as the wife came to see me quite infrequently and then only for fairly minor illness. Her husband I knew even less well as he was a fit elderly gentleman.

Unfortunately, quite out of the blue he developed a stroke, which was not too serious but it certainly prevented him from leaving home unless he was accompanied, and driving was completely out of the question.

Even worse was to follow as she slipped on the path and sustained a Colles fracture of the wrist. They did, however, cope reasonably well for a week or two then a request for a house call was made.

I visited and discovered a beautiful home full of wonderful souvenirs and furniture from foreign countries. They had owned a licenced grocer and done very well and travelled widely abroad in the days before foreign travel became popular.

Her main complaint was of a tremor so severe that she could not cook and this coupled with her broken wrist made household duties very difficult.

"Who will get our groceries?" she moaned, "there is no one to help."

I discovered that the fridge and freezer were both stacked full of food so I could not understand their worry. I offered to help if there was something special they needed and discovered the cause of their dismay.

It appeared that they required to top up their wine supply. Only, it was not wine they drank, but brandy, and indeed they consumed a case of brandy every week. She had managed to drive and obtain the necessary supplies until she had broken her wrist and the brandy ran out.

And the cause of the tremor – it was my first but certainly not my last, example of the DT's!

The Sewing Box

She was reading the French edition of Paris Match at the age of 93 and alternated this with the German version just to keep her languages up to scratch! This should have been enough to warn me how next to handle the consultation to follow.

I was obliged by government regulations to carry out 'an over 75 assessment' each year on those patients in that age group. One of the mental tests was known as serial 7s, i.e. subtracting 7 from 100 and then 7 from the remainder and so on.

When I requested her to do this she looked at me in astonishment. After at least 30 seconds she rapidly uttered 100, 93, 86, 79, 72, 65, etc without pausing for breath!

The next question was: "Who is the present and last Prime Minister?" Without hesitation, she named each and every one back till 1940.

She paused then looked me straight in the eye. "I have never been so humiliated in my life, do you think I am senile?"

I rapidly apologised and blamed the present government for submitting patients to these tests. When she discovered my feelings about the Prime Minister of the time, she relaxed and opened her sewing box.

Not knowing what next to expect, she produced a bottle of Chivas Regal Whisky and two glasses. "Doctor," she said, "let us drink a toast to good health and happiness and to a change in government!"

The Room

Not quite as gruesome as the John Grisham novel, *The Chamber*. Hopefully in this case the ending will be happier and no shrunken body has to be carried out wrapped in a white sheet.

Thankfully, the area of living space is somewhat better, and, in death row, Grisham makes much of restrictive size. Here, although slightly crowded with all the paraphernalia of surgery there is room to move.

Grisham's toilet facilities were crude in the extreme, but here I have a very adequate shower, albeit with a fairly poor flow, a flushing W.C. and ample rails to grab if necessary.

Some privacy is ensured by a sliding door, but it is quite amazing how modesty and embarrassment, totally disappear when it comes to being given whatever help is necessary for your own benefit and progress towards recovery; a luxury never available in that inexorable progression towards demise.

On the subject of basic body functions, and especially in the post-operative period, there appear, those two charming crushed and reinforced cardboard containers – the 'bottle' and the 'bedpan'.

I am not certain if a study has ever been carried out as to the stress, anxiety and anguish these objects cause. Perhaps some final year student or even better a retired doctor (? GP) could obtain views and opinions in this, which surely is of critical importance. I can see an MD thesis looming.

The window, of reasonable size, overlooked an internal hospital road, but unfortunately the general public had discovered it to be a very effective 'short cut' between two parts of the city. This, not surprisingly, led to boy racers revving up late at night and disturbing the patient's sleep. Grisham's view was of course over cotton fields in wall-to-wall sunshine and blistering heat during the summer followed by very cold nights and torrential winter rains. OK, the temperature in the room might not be quite to everyone's liking, but it is comfortable.

I have deliberately left till well into my narrative, those persons in uniform at the other side of those restrictive obstacles which hinder free flowing movement from one area to another. I am not saying there is an inability to move, but certain confines are unfortunately in place to deter this, which may lead to anger and frustration.

In one group are those who because of mental, physical or general infirmity cannot, however willing they try, traverse those seemingly impossible hurdles. Thankfully, most conquer the foe and progress, onwards and upwards thereafter.

The Retirement Home

Sitting together in their usual chairs, they chatted happily. Discussing their families, especially the grandchildren whose names they cannot remember accurately and whose birthdays are largely forgotten. The fact they have exactly the same conversation every day was immaterial.

The retired Major who still dressed as nattily as in his Army days, hair neatly parted, shoes gleaming. His memory however, revolved round his army adventures in Malaya, Kenya, Aden and Germany. Despite the fact he had been in a desk job all his career and never faced the heat of battle did not prevent him from giving the impression that he had saved the British Empire from collapse. The fact that he could not remember what he had for lunch did not detract him.

There was the retired physician who, every morning, conducted a 'ward round' of his fellow companions, and stood by the end of each bed and pronounced which treatment should be prescribed.

A lady who could only be called a professional patient, whose hospital notes were too bulky to be carried without a trolley, and who conjured up wonderful symptoms not found between the cover of even the most learned textbook. She made the staff's life a misery as they were almost obliged to request a visit every time she complained of a new and potentially serious symptom. What made it worse was that she was mentally alert but still required nursing attention. She was the epitome of the 'heart sink patient'.

I had never been aware of the hierarchy in certain religious orders. However, the first occasion I visited a retired but senior clergyman I was amazed by how he expected those below him to jump to his every need. He did indeed expect me also to comply and was quite taken aback when I did not conform. It was a classic case of 'do you know who I am'?

Having observed his behaviour towards those attending him, made me more determined not to kow-tow to his demands. Suddenly his commands were being questioned and he did not like it one bit. I stood my ground however, and in turn explained quite forcibly that I was in charge of his medical condition and no matter how much he hectored and shouted, it would not make the slightest difference.

Eventually after one or two difficult and even unpleasant consultations he relented although there was always a certain chill in the air when we met.

In contrast, there was the retired professor, whose physical ailments (and they were many) finally caught up with him, and he required too much nursing care for his wife to cope with. His mind was sharp as a tack, his demeanour delightful, his complaints non-existent and his popularity high.

Visiting him was often the highlight of my day /week / month. Entertaining and humorous he made light of his not inconsiderable multiple illnesses and of course this was reflected in the way the staff treated him. A truly charming man and whom I considered an honour to have met and attended.

Visiting a Retirement Home was often an eye-opening and revealing experience.

The Post Mortem

No, not the opening chapter of a Patricia Cornwell novel involving Dr Scarpetta the Forensic Pathologist. This is the occasion after a football match when the manager gives vent to his feelings and thoughts about the game.

This is not for the faint-hearted; the language is expressive, vivid and usually rude, crude and often nasty, delivered with a venom, which would blister the paint on the dressing room walls and would make a marine blanch.

There is a fearful atmosphere as everyone takes his seat. The physio and occasionally the doctor scurry about treating injuries and various players are clutching ice packs on ankles, knees or groins. No one dares to start stripping off their kit.

Then the onslaught begins. Every misdirected pass, cross, shot, missed tackle or wrong positioning is recounted, criticised and blame apportioned. Excuses are not tolerated or accepted; it was your fault and you will accept responsibility. The implication being that your mistake cost us the game.

The combination and repetition of swear words and imprecations are incredible. We all know all the words, but the recurring phrases, with four letter words used as nouns, adjectives, verbs and even adverbs is mind-boggling.

This may destroy some players, especially younger members of the team, cause indifference in many who allow the tirade to wash over them, and perhaps motivate a few but possibly fewer than the management thinks.

The non-players also in the dressing room shrink to their smallest possible size and try to appear inconspicuous as gratuitous insults and unpleasant home truths hit home.

But, how effective is this exercise? Does it really influence the next performance? I somehow doubt if it does. Perhaps a one to one discussion might be more beneficial. However, will this ever change? Somehow I think not and this may be part of the 'psyche' of football managers. Perhaps a Sport's Psychologist would be able to analyse the behaviour, but even such a professional may be flummoxed.

The New Motor Cycle

He had been so proud of his new Harley Davidson, gleaming black paintwork and shining chrome. His new wife was not as enthralled as she would rather have had a car for the money, but she accepted his new toy as some reward for his recent promotion in the oil company he worked for.

Not many days later, his mother-in-law requested a house call for her daughter.

When I arrived, everyone seemed to be crying and tearful and it was only with difficulty I extracted the story.

Her husband and her brother had gone 'for a spin' with the new bike and unfortunately he had failed to negotiate a sharp corner due to his speed and he had been flung over a fence and into a wall and broken his neck and both legs. He was in intensive care, unconscious and critically ill.

His brother-in-law had been less fortunate. He had been thrown against a newly erected barbed wire fence, with such force that he was literally minced flesh and bits of bone scattered across the ploughed field.

I was unfortunately left to pick up the pieces in a completely devastated family.

The Medals

He really was a pathetic patient who always complained and seemed incapable of coping with even the most minor illness without drama.

He had requested a house call for some trivial reason and it was with bad grace that I visited.

On entering the house, he was in the bathroom and asked me to wait in the living room. He seemed to take ages in the toilet so I wandered around the room looking at his pictures on the wall. In one corner was a small glass covered casket containing two medals.

Closed examination revealed these to be a Military Cross and a Distinguished Service Order medal, both awarded to my patient in the First World War.

I reversed my opinion of the gentleman very quickly as anyone who received these awards for gallantry must have been very special.

The Manager

He is god or the nearest thing to him. He is the boss. Whatever decision has to be made, he makes it. Control of the players is total. Racial equality and sexual discrimination are unheard of. Woe betide the player who summoned the help or advice of these two bodies. He might win his case but he would never play football again. He would win the battle but lose the war.

The way a team, plays, eats, dresses and lives is controlled by the manager. Truly a position of power.

A good manager does of course listen to those around him. The assistant manager has a large contribution to make. The physio should be, and usually listened to, but some managers override their advice.

The doctor's opinion again is usually heeded, but pressure, sometimes subtle, sometimes blatant is occasionally brought to bear, to play a player, not fully fit if the manager wants it.

Confidential medical facts and findings are often given to the media, and it is only a matter of time before a player will sue the doctor (not the manager) for disclosure of information, which might be detrimental to the player's career in subsequent years.

A successful manager makes money, wins accolades and popularity. Everyone wants to shake his hand, speak to him, get his autograph, have a photo taken with him, He can do no wrong in the punters' eyes, life is good. He is feted wherever he goes, and doors, hitherto locked and barred, open miraculously for him. 'Jump' and the query is 'how high?' and many people jump very high.

But, when the team starts losing, the goals dry up, and there is an inexorable slide towards the foot of the table, and relegation looms, then things change and often very quickly. The supporters (or so-called supporters) get on the manager's back and the call 'give us a wave' is replaced by booing and shouts of 'get out'.

The chairman then publically backs the manager and that effectively is the kiss of death. He might as well clear his desk and negotiate his cash settlement, for he will not be there much longer.

The silver lining of course is that despite perhaps being a failure, he gets a handsome golden handshake. He does not have to immediately rush to the Job Centre for his giro to buy a crust for his family. He merely sits tight and waits for the phone call from another club and the whole cycle repeats itself.

The Lonely Widow

She was a tiny lady with a waspish tongue and really not the nicest person to know. She was widowed and seldom left her small flat, spending most of her time reading the broad sheet newspapers.

House calls inevitably ended with her complaining bitterly about the cost of living, the profligation of the government and the detrimental effect this had on her standard of living.

Admittedly her flat was not too luxurious but she seemed unwilling, or unable, to alter this. She ate very frugally and her clothes although neat and tidy were well worn and had seen many winters.

She did not go on holiday and judging by the paucity of Christmas cards she did not seem to have many friends and apparently no close relatives. In essence she seemed a lonely, rather miserable, rather unfriendly old lady.

It appeared I was her only regular visitor as I visited her every 2-3 months to monitor her quite severe heart failure due to aortic valvular disease. In those days heart surgery was in its infancy and she was definitely not a candidate for operation. Admittedly, today this would be much more amenable to surgical intervention.

However, she read her newspapers assiduously from cover to cover, missing nothing and including the crosswords. She did not possess a TV, which she thought was socially diversive.

I attempted to make my house calls as short as possible as they were not enjoyable and any happy feelings were quickly dissipated after a few minutes in her company. She epitomised the 'my glass is half-empty rather than half-full' sentiment which of course contributed to her social isolation.

One day I received a request for an urgent home visit but when I arrived at the house, all the doors were locked. I obtained the help of the police and we broke into the flat. There she was, still in bed, and quite dead. Her heart failure had eventually caught up with her.

The police meantime were sifting through her papers trying to find evidence of any relative or her solicitor's name. One officer then made the strange remark: "I hope you are in her will, doctor!" He had come across a financial statement from her accountant for tax purposes and this little lady was worth well over a million pounds. Evidently, she had spent her days playing the stock market with obviously great success.

I did indeed receive something in her will – a 1920's Doulton figurine – called 'June' – which still adorns our mantelpiece.

The Cook With The Cleaver

The ship was 42,000 tons and too large to berth in Aberdeen harbour. I received the call via two-way radio from the ship to state that there was a problem on board as the cook had gone berserk with a meat cleaver.

The pilot boat, all 42 feet long, took me alongside the ship which was proceeding slow ahead through Aberdeen Bay. The Pilot boat was bobbing up and down as I stood on the gunwale and attempted to catch and climb the rope ladder dangling from the ship's side.

With difficulty I climbed up trying to keep above the waves, which threatened to wash me away. Reaching the top I retrieved my medical bag and was shown my patient.

His eyes were wild and bulging with malice and anger but thankfully the crew had managed to put him into a straitjacket, but he could still kick, spit and bite and there was the small problem of getting him overboard and down a rope ladder while still wearing his straitjacket!

It was decided to lower him over the side while I guided his feet into the rungs of the rope ladder and goodness knows how I agreed to that scenario. I was in grave danger of getting my head kicked in but we managed to get him onboard the pilot boat despite these difficulties.

Never was I so glad as to see the lights of Aberdeen Harbour and the waiting ambulance, which whisked him away to The Royal Cornhill Hospital – the local mental institution.

My fee for this escapade was a miserly £15!

The Convent

The novice nun opened the door in response to me ringing the bell. This was my first visit to a Convent and I was not sure what to expect. "Please have a seat and I will fetch Mother."

I was shown into a waiting room with polished linoleum, two hard upright chairs and the lid of a tin presumably as an ashtray.

The reason I was there was in response to a call stating that one of my patients had become ill while visiting the nuns which she apparently did quite frequently. I sat on one of the chairs and waited.

Suddenly the door burst open and there stood a tiny round faced happy nun. "Dr Gray thank you for coming." This I gathered was Mother Superior.

She sat down beside me and said in a rich Irish brogue, "I'm afraid your patient is not very well! She's had far too much gin and is drunk out of her mind. We have filled her full of black coffee and walked her up and down the corridors but to no avail so we thought we should get some higher help."

Well I thought no beating about the bush or pretending she had some dreadful illness and I admired the honesty shown.

My patient when I examined her was definitely the worse for wear with alcohol so I requested a couple of nuns to assist me in taking her home in my car and we would put her to bed. We bundled her into the car with difficulty and drove the relatively short distance to her home, a large house in the west end of the city.

Once inside we found there were no sheets on her bed so we searched the cupboards and on opening one we found every shelf laden with bottles of Gordon's gin! Quite nonplussed the nuns found some sheets in another cupboard.

She was undressed and placed in the bed and the nuns kindly stayed with her for some time and I proceeded to another call.

My impressions of the Catholic Church certainly rose after this experience.

The Collection

His home would have been a delight to anyone from Sotheby's, Christies or the Antiques Road Show. Never have I seen so many exquisite antiques in one place. There were delicate porcelain figures and plates, first edition books and pieces of jewellery and pictures by some well and some not so well-known artists.

I never did discover how he had amassed such a magnificent collection, but obviously it had taken a long time, a lot of money and lots of patience.

He was a bachelor and a milder, meeker and delightful man you could never meet. Not long after I knew him, his sister, recently widowed, had moved in. She fussed around him like a mother hen and pampered and cosseted him and especially with regards to his health. The slightest upper respiratory sniffle and he was packed off to bed and a demand for an immediate house call made.

He himself did not have the strength of character to stand up for himself, and he was completely dominated by his elder sister. She herself was not a patient and I knew little of her background or of her late husband, but I suspect he might have been similar to his brother-in-law.

Gentle guidance as to the necessity of house calls for simple self-limiting illnesses was met with stout resistance and occasionally with lightly veiled threats if her demands were not met.

Inevitably her attitude meant that no doctor wanted to visit, as his sister harangued and harried and complained and moaned. All this of course rebounded on our poor patient, as he suffered for his sister's behaviour.

Previous to her arrival it had been a pleasure to visit him and admire and discuss his beloved snuff boxes, silver thimbles and spoons each of which he could give a full history and description.

When his sister descended on him, and I am not certain if he invited her, or she simply made the decision herself, but his gentle cloistered way of life was shattered. He withdrew into himself more and more, and it was almost impossible to engage him in conversation.

Always his sister hovered in the background, ready to intervene with a barbed comment or criticism about his medical care, and one of my young female assistants was quite traumatised by the experience.

He was literally fading away in front of us as he almost seemed to lose the will to live, when, quite suddenly, his sister collapsed with a cerebral haemorrhage and died 48 hours later.

He, to some degree, almost blamed himself for her demise, but I pointed out that this was something which could not be predicted and that she had not suffered.

He took a little time to recover but gradually he regained his confidence. He, once again, enjoyed his wonderful collection of beautiful objet d'art and he lived happily for many years.

When he died he presented some of his antiques to a museum and some to his favourite charity. Thankfully others were able to enjoy what he had enjoyed for many years, something which would have pleased him enormously.

The Briefcase

He was well dressed in a dark blue suit, polished black shoes, discreet tie and carrying a briefcase. He was a new patient to the practice and had asked for his repeat prescription but I thought it important to meet him and discuss his medication.

He smiled pleasantly as I enquired how long he had been taking the requested tablets, as normally, these were drugs given for short periods only, both having marked addictive properties.

He prevaricated and asked if there was a problem in continuing the medication and when I hesitated he bent down and picked up his briefcase. Opening it, he placed on my desk a bottle of well-known single malt, and a bottle of liqueur whisky.

I stared in amazement at this obvious bribe and still remained silent. It then appeared that his previous GP had accepted the bottles in exchange for ongoing prescriptions and he thought the same arrangement would continue.

He was the senior representative of a well-known whisky firm and a constant supply of alcohol was not a problem. Unfortunately for him, a constant supply of the drugs he wished was a problem.

He gathered up his bottles, stomped out of my room, slammed the door and I learned later he had left the practice.

I have since then tasted the brand of whisky he had proffered and the malt really was very very nice!

The Alternate Answer

The epitome of Joyce Grenfell's song 'Stately as a galleon', she swept across the floor, into my consulting room. Larger than life, flowing dress with a bold pattern, she greeted me effusively like an overpowering aunt speaking to an unsuspecting nephew.

"Now," she said, "my body is out of balance and equilibrium, you must assist me in correcting this."

She then listed all the treatments she had received recently, from energy giving crystals to the food supplements she required for her multiple trace element deficiencies, interspersed with advice from weighty tombs on alternate medical practice, the titles of which meant absolutely nothing to me.

Conventional medicine had apparently no place to play in the maintenance of her health, until a crisis such as this arose and she reluctantly sought her GP's advice, and I was her listed doctor.

Taking a history was a nightmare as she only admitted to those symptoms which she thought were important. She then compounded this by making her own interpretation of these and also the treatment she had decided she required. Unfortunately this treatment defied the principles of accepted Materia Medica.

Her extroverted manner meant it was difficult to get a word in edgeways and consultation took an eternity followed by interminable discussion's which of course centred round her internal imbalances.

Occasionally after examination and investigations I was able to suggest treatment which might help and thereafter I was able to bring the consultation to a close (until the next time).

The net effect was one exhausted GP and one only semi-satisfied patient. Truly a challenge for any doctor especially one newly qualified and who I feared might be totally overwhelmed and never recover.

Someone Lost Their Head

Every lunchtime I attended the football club for a consulting room session to deal with injuries and illness and if necessary refer players to appropriate consultants.

Each Wednesday our attached Consultant Orthopaedic Surgeon visited to examine any players with orthopaedic problems which of course are the commonest injuries affecting footballers especially of the knee and hip.

The injured players would assemble around noon, his usual time of arrival, prior to lunch, and our physiotherapists and myself would be in attendance.

He was a tall extroverted gentleman who was popular with the players as he was inevitably straight and honest and did not suffer fools gladly. Coupled to that he was an excellent surgeon who had a great reputation and high success rate in dealing with typical football injuries.

On one occasion all were assembled waiting for the great man; 12.30 came and went as did 1 o'clock and 1.30 and everyone was becoming a little fraught with the delay.

Finally he arrived; a little dishevelled having driven from the hospital where he had been operating, which was about 30 miles from town, at great speed to keep his appointment at the football club.

He then proceeded to explain his late arrival. He had finished operating in plenty of time to arrive as usual at 12.00, when, whilst exiting the hospital gates, an accident occurred when a motorcyclist travelling at great speed northwards had crossed the central reservation and collided with a car containing an elderly couple driving southwards.

Of course he had to attend the accident although there was little he could do, as all were fatally injured. The motorcyclist has hit the car windscreen and killed both driver and passenger before he exited the car through the back window and ended up 50 yards from the collision.

He had of course to certify death and allow the emergency services to deal with the obvious carnage and vehicle wreckage.

And the cause of the delay? The driver was decapitated by the force of the motorcyclist as he crashed though the windscreen and no one could find his head. After much searching it was found below the driver's seat having obviously bounced off the back seat before coming to rest out of sight of all.

No one felt much like eating that day although the surgeon and myself, perhaps made of stronger stuff, enjoyed a late lunch of tasty stew.

Sherry En Frappe

Born in 1900 she lived in a huge house, one of three in line built by her father. In the garden a stream cascaded from pool to pool and in each were golden bass protected from predator birds by caves. Opposite were the gravestones of her numerous Skye Terriers.

Inside were the models of famous sailing ships her family had built and also many antique articles from those ships. The porcelain was delicate and rare, having come from China and the Far East and she had the most beautiful silver trays and tea sets from the 17th and 18th centuries.

My patient was a gentlewoman from a bygone era with remarkable style and elegance and visiting her was always a pleasure.

On that extremely warm summer day when I visited her companion, who was ill, she was sitting on the patio and asked me to join her. It was my last call and I had plenty of time to talk. She was a most interesting lady telling wonderful stories about her family who sailed to Australia, a journey taking nine months in those days.

She offered me a sherry and produced two large glasses, which I learned later were George IV, filled with ice, and a decanter of sherry. She told me her father had drunk sherry en frappe back in the nineteen twenties. I suppose they were lucky to be able to produce ice in those days but it was interesting that sherry on ice was being actively promoted on TV.

This was only one of many surprises I got with this delightful lady whose family bequeathed many wonderful things to the city of Aberdeen, lasting memorials to this day.

Seen From Any Angle

The house was in one of Aberdeen's wealthiest and most sought after streets there being a North variety and a South variety.

The call was to a young married lady aged about 25 years. Apparently, she was so unwell that she was confined to bed.

The front door was ajar when I rang the doorbell so I entered and called as I usually do 'doctor'. A voice asked me to proceed upstairs, which I did to the master bedroom on the first floor.

Most doctors are familiar with bedrooms as these are one of the commonest rooms we visit on house calls but the sight, which greeted me, was a little unusual. The patient, who could only be described as voluptuous, was wearing a tiny wispy white nightdress and lying on black silk sheets.

She indicated that I should sit on a chair beside the bed and I did so.

All during the history and examination, I was aware that there was something else unusual about the bedroom apart from the black sheets.

Casually looking around I noticed that two sides of the room had floor to ceiling mirrors but most surprisingly the ceiling was a wall-to-wall mirror also!!

Saving For My Rainy Day

She lived in a large semi-detached house in the west end of Aberdeen. Her late husband had a very successful and excellently remunerative occupation and when he passed on at a relatively early age, he left her in a very secure financial position.

She did not call us very frequently, but I was asked, one December day to call, by the Health Visitor who was a little concerned about her general health.

Getting into the house proved a little difficult as she religiously kept her newspapers in neatly stacked piles along the corridors of her house and over the years these had grown to a prodigious number.

Entering her living room revealed a tiny black and white television dating from the 1950s and one glowing bar of a pathetically small electric fire which barely raised the temperature of the room above freezing.

On questioning her about her health I was struck by her lack of reality regarding warmth and comfort. I suggested that she increased the heating by turning on all the bars of her heater but this was met by stiff resistance.

"I am having to save for my old age and a rainy day," she told me. Initially this was quite comical as she was aged 80 and I felt her 'rainy day' had come.

Through a little judicious and perhaps slightly unethical questioning I discovered who her solicitor was. It transpired I had been about 3 years ahead of him at school and so I decided to call him after I left my patient.

"Can she afford better heating and perhaps a more modern TV?" I asked. "I am sure it would improve her quality of life."

There was a pause and I felt I had breached ethical guidelines. Then came the reply.

"She could afford to spend £20,000 a year of her capital for the next 20 years and still have a very comfortable income."

So between us we devised a plan. We bought a new colour TV, hired a cleaning lady, who disposed of all the newspapers, installed gas heating and a simple microwave and appropriate meals and very surprisingly she accepted everything and had a wonderful last few years of life.

She became almost addicted to Game shows and Countdown and

simply loved Richard Whitely.

She never really suspected how the transformation occurred but she did once accuse me of having some part in the change.

She still left a huge amount of money to charity and a very small legacy to her lawyer and GP.

The Flying Stone

Struggling into my survival suit at the heliport, I wondered exactly how I would enjoy my first helicopter trip. I had always viewed the flight of a 'copter as akin to a flying stone'.

Being relatively of short stature I did not find the space too cramped, but it was noisy despite earplugs, and the regular shadow of the rotor blades made reading almost impossible.

When the rig came into view it appeared like a dot in the ocean and it seemed impossible that the plane could land there. But land we did, safely but stiff and tired. On the helideck the wind snatched and tore at our clothes as we struggled to the edge, the sea churning and lashing the legs of the rig 150 feet below.

I was shown to my cabin and prepared for work. I was there to examine all the crew from one company for their annual medical examination. Over the course of three days 100 men would pass through the examination room; hard work but financially worth the effort.

Breakfast the first morning was an experience. As I stood in one I upset the chef somewhat by declining steaks, chips and fried eggs, opting for coffee and toast only.

"Come on doc, don't you like our cooking?"

I of course had not just finished an exhausting 6 hour shift on the rig and my activities were only beginning.

That first day on board I was lucky to observe the rare sight of a completely mirror sea reflecting the clouds and the sky like land and inland loch. But this was the calm before the storm. The next day blasted in with low scudding clouds, driving rain and howling wind. I was enormously grateful to be snug inside doing my medical examinations and not being on the drilling floor.

The storm grew more intense as the day wore on and the rig began to sway ominously. There was a gauge and when it reached 8° from the vertical it was time to abandon ship. We watched and waited as the rig tilted nearer and nearer the critical mark. None of us fancied a helicopter ride in that gale and indeed a 'copter' went down a few weeks earlier in a similar situation when making only a 150 yard trip from one rig to another.

Nerves were taut and I would be less than honest if I did not admit to a fair degree of anxiety. Luckily the storm blew over and the next morning was all calm.

After that, every trip to the rigs reminded me of my first and most dramatic encounter with the North Sea oil fields.

A Wonder Drug

He limped slowly into the consulting room and lowered himself gingerly into a chair. His face grimaced with pain as he requested more painkillers for his excruciating back pain, which despite treatment had been present for more than a year.

Pills, physiotherapy and an orthopaedic opinion had not managed to control the agony which was devastating his life! He could not walk, climb stairs and certainly not accept remunerative employment.

He berated the medical profession for its failure to cure him and insisted on a medical certificate for incapacity to work for at least another 6 months. He also demanded to know which immunisations he required for Phuket. It would appear his backache would not prelude him from a 12-hour flight, but I bit my tongue and said nothing, his attitude always left me with a sour taste but today I was quite annoyed by his aggressive manner.

Over the next few days I forgot about the incident but a chance meeting a few days later brought the consultation vividly back to mind.

I was driving along the far end of George Street where we have very few patients, when, there he was, balancing on top of a ladder, cleaning shop windows.

I stopped and took great pleasure standing at the foot of the ladder and calling to him.

"These new tablets must be wonderful; you have made a miraculous recovery."

He almost fell off the ladder as I waved gaily to him as I drove off. I did not see him again for a very long time.

May I Leave?

Every time I read a Patricia Cornwall novel I remember my first and short lived experience of Forensic Medicine.

One of my partners who was assistant Police Doctor unfortunately became ill and his senior colleague asked if I would deputise whenever two doctors were required at a forensic post mortem.

Promptly at 9am one cold December day, the duty police constable and I assembled outside the morgue where two post-mortems were scheduled.

I had of course experienced post-mortems during my medical school course in pathology but nothing quite prepared me for what was to follow.

I had watched dissections of hospital patients who had either died undiagnosed or perhaps there was an uncertainty as to the extent of the disease. These patients had been clerked after admission and investigated prior to death.

Our patient today had been found behind a dyke in the country near Inverurie and he had been covered with snow and laying invisible for at least three weeks. When the snow melted, a farmer found him and reported the matter to the police. At this point I noticed the young constable seemed a little nervous. He admitted that this was a totally new experience for him and he did not know exactly what to expect. The body was lying on the table under a sheet and we waited for the Senior Police Surgeon to start the proceedings. The inspection preliminaries over, i.e. noting and measuring scars, bruises cuts, etc, the examination proceeded. The first cut was made in the chest and abdomen and caused a dreadfully smelling odour to assault our nasal organs. Worse was to follow. Inside the abdominal cavity were hundreds of wriggling white maggots; they were everywhere. At this point the police constable gagged and stammered, "Please may I leave?" he dashed from the room with the most ghastly almost green complexion.

I must say, it took lots of will power and self-control to remain for the duration of the examination.

My 'Friends' The Pressmen

"Now doctor, just tell me exactly what the injuries are, and how long he will be out for." A common opening line from the sports journalists. I use that term advisedly, especially in my young, innocent, days as the club doctor, but thankfully not now.

Only once or twice did I give diagnosis and prognosis to the press. When I realised that this was really none of their business, I refused to issue medical details, but I was harassed and almost threatened.

'It is in the public interest', I was told, and 'You must tell us'.

Still I refused and the conversations and phone calls became more heated. Finally, to one very persistent tabloid reporter, whose allegiances lay far more strongly in the Central Belt for Scotland, and most specially with the Govan team for Glasgow and I don't mean Patrick Thistle, I requested he carried out an anatomically impossible task on himself and slammed down the phone.

I was quoted on that occasion as 'having no comment' but that put a stop to face-to-face dealings with the press.

However, worse was to follow, I discovered that the management and even some players were quite happy to give out medical details. I managed to reduce the activity by telling management when asked about a player's injury or illness to tell them he got VD. The reply came back. "But that's confidential I can't say that!"

"A groin strain is confidential," I replied – end of problem.

The Mobile Phone Call

I hate mobile phones! They are intrusive and liable to ring at precisely the wrong moment. Patients are meant to switch off their mobile phones when they enter the practice. During consultation there is nothing more annoying than their phones ringing and interrupting the consultation. I was halfway through a consultation with a 40-year-old patient when her phone rang. She answered and much to my annoyance, she did not ask the caller to ring back or suggest that she would return the call. She listened and did not speak very much, except for the few 'ah', 'oh' or 'I see' and after about 3 minutes she ended the call.

She sat with a vacant look on her face and tears silently rolled down her face.

"Bad news?" I asked, but she did not immediately reply.

Slowly turning to me she said, "That was my husband, he is or supposed to be golfing with the boys, he is, however, away with his secretary in Malaga and he is not coming home. He is leaving me and filing for divorce!"

As expected the rest of the consultation was difficult as she spent most of her time weeping and wringing her hands.

This made me hate mobile phones even more.

Every Time A New Experience

Late September when the fruits of the cold December nights come to fruition and I was in my final year of Medical School. It was time for midwifery and the practical part of our obstetrics course; something you either loved or hated.

We lived in and were on call day and night to deliver babies and each of us had to deliver twelve. We took it in rotation and had to be prepared to stay up all night if necessary. Eventually it was my turn and I was assigned to a Mrs A from Peterhead. I introduced myself and checked the medical records. This was her third baby so at least one of us knew something about it. Her contractions were a little erratic so the birth was not quite imminent.

I chatted to my patient, periodically checked the contractions and monitored the baby's heartbeat. The midwife popped her head in every so often to check that all was well.

That evening the labour ward was extremely busy. Babies were popping out in every room and everyone was involved apart from me. Nothing seemed to be happening and I was rapidly running out of small talk.

Suddenly everything changed. Mrs A's contractions became more frequent and stronger. Then she said the words I dreaded, "I'm starting, and I'm coming!"

Then the difference between theory and practice became apparent, reading how to deliver a baby and suddenly having to deliver one were worlds apart.

I whipped back the sheet and examined the abdomen, the contractions were long and strong, the baby was coming.

Desperately I called the midwife but everyone was busy. Panic gripped me, think, think, keep calm, I said to myself, desperately attending to Mrs A.

Head crowning, head coming, head delivered, pull gently down, one shoulder out, and gently deliver the rest of the baby. At this point a voice at my shoulder said, "Well done, now clamp cord, cut cord, stimulate baby." The infant, a boy, cried lustily so all was well. "Quick check, then give him to mother."

I turned to sister, "How long have you been here?"

"Just a few minutes, you seemed to be coping well, so I left you to get on with it."

Thank you very much, I thought. I was panicking from fear and inexperience and you left me.

Then Mrs A spoke. "That was my easiest and best delivery, thank you doctor." Then the question I did not want to hear, "How many babies have you delivered?"

Fearful of saying this was my very first, I prevaricated. "Each delivery and birth is a new experience, I don't keep count!"

Understood By All Races

It was Easter weekend and the weather was glorious in the Burgundy region of France. The game was the under 19 International between France and Wales.

Play was fast and furious and flowed from end to end. The Welsh had fought back from 27-6 down to level at 27 all and were pressing for a winning score camped on the French line.

Quite out of the blue and well away from the play the French right winger (who was later to become a full International) suddenly 'collapsed' near the touchline. The whole episode smacked of a tactical injury. He was writhing on the ground apparently in great agony but there seemed very little wrong medically.

"Levez vous monsieur," I suggested but the writhing and groaning continued.

"Get up," I ordered but still he lay prostrate.

Bending over him so that no one could overhear I whispered in basic Anglo-Saxon vocabulary to get to his feet.

His response was instant, "Oui monsieur." He stood up, his injury apparently miraculously cured!

The Mistake

I had made a mistake. This was evident from the voice on the phone.

"Where is Dr Gray, I expected him to call yesterday!"

This was a patient I had visited 3 days earlier and promised to revisit yesterday. For some reason, perhaps involving the pretty final year student whose attachment to the practice had only started that day. I had forgotten to enter it into my diary.

The lady in question was not the most patient at the best of times and was one of these ladies who expected everyone to jump (and also to jump as high as she wanted) whenever she demanded!

I warned the student that the consultation might be rather stormy as we set off to visit her at home; but I thought it would be an opportunity to demonstrate the art of General Practice.

I parked the car and rang her doorbell. The apologetic face with literally steam coming from her ears would have scared the strongest of men. She took a big breath, but before she could speak, I said, "Mrs B I owe you a sincere apology. I promised to visit you yesterday but for some unknown reason I omitted to write the call in my diary. It is my fault entirely and please accept my humblest apologies."

The change in my patient was as swift as remarkable. "I understand completely doctor, you must have been very busy yesterday. Please come in."

She was in fact much better but I promised to visit 3 days hence to make absolutely certain that she had totally recovered and on this occasion I made certain that I did not forget that call.

Dietary Indiscretion

One of the most enjoyable parts of General Practice I found was the Well baby clinic. This was for immunisations, weighing, feeding problems and periodic screening. I undertook this clinic along with a health visitor and it was always busy, enjoyable and occasionally entertaining.

One morning towards the end of the clinic, a rather anxious mother appeared with her twins who were by this time a few months old and had just started weaning. They were developing normally, height, weight and immunisations all normal as expected.

However, mum was rather agitated to say the least. "You must help me," she said as she sat down with a very worried expression.

I glanced at the twins, then glanced again looking more carefully and then observed them in greater detail.

This was something I have never seen during my paediatric training or my experience in a medical practice. The twins were orange in colour. Not jaundiced, not red, not sunburned but normal Caucasian children with orange skin.

They were happy and appeared perfectly healthy apart from their skin. Wow, I thought, what is going on here? I examined them very carefully and I could not find any abnormality in them.

Then I had a brainwave. "What have you been feeding the twins?" I asked.

"Just normal milk, and fruit and vegetables," she told me.

"Which vegetables?" I asked. "Not carrots by any chance?"

"Yes," was the reply. "I thought it was good for them to have plenty of vegetables so I give them carrots every meal."

This was the cause of the skin colour. Mum had fed them so many carrots that it was appearing in the skin. These children were bound to see in the dark!

Not exactly one of the commonest problems encountered in paediatric practice.

(The twins returned completely back to normal, when the carrot intake was reduced.)

Embarrassment

She had just reached forty and her two girls were teenagers. She was small and neat with a pretty face although when she consulted me she looked rather sad.

Taking her history it was obvious she was depressed. I asked about her sleep pattern, her appetite, her interests, and her energy all of which may assist in reaching a diagnosis. Another question asked is about her libido.

Her answer was a little surprising.

"I know we should be making love regularly each week. I should love to attain that, but my husband (a professional man) would happily not have sex at all except for birthdays and occasionally on holiday." Then an even more amazing statement.

"I am thinking of encouraging a colleague who seems attracted to me. Perhaps he will fulfil my need? Are you shocked?"

I found it difficult to reply honestly.

7 Stitches

This was a big, big game for the club. The semi-final of the Scottish cup after a disappointing season in the league. It was a filthy day of pouring rain, a muddy pitch and a tight game.

Halfway through the second half, leading 1-0 against Rangers, and two of our substitutes already used, our talismatic centre half went down after a head clash.

Davie, our physio, ran on and then led the player off holding a wad of gauze to a large gash on his forehead just at the hairline.

Now the quandary, do we put on out last substitute – a forward – or pitch up our centre half?

I raced to the dressing room with my medical colleague in tow, followed by the player and the physio. While I ripped open a stitch pack, Davie liberally splashed saline on the wound to clean it. I injected local anaesthetic and my colleague started stitching. I cut the sutures, David prepared a dressing, and one, to three... seven sutures inserted, dressing on, player back on the pitch, total time 3 minutes!!

We won 1-0.

The Count

He really was the most miserable specimen of man, small; thick horn rimmed spectacles and surprising aggressive manner. He worked as a clerk in a lawyer's office and almost acted like a lawyer. He had a 19-year-old girlfriend or fiancée, I am not exactly sure which. She was the most attractive young lady with a neat figure and pretty smile and a manner quite the opposite of his. I could not fathom how she became attached to him.

One day they consulted me together and the problem was of her inability to become pregnant. They were not married but had been trying for a baby about one year.

I did advise that one year was not an abnormal time for the pregnancy to occur but he in his usual aggressive manner demanded that she be investigated.

I carefully explained that both need basic investigations as it might be one or either who require treatment.

I took a full history and examined them both and then advised him to have a sperm count analysis and I carried out random blood tests on her. At this, he flew into a rage and demanded that only she must be checked, as it must be her fault. I refused to undertake any further tests until he provided a specimen of semen. He point-blankly refused so there was an impasse. I suspect he was worried that he might be the culprit...

She became quite distressed about the whole situation but he still prevaricated and prevaricated for weeks and weeks.

However, one day he appeared and he admitted he was prepared to have this test and I supplied him with the necessary specimen jar and instructions how and where to take the sample. I advised him to make an appointment to see me in a week's time.

He duly appeared, very downhearted and morose and not his usual nasty manner. It appeared his girlfriend had left him for someone else after his unwillingness to be tested. (Personally, I feel it may have been the excuse she was looking for.)

And his specimen? It was one of the highest levels I have ever encountered!

Recognition

Every doctor knows how difficult and embarrassing it is not to recognise a patient out of the consulting room, or to forget their name when face-to-face especially someone who has recently consulted you.

I am always anxious I will meet a patient when I'm with my wife in some store like M&S and am unable to introduce her as I have forgotten the patient's name.

My wife now knows that it I have made the introductions within about 30 seconds that I am struggling and she promptly introduces herself. Recently I was in surgery when a new patient consulted me. Her face was very familiar but I could not place where I had seen her.

"Have we met previously?" I asked.

"No," was her reply and still I pondered.

"Your face is very familiar," I said.

"Perhaps because I appear on your local TV station," she said.

I then wanted a hole to swallow me up!

A Sorry End

I had seen him frequently over the years from about the age of 5 when his family joined the practice. He was a frequent attendee as he suffered from recurrent chest infections and he was a thin scrap of a boy with a typical peeri-wally look. Things improved however, and he did reasonably well at school and left with some qualifications and went to college and obtained a diploma in accountancy and secured a job in an oil related service company office.

A year or two passed then he attended with vague ill health after many consultations with myself and my partners, it emerged he was taking illegal drugs. At first, there were only 'recreational' drugs which mistakenly are thought to be quite harmless but in reality, as in this case, led to a progression to heavier and more addictive heroin and cocaine.

For a while he managed to control the amount and frequency of his habit and indeed got married and his wife had a little boy who was the apple of his dad's eye.

Disaster was, however, around the corner and he lost his job due to frequent absences due to unfortunately, to an escalation of his heroin intake.

He sought help and after a long, painful and difficult period he managed, with our help to carry through a methadone reduction programme and finally kick the habit. He left the surgery happier than I had seen him for a long time and I congratulated myself and my partners for the success in helping him finally get his life back on track.

However, this story did not have a happy end. He returned to his flat, in a multi-storey block at the other side of town to find that his wife had left him and taken his son with her. The note she wrote and left on the kitchen table said that she had met someone else and she could not put up with his drug habit any longer. She would not be coming back and he would never find her or see his son again.

This was a devastating blow to him and obviously he could not cope with the news. He opened the living room window and jumped from the 16th floor to the concrete path below.

Truly a sad end to what seemed a good day for us and our patient.

Try A Different Position

She was a large lady, a psychologist by profession, but also the bearer of many medical problems and quite a few psychosexual hang-ups. Prior to becoming my patient she had extensive investigations for many gynaecological problems, and now she presented a history of infertility.

As mentioned she was large, weighing about 26 stones (that being the maximum weight my scales could measure). There appeared to be no problems with her husband's fertility but she did admit to anatomical difficulties during coitus!

Not surprising I thought and offered the advice that perhaps a different position during intercourse might help.

"What position would that be doctor?" she enquired, "perhaps you could demonstrate it to me more fully!"

At this point my nerve failed me so I suggested that she buy the book 'The Joys of Sex' and perhaps experiment.

She was not too happy at that but promised to try and then stated, "If this is not successful we will be back for some more practical advice!"

I do not know the outcome of this saga as they moved country and changed practices.

The Disappearing Willy

He was a regular attendee at the surgery, usually with weird and unusual symptoms. He was, however, not too willing to take any medication or other treatment but spent all his time worrying that he had some serious illness.

It was the state of his teeth that caused most concern. He was terrified of the dentist although he had once managed to finally sit in the chair he steadfastly refused to allow any treatment; indeed, he hardly consented to an examination of his dreadful caries.

He frequently consulted me and with difficulty I was usually able to convince him he was not going to die that day, he departed a little calmer which would last a few days.

One summer afternoon just before the surgery closed he dashed in and demanded an immediate appointment. He was very agitated and sweating profusely.

I agreed to see him and resigned myself to a long consultation, which was going to delay my golf match that evening!

"I thought you were supposed to be on holiday in France," I exclaimed.

"Well yes," he replied, "but I could not go."

Then the story emerged. He, his wife and two boys had driven almost to the outskirts of London when he visited the toilet in a motorway service station. There to his chagrin and despair he convinced himself that his 'willy' was shrinking inside him and almost disappearing from view. In sheer terror and desperation he about turned and drove all the way back to Aberdeen and made straight for my surgery.

On examination, however, I was able to convince him that everything was absolutely normal and that he had not lost his manhood and that his genital functions would perform as normal.

Every time he consults me, I remember this story and smile inwardly, although he had never mentioned that emergency consultation.

The Experts

They really were the experts. Any claim or benefit, which required an encyclopaedic knowledge of the Social Security regulations, they could quote chapter and verse.

He was a long time unemployed building trade worker (labourer) who suffered, he claimed, from crippling arthritis, due to working (?) in cold damp conditions.

Unfortunately, although he used elbow crutches, which certainly helped to keep him upright when he had had too many Carlsberg Specials, exhaustive medical tests revealed no arthritis or indeed any cause for his periods of sudden unconsciousness.

His wife was mentally disabled apparently after pertussis vaccination, given in infancy, but she had an amazing natural wit and cunning and was not as foolish as she made out.

Neither had a great predilection for soap and water and their clothes were seldom without food stains, and an air freshener was needed after every consultation.

Their home reflected themselves – and overgrown garden complete with rusty Lada, (they could not persuade the Town Council to tend it for them) – a filthy house with foot sticking carpets, two dogs, one the inevitable German Shepherd and a lovely looking but vicious collie. An open cage housed a dirty yellow budgie. They both smoked heavily and the walls and ceilings were stained brown and the atmosphere was foul.

Dealing with them was a nightmare, but after many years of lawlessness, he was convicted and sentenced to a year in prison. She was ejected from the house and luckily moved out of the area much to everyone's relief.

The Streaky Mascara

The five o'clock shadow somehow spoiled the appearance in the blue dress and white high-heeled shoes.

No, it was not a hirsute female, but one of the few transvestites I have encountered in my professional career.

He/she was a pathetic figure, shoulders hunched, head down staring at his feet, and sitting on the edge of the chair wringing his hands – the classic picture of depression.

Gently I asked him his problem and the tears left mascara streaks down both cheeks; he was inconsolable.

Depressed he certainly was, but the cause was surprising. His partner, a very nice boy, called Simon had left him, because as he put it, "I can't manage anymore!"

So, for the first time ever a depressed, impotent, transvestite – not an everyday occurrence, consulted me.

Quite A Lady!

I suppose I came quite late into the life of the elderly patient who had been in the practice for only a few days. Her medical records were not available prior to my first contact with her, which was an emergency visit for acute heart failure.

Fairly vigorous treatment was required for her condition but she responded beautifully and I was able to keep her at home with new medication.

She was a pleasant if garrulous lady with a certain old-fashioned grace and style. Her manner was perhaps, however, a little 'uppity' and she gave the impression she should be treated as someone special.

I visited her regularly for a few days and arranged for an out-patient consultant cardiological appointment. She demanded to go privately, which surprised me a little as her home or clothes did not suggest too much spare cash.

She had been a patient of a neighbouring practice but had apparently had a disagreement with her regular GP and I was not certain if the change of GP was suggested or if she decided herself to move practices. In those days it was easier to 'score off' patients and also much easier to join a new practice without too many questions, if the patient wished. She continued to exercise that air of superiority and hinted that she had really come from a wealthy, socially superior family.

She saw the Cardiologist who confirmed Aortic valvular disease and advised her to continue with her present treatment.

Around that time, her records were received from her previous GP and very extensive they were.

I decided I should familiarise myself with her past medical history and settled down with a heavy heart to plough my way through many hospital letters and hand written General Practice notes.

What I discovered surprised me somewhat. She had had a very chequered career. Before the first of her three marriages, she had been what could only be described as a 'high class call girl'.

In between marriages she had developed a fondness for Scotland's amber nectar and her liver had obviously been heavily assaulted although she did not appear to have reached the stage of cirrhosis. There were, however, descriptions of typical Delirium Tremens (DT's) with anxiety, sweating, tremor and vivid and terrifying visual hallucinations, leading to hospital admissions to be dried out.

Her second marriage was to an older man who was a born again Christian, whom she met at Alcoholics Anonymous and who persuaded her to give up the alcohol and involve herself with the church.

Unfortunately this monastic existence of regular church attendance and the change from her previous lifestyle proved too much for her and she divorced him and for some months she literally disappeared and certainly did not require medical attention.

She then, it appears, met a male friend from schooldays and he rapidly became husband number 3. Unfortunately, he also liked the liquid refreshment and it would appear that their intake became heavier and heavier, until one evening, while holidaying in a remote highland cottage, he haemorrhaged from a peptic ulcer and died before medical help arrived.

When she consulted me again I wondered if she suspected I had found out about her earlier life, or realised where her money had come from, but she still acted in a superior and lofty manner.

Playing Away From Home!

Our football players are role models even although they are not superstars. Inevitably if they step out of line then the media certainly make the most of their error of judgement. Not for them the privacy and anonymity of the man in the street. The headlines scream out lurid details designed to attract attention.

I received a phone call from one player who had been transferred to another club, and who had unfortunately picked up an infection and he asked for some antibiotics, which he had had previously. He was coming back home that weekend, so could he get a prescription for the drugs? He had not yet registered with another GP and I prescribed medication and left it at the surgery for him to pick up and thought nothing more about it.

The next thing I knew about it was headlines in a tabloid paper along the lines 'Love cheat' or 'Caught playing away from home'. The papers revealed that his wife had picked up a STD and claimed her husband had contacted the disease from another woman.

I felt a little embarrassed that I had prescribed drugs for what obviously was a sexually transmitted disease not having questioned him more fully. His wife was not a patient of mine and I had not known that she had not travelled with him to his new club, but had remained at home.

Somehow I felt his career was taking a downward turn and the media certainly did not help.

Peace Not Guaranteed

Just how, can anyone sleep, but sleep they do, and that included me.

I never realised how loud and strident a female voice could be, but it appeared and sounded like a meeting of fish wives all speaking at once. This was the sound emanating from the female side ward and just exactly why they had to chatter and gossip so late at night when sleep was beckoning, amazed me.

The cacophony of sound emitting from various beds was breathtaking both in variety and volume. Snoring, snorting, wheezing, grunting; all were present in varying intensity and persistence. Sometimes it seemed as if the whole ward was reverberating and echoing. Adding to this was the creaking of the beds as the occupants tossed and turned, accompanied occasionally by groans and moans.

As expected, visits to the loo were necessary and the tip-tap of the zimmer frame or squeaks of the crutch ferrules was evident as progress was slowly made to the little boy's room. Then the flush of the toilet and the occasional inconsiderate banging of the door on completion of the toilet.

Returning to bed was amazingly noisy. The walking aids clattered against the bed frame and the monkey frame creaked as entry to bed was accomplished.

Then peace, for a short time as least, but the ward clock could clearly be heard, ticking away continuously, time not standing still for any man. Suddenly the peace was broken, as the piercing ring of an alarm from a completed intravenous drip, rang through the ward. On and on it went till eventually a nurse turned it off and silence ensued again. As if that was not enough a gentleman with sleep apnoea disorder repeatedly set off his warning bell and again the noise shattered the peace.

Somehow, however, we all got some sleep, one or two more than others. A long lie was precluded as of course everything starts very early in the ward activities. The bustle and clatter of a new day made certain of this. Patients are being prepared for theatre; drugs are being issued and routine measurements of pulse, BP and temperature taken; all part and parcel of a day in the life of a hospital patient.

Of course, those lucky souls in a single room are denied this experience, and blissfully pass the night safe in the arms of Morpheus.

Passing Thoughts

As senior medical students we spent long hours in the wards clerking, examining, and discussing patients who were admitted to the ward. We would often still be present in the early hours of the morning if 'our' ward was on call for emergency admissions. This was often where the most useful experiences were learned as the registrars, senior registrars and even consultants would conduct impromptu teaching sessions on patients admitted.

One such consultant was always keen to teach and after examining the patient, discussion often took place over tea and toast in the resident's room as to the examination, possible investigations and management of the case. When you were in a one to one or two to one situation with the consultant there was no place to hide but it made you think on your feet and justify your suggestions.

Once the initial fear of being put firmly on the spot disappeared these sessions were most enjoyable and worthwhile and much useful knowledge, some of which I have to this day was tucked into the grey cells of the brain.

One morning those 8-9 students who were attached to the medical wards were being taught by the very consultant whose teaching I had experienced in the early hours of the morning having not got to bed till about 5 a.m.

Thinking we would be examining and discussing those patients who had been admitted the previous day I was confident about my diagnosis and investigations and was ready to display my 'superior' knowledge to my peers.

However, this was not to be. The consultant who was perhaps a bit of a maverick when it came to teaching decided not to enter the ward but directed the students to follow him to the sluice room where the tutorial would be carried out.

On entry there laid before us, were about 15 bedpans filled with the bowel movements of patients in the ward. Yes, we were experiencing a 'bedpan' round.

Each of us in turn had to examine a fresh specimen and explain the abnormal findings, if any.

If the contents of the pan were particularly interesting then each and every one had to make a more detailed examination by viewing it, smelling it and occasionally prodding it with a spatula.

The room was small and rather crowded and the odour was pervading and getting worse by the minute. As it neared lunch time the thought of food was the last thing on our minds; fresh air was what we needed.

At last we were dismissed, my dreams of intellectual glory gone. I do not think I will ever forget my first bedpan round.

On Traffic Duty

There is never a good time to have your first epileptic fit, but when it happened to my policeman patient it was unfortunate to say the least.

He was on duty at the busy Tollcross junction in Glasgow during the late afternoon rush hour. Everything was proceeding smoothly despite the very heavy traffic. Suddenly this all changed and he directed traffic to come from all directions at once. This of course, caused the most almighty snarl up.

Everything was chaos and during this time, he suffered a full major epileptic seizure. Of course, an ambulance was called to the scene, but it also became enmeshed in the traffic despite siren blaring and blue lights flashing.

Horns tooted, drivers became very angry, and as a scene resembling the traffic jams in the film, *The Italian Job* ensued.

Despite the fact that this happened more than 25 years ago, there were probably many cases of the modern equivalent of 'road rage'.

Not Too Little, Too Late, But Too Much Too Soon

"My son is very sick, he is vomiting all the time, he is unsteady on his feet, please come quickly." I was unable to obtain further details apart from the address, as the phone was put down immediately.

When I arrived, I did indeed find my patient bent over the toilet vomiting profusely; his parents looking on anxiously.

When at last he stopped, I helped him to his bed. He was very unsteady on his feet and looked ghastly.

I ascertained that when his parents had welcomed their next-door neighbours in for a Christmas drink he had been lying in his bed watching TV. His parents had proceeded on to supper after a drink or two and his father had called upstairs and checked that all was well.

An hour or so later the guests had departed and then the fun started. He literally staggered from his bedroom and thereafter retching was heard from the bathroom followed by violent vomiting. It was then that I was called.

After questioning him alone and examining him I made quite an easy diagnosis, helped by discovering the empty wine bottle under the bed. Whilst his parents were entertaining downstairs he was quietly consuming a bottle of rather nice Merlot which he had 'acquired' from the wine rack in the dining room.

Unfortunately one whole bottle drunk in a couple of hours was rather too much for an eleven-year-old boy. And gosh was he unwell later with his first but probably not his last hangover.

Not Quite A Lady

First impressions on meeting someone new are often correct but sometimes can be widely wrong.

When my Senior Partner retired and I took over his list (at that time I was an Assistant), I quickly discovered that certain patients would definitely not be consulting me, some were happy to attend me and most were quite indifferent to the change.

I received the most charming letter from a lady who flattered me by stating she had heard good things about me and that she would be delighted to consult me. She elaborated how little she required a GP and that her needs were minimal. All this was written on heavy vellum paper using a fountain pen and immaculate copperplate script. Duly impressed, I looked forward to meeting this patient who was obviously living in a bygone era.

Over the ensuing few months I dealt with spasmodic requests for some analgesic tablets which she took for her 'rheumatism'. After some time I felt I should meet this lady rather than continue to dish out medication, and I requested her to make an appointment. Evidently she responded to my request by being quite shirty on the phone to the receptionist, muttering how unnecessary this was.

When I admitted the thin, quite haughty but strangely elegant lady dressed in a rather old-fashioned style, with a hat similar to that worn by Mary Poppins in the film, I felt I was being transported back in time to the Edwardian era.

She extended a bony hand wearing lace gloves and wished me 'good day'.

I invited her to sit down and tell me about her rheumatic aches and pains, but she ignored this and immediately informed me she had been a close personal friend of the original founder of the practice (now long since dead) and she should be treated accordingly. She would of course not be expected to wait for an appointment and if it was more convenient to her she would demand a house call at a time which suited her. In her working life she had some tenuous connection with the University and of course it went without saying that she was on first name terms with the Principal and senior professors and that somehow gave her carte blanche to any medical services she required.

She informed me quite forcibly that her attendance at the surgery was quite unnecessary. I obviously knew nothing about medicine and how to handle patients. Even more pointedly she warned me she would be keeping an eye on me and any indiscretion no matter how slight would result in a letter to the GMC and of course she knew several of the committee intimately.

I sat back in amazement as this tirade was thrown at me and thought that this has resulted from a simple request to review her medication; what would it be like if it was really important. Now came the difficult bit. How did I handle things now? I decided to make a stand or else I would be in an impossible position. Very pleasantly but quite forcibly I explained how things had changed. I told her that her threatening behaviour was quite unacceptable and any evidence as such would result in her immediate removal from our list. My hand was strengthened here by the fact that she lived outside the established practice boundary and I was entitled to ask her to leave.

Over the years I attended her we never really had a great rapport and I never warmed to her. She continued to act in a manner above her station as Gilbert and Sullivan would have said. Her airs and graces were so phoney that no one took any notice.

Her parting shot in our relationship was spitefulness itself. She requested a house call and when I arrived she gleefully told me she was leaving me and had joined another GP. He evidently was expected soon so I could leave right away.

Rather naughtily I sat in my car and waited till her new GP arrived. I knew him well and in full view of her front window I spent some time filling in some background details for him with more than occasional glances at her house.

About six months later she asked to come back to our practice. It gave me great pleasure to regretfully decline.

Not For Eating!

Sometimes as a young doctor a once in a lifetime case comes along.

It was an exceptional afternoon. There was a most important Extraordinary Meeting of the senior consultants and the Health Board.

I was on call for the ward and all was quiet until mid afternoon when I took a call from a GP. One of his patients, a six year old, had swallowed approximately 6 pods of Laburnum. Vaguely at the back of my mind were the dangers of Laburnum from my lectures in toxicology.

By the time the child arrived in the ward I had ascertained the fatal dose which was 3 pods i.e. half what my patient had taken.

Slight panic took over and I felt I required Consultant opinion or else I might have a fatality on my hands. However, for some reason I could not reach my chief (no pagers or mobile phones in those days) so I had to deal with this potential time bomb on my own.

I read the textbooks and treated him appropriately. Then the wait until the success or otherwise of my ministrations was revealed. Would the child survive?

Thankfully, these were successful and the patient was sitting up bright and breezy on the ward round the following morning.

Interestingly, 30 years later, while I was in General Practice, the parents of the little boy became patients. At the first consultation his mother reminded me of the occasion when he thought she was going to lose her 6 year old son. Thankfully, he was now married with 3 children and was a successful TV producer.

No Taste

She was a middle-aged spinster who had led a relatively sheltered life and had suffered few illnesses and certainly nothing serious. She looked after her elderly parents, both of whom were failing, her father mentally and her mother physically, but she was determined to keep them at home as long as possible.

Unfortunately, one weekend she developed flu and being of the old school who would never call a doctor out of hours, she struggled on trying to care for her parents and herself.

Things got progressively worse and finding that hot drinks and paracetamol were not having much beneficial effect, her mother suggested that she try old-fashioned toddy and go to bed.

My patient had never made toddy before and in fact, she was virtually teetotal, a small sherry at Christmas being her annual intake; but, she followed her mother's instructions and mixed the whisky, lemon, honey and hot water and sipped it.

"It has no taste," she informed her mother and thinking she had not used sufficient whisky she added a further 'tot'. This, however, made no difference so in desperation she added some more of Scotland's amber liquid and drained the glass.

When she woke up the drama began. She was seeing spiders on the bed, pink elephants on the ceiling, and when she sat up the room started spinning.

Her poor mother could not cope and called one of the neighbours. She assessed the situation and called me.

Luckily, there was nothing too serious to find. My patient had flu, and had lost her sense of smell and taste. She had added so much whisky to her toddy that she drank the equivalent of a quadruple measure. Poor woman was drunk and having visual hallucinations, followed unfortunately by a nasty hangover.

I do not think she ever tried toddy again as a cure for flu.

No Snow!

It had been snowing quite heavily during the night and a neighbour made a request for a house call to No. 47 at around 10 o'clock.

An elderly couple lived there; he with senile dementia and his wife who looked after him very well was a tiny lady with a waspish tongue and an exceptionally brusque manner.

I arrived and was greeted by the neighbour who stated very forcibly 'something must be done'. These four words bring dread to any GP as inevitably it heralds problems, usually of a social, and not a medical nature.

"What exactly is the problem?" I asked.

"Her, your patient!" he replied.

"And, what has she done?"

He gestured at the pavement. "She was out at 7 a.m. in her nightdress and slippers clearing the snow."

Strange though that was, more amazing was that she had swept both pavements for the whole length of the street!

Misguided Pity

The accent said it all. It pierced the genteel air, but, it was phoney; surely no one actually spoke like that, but, they did. Loud and strident, confident but condescending to those around, the opinion was given. The pronouncement was uttered and no one could dare doubt the veracity. A superior English accent from an (allegedly) superior being.

Equally the reply; in similar tone and inflection and inevitably agreeing with the first speaker. If these two were in accord then consensus among the company was not in doubt.

And the cause of their distress, it was the ethics of confidentially. Why should she not know the details of her 16 year old daughter's latest consultation. Just who, did the doctor dealing with the case think he was; after all, her father was very friendly with Professors 'this' and 'that' and they would quickly put this young doctor (me!!) in his place.

However, to the discerning ear, the arguments proposed were often flimsy and ill conceived. But, when contra opinions were expressed there was shock and horror. How could someone possibly question their statements? The fact that a horse and cart could be driven through the postulation was greeted with dismay and annoyance. The volume increased and the accents became more pronounced, but instead of raising their voices they should reinforce their arguments and that they were unable to do.

Then the superior attitude kicked in. The haughty gaze down the nose, the sneering almost sympathetic look at someone who in their opinion, was definitely an inferior individual, who required pity before they were dismissed as a nobody. They had more important things to discuss, so they sought out like minds, who, would agree with their views however powder puff and incorrect they might be.

Shallow minds in frivolous and inconsequential people.

A 'No Win' Situation

She lay in the hospital bed, her make-up a mess, mascara running, vivid red lipstick a little out of place in an acute surgical ward, and blonde hair dark at the roots. It must have been so different 12 hours earlier.

The cause of her appearance was interesting. She was a 'lady' who had arranged to meet a male 'client' for mutual benefit, (one financial, one gratification) at a pub in Whiterashes near Aberdeen.

Unfortunately her geography was rather faulty and she went to Whitecairns, a village approximately 3 miles away. Realising her mistake after waiting in the bar for about an hour and having 3 large vodkas she started walking to the correct destination.

However, it was wintertime and the snow lay thick on the ground. The frost was hard that evening and dainty court shoes offered no protection in these conditions.

The outcome was disastrous and she presented with the very first case of frostbite I had ever seen.

She required the amputation of several toes, so this was an expensive mistake. Lack of financial gain for one and hormonal gratification for the other.

A Beautiful Accent

They were the quietest couple you could imagine. He was a retired carpenter and had built their retiral home to their design. While he pottered in his greenhouse or garden, she embroidered, knitted, made jams and jellies all for the benefit of the local church and local charities.

They seldom consulted although she suffered from winter bronchitis and a visit there usually resulted in a pot of her latest jam to take home. They were both typical Grampian folk having worked and raised their family some way out of Aberdeen and then retired to the city. Their accents were typical 'Buchan tongue', which is a fairly broad accent with many words similar to German.

One day I received a call to visit her at home. She had been preparing the evening meal when she developed a severe headache and collapsed. When I examined her, she was deeply unconscious from a cerebral haemorrhage and I feared the worst when I admitted her to hospital.

She remained unconscious for a day or two and the next I heard of her she had made a miraculous recovery and was discharged home.

In those days we always visited patients after hospital admission and so I popped in to see her review her treatment.

She was sitting in a chair looking remarkably well and I could hardly believe it was the same patient I had admitted several days previously. But there was one incredible change. She now spoke with delightfully musical accent typical of the Scottish Highlands, and so unlike her previous voice. She knew it was different but no one was ever able to explain the change. It never varied in the ensuing years and she passed away peacefully many years later.

A Man to be Pitied

I had never been in a house with so many wonderful antiques, furniture, porcelain, silver, painting and much, much more. They were everywhere and must have been a nightmare to dust.

The house was enormous, the garden huge, the chauffeur driven Jaguar in the garage and wealth very evident.

His 'man', however, kept everything immaculate, despite being paid a pittance, but was powerless to influence his boss.

A more pernickety, parsimonious and petty man it would be difficult to meet. He moaned, complained, expected the best for himself but without spending any of his money, and he was a nightmare to treat.

He had been married but this had only lasted one month, and I believe his wife could not cope with his selfish behaviour and also the attention given by him to his mother who behaved exactly like her son.

His father had been an exceptionally successful doctor who made a fortune in the days before the National Health Service, augmented by shrewd investments.

Unfortunately, his son had neither the charisma nor brains of his father and had started several businesses, all of which had sunk without a trace. He still, however, thought he was someone special and expected his doctors to jump at his command.

He was a very close personal friend of the soon to retire Senior Partner and when he departed he expected me to take over his care.

I was introduced to him and he set out his expectations for his medical care, which seemed to consist of me visiting at whatever time and place he chose.

To say he was not pleased, was an understatement, when I declined to conform to his plans.

"But, this is what I expect and your Senior Partner assured me it would be so," he told me forcibly.

"He has retired, as you are aware, and things have changed."

I did continue to look after him for many years and he never tried to lean on me again. However, his help died and he was left alone, unwilling to spend his money to make his life more comfortable. He died a lonely, sad man still with all his baubles but with no one willing to give tender, loving care when most required.

A Step Too Far

It all started so innocently. My patient, an amiable bachelor of 50 but with a rather anxious and nervous disposition, was delighted to help the 70-year-old widow with her garden, and various odd jobs around the house. They were both members of the same church where mutual help was given and received.

Whenever he was stressed, he inevitably appeared in the surgery to discuss those forces of nature, which affected his 'id' and equilibrium.

He was quite a fan of alternative medicine and we discussed homeopathy, aromatherapy, hypnosis, etc., but I was out of my depth with transcendental meditation and various Eastern mystics, most of which I had never heard of and certainly knew nothing about.

This day he was upset and stressed more than usual.

"I have been victimised and violated," he cried, an anguished look on his face.

"Tell me about it please," I requested.

There followed a sorry saga of giving help in the garden, help in the garage, help in the kitchen and then the bombshell.

"Please come tomorrow, I need help in the bedroom," the lady said.

Quite innocently, he appeared to find this 70-year-old apparently helpless widow lying on her bed in a rather inappropriate nightie. She then encouraged him to join her in bed. It would appear that this was the 'help' she needed.

Unfortunately for my patient he could not and would not provide the assistance required. His 'id' definitely could not cope.

All Shades Of The Rainbow

I have never seen bruising so severe as on the back of the 70 year old patient. He was a typical Buchan farmer who tended 100 acres of arable farmland by himself and his farm was neat and tidy and obviously profitable.

His wife had called me because he had 'a sore back'. Surprisingly for him he was in bed when I called, totally immobile and unable to walk.

When he removed his shirt, I was amazed. The whole of his back was bruised and cut and the skin was turning all the shades of the rainbow.

The cause was strange. He had been in his barn where a machine was being driven by a belt drive. He was wearing a loose fitting jersey and the sleeve had caught in the belt and swept him off his feet. He had repeatedly been thrown against a supporting pillar set in the floor.

By some miracle, he had managed to free himself but not before he had received several severe blows to his back. When he had not appeared for lunch, his wife had gone to investigate and found him on the floor.

I prescribed some analgesia for him and instructed him to remain in bed until I revisited him 3 days later knowing full well he could not move.

I duly visited him as arranged and his wife answered the door. "I'm afraid he is not here," and pointed to the 10 acre field behind. There was my patient sitting on his tractor ploughing prior to sowing his winter barley!

I wonder just how long a young city dweller would have been off work?

In A Measured Manner

He was a professor at Aberdeen University and absolutely brilliant in his field, a world authority, he had written many textbooks and numerous articles about a subject that was beyond my comprehension. He was a real intellectual giant.

My first meeting with this patient set the tone for future consultations. He requested a house call because of abdominal pain and although there was little to find clinically, something made me suspect there was a more serious cause for his pain. I arranged for him to be seen immediately by a consultant gastro-enterologist who rapidly referred him to a surgeon who operated that afternoon and removed a malignant tumour from his bowel. From that day, he would consult no one but myself.

In the consulting room he would sit sometimes for at least a minute before telling me his problem. He spoke in an extremely slow, measured manner, with long pauses. He used no unnecessary words and was extremely precise. However, each consultation took a considerable time and there was no way to hasten the procedure.

This had a strange effect as I found myself replying to him in the same precise manner and I was determined to use the correct word in the correct context.

His operation was a complete success and he lived for many years and died from a totally unrelated illness still as alert mentally as in his younger day.

Caught out

It was a very agitated voice who called late one evening asking for an urgent house call to someone who had collapsed with chest pain.

The address was not familiar but the patient's name was. I knew him and his family quite well.

The house was fairly close so I was there in a very few minutes. The door was opened by a worried looking young lady in a fairly revealing negligee. She ushered me through to the bedroom where a familiar patient lay on the bed, pale and sweating and looking very unwell.

When asked, the young lady said they had been 'talking' over a glass of wine when suddenly he had complained of chest pain.

Unfortunately, that did not exactly explain why he appeared naked under the sheet and she seemed to have very little if anything on beneath her gown. Perhaps there had been rather more physical activity than sipping wine. After all, he was not in his own home and she was not his wife!

Mentally raising my eyebrows, I proceeded to examine him. He had the classical signs of a myocardial infarction (i.e. heart attack) confirmed by cardiograph and so I gave him the appropriate treatment and arranged for his admission to the Coronary Care Unit of Aberdeen Royal Infirmary.

Now there came the problem. Who would inform his wife of this present illness? Would it be the hospital, his lady friend, or someone else? That was not a decision I was happy to make.

'Can I Help?'

Team doctors have their own 'union', like the goalkeepers and the front row forwards although it is never called this, usually more a sign of professional ethos, ethics and respect.

When a visiting player is seriously injured it is normal for the 'home' doctor to offer assistance in a non-clinical way. Knowing the local set up for ambulances, X-rays, directions to A&E departments or private hospitals smoothes the path for further assistance if necessary.

One team which seemed to be composed of mainly foreign (European) players, plus a foreign manager and a foreign doctor, were playing Aberdeen in a cup game.

Their left back broke through and headed for the by-line. Suddenly, just as he was about to cross the ball his studs caught in the turf with no one near him and he crashed to the ground with a shriek. Obviously this was a potentially serious injury so while he was being stretchered off the pitch, I made my way to the 'Away' dressing room to offer any assistance I could.

I was met with what can only be called a foul-mouthed rant by their doctor.

"Where is the f****** ambulance, I need it now! You are the most incompetent medical team I have ever met."

I thought I was familiar with most of the swear words in the English language, but I have never heard such a fluent stream of invective as I was subjected to that evening, by my European medical colleague.

At this point again I offered to help but he swore again this time at my assistant. I have never experienced behaviour quite like it and certainly not from another doctor. I was flabbergasted.

At this point, having ascertained that the ambulance was on its way, I decided not to direct it to the private hospital we used, but let them suffer the delays, drunks and drop outs at A&E. A fifteen minute wait for an X-ray at the private clinic was converted into a four hour wait at A&E, and it was not the player's fault.

Blind As A Bat?

Although of poor intelligence, indeed, she verged on the borders of mental deficiency, she had a native wit and cunning which she used especially to her advantage.

She visited various opticians whom she managed to convince by fair means or foul that she had a serious eye complaint and that she was almost blind.

The opticians felt that she required Consultant Ophthalmologist opinion and examination and duly referred her to hospital.

She turned up at her appointed time and tried to fool the Eye Specialist much as she had done to the opticians. She could not even read the topmost largest letter on the eye chart and she was delighted when the consultant expressed the view that she must have serious eye problems not to be able to read even the top letter.

"Please have a seat outside while I arrange further tests," he explained and she patiently sat outside the consulting room feeling very pleased with herself.

Moments later the door opened and she was invited back into the room.

"Please take a seat and I will proceed with the rest of the examination."

Without any hesitation she walked across the room and took her seat and waited expectantly.

"Right, I think you can go, I do not need to do any further examinations."

"But I am blind!" she cried in anguish.

"No I don't think so. You managed to reach the examination chair despite all the obstacles I had placed on the floor. You can see as well as I can. You are a fraud and you are wasting my time. Leave now and do not try to trick us again."

The Consultant had placed chairs, tables and lamps between the door and the chair and she had successfully manoeuvred her way past all obstacles to reach the chair.

Cunning she might have been but not as smart as the Specialist.

Before The Mast

The pilot boat edged away from the quay and headed out of the harbour. I stood on the deck one beautiful summer morning as the sun rose and the first beams caught the brilliant paintwork and rigging of the elegant 3 masted barque anchored in the bay.

I was mildly apprehensive as we approached the ship, as the call on the ship to shore radio had been slightly difficult due to the foreign accent and also lack of medical details presented to me. There had been some evidence of panic as the 1st Officer thought that the 16 year old on board might be suffering from Typhoid fever! Evidently he had complained of general malaise, headache and a rash on his trunk, and the first diagnosis made via the Nautical Medical Handbook was that rare infectious disease, which most UK doctors will never see in their whole professional career.

However, this Polish sailing ship was unwilling to come into port in case it was an infectious disease, which would immediately place it in quarantine for an indefinite period.

So the shipping agent called me and arranged a 'home visit' 2 miles offshore, via the pilot boat. Thus at 4 in the morning in late June and the sea flat calm we proceeded towards this wonderful reminder of the bygone era of sail.

I was surprised how easy it was to board the ship and it did not involve climbing up a long ladder. I was led to the patient, a young man splendidly isolated in a cabin far from the rest of the crew. He was fevered and headachy but not unwell and examination revealed little apart from a classical rash of Rubella, better known as German Measles, and certainly no evidence of Typhoid fever which of course I had encountered during the 1964 Aberdeen outbreak.

I was able to reassure the Master of the ship that there was nothing to be concerned about. This being a training ship with 30 young men learning the craft of sailing these marvellous vessels and watching it in full sail as it sailed away to the next port of call was a magnificent sight.

58 Years Ago

Her medical notes were wafer thin and contained only one page. The last entry was when she required immunisations for foreign travel. Previous to this there were no medical records, but this was I recalled, a family, who did not attend the doctor unless it was something fairly serious.

However, she appeared one day, somewhat hesitant in her manner and rather reticent about her problem. By this time, she was 85 years old and remarkably sprightly.

Eventually she admitted she had some rectal bleeding but was rather unwilling to be examined in the surgery and I did not press this point. I knew she required investigation so I referred her to one of the General Surgeons. In my letter I stated that she had been a very fit lady with no medical history of note.

When the Consultant saw her he was a little upset at the lack of information in my referral letter. He questioned her regarding her previous medical history and became rather frustrated when she kept repeating that she had no history of illness. He, thinking she was a little senile and forgetful when he received yet another negative answer to his questioning finally asked, "When did you last consult your GP?"

Her reply, "When my son was born, and he is now 58 years old."

Yes, truly a very fit old lady.

Annoyance

I was never upset about doing house calls. To me, they were part of General Practice as I knew it. However, certain little things sometimes made me quite annoyed.

Perhaps the most common was the failure to switch off the TV. I had sometimes to request this and very occasionally this was refused. On these occasions I lowered my voice to a whisper so that neither patient or parent could hear me above the noise of the television.

Sometimes the TV would be switched off, only for another child to switch it back on again and often refuse the parent's request to switch it off. On one or two occasions I simply picked up my instruments, placed them in my bag and got up to leave. This usually did the trick.

Almost as annoying was when the patient continued to drink tea or coffee during the consultation. This was usually a good time to have them lying flat out and examining the abdomen even though it was completely unnecessary. It is very difficult to drink anything lying flat on your back.

Patients who would not stop talking when you were trying to examine them were quickly silenced by placing a thermometer in their mouth and leaving it there for 2-3 minutes. These new instant models unfortunately preclude that manoeuvre.

However, the most annoying feature of house calls was when the patient stipulated a time for the house call to be made because they have a another appointment such as going to the hairdresser. On these occasions I sometimes deliberately made the call when I knew they would not be there. I then left a note saying I had called and inviting them to make an appointment at the surgery. This occasionally attracted an objectionable phone call, but I took great pleasure in reminding them that if they were fit enough to go to the hairdresser they were certainly fit enough to come to the surgery.

Animals in the bedroom can sometimes cause problems. On more than one occasion I was totally unable to examine a child because her pet dog/cat/parrot, etc., refused to let me near my patient.

In 'uppity' households, who thought they were superior, I always requested a clean towel to dry my hands, giving the impression that the present towels were less than acceptable. The final indignity was then to drop it on the floor and walk out.

An Unusual Rash

They were a slightly odd couple. He was confident, extroverted and bossy. Rather overfriendly with doctors and nurses in the practice and took liberties in his conversation.

He consulted me occasionally but his wife had severe Irritable Bowel Syndrome and Chronic Bronchitis and consulted frequently. Her family of three girls grew up, married and moved out and then the problems surfaced.

In addition to her ongoing physical illnesses as mentioned she started showing signs of stress, anxiety and depression. I had always known there were problems between them and now that the family had left, tensions obviously became more apparent.

The actual cause of their marital disharmony was never really discovered but a hint of the reasons was revealed one day.

She consulted me with yet another nasty chest infection. She was wearing a high necked dress with long sleeves and when I wanted to auscultate her chest there was no problem as the zip was down the back of her dress.

Having completed my examination of her chest I decided opportunistically to check her BP, which had not been recorded for some time. I asked her to roll up one sleeve so I could apply the sphygmomanometer cuff to her upper arm. She hesitated then virtually refused saying it was not necessary.

I was a little surprised and gently insisted that I needed to note it in my records. Very reluctantly, she complied and then as I wrapped the cuff round her arm I noted an unusual red raw abrasion on her wrist. Having checked her BP I enquired about the abrasion. She was very unwilling to explain but by now I was quite intrigued as to the cause.

For some reason I glanced at her ankles and noted despite her dark coloured tights similar lesions on each ankle. She saw me looking at her wrist and then her ankles, blushed and hung her head. She realised I deserved an explanation.

I recognised rope friction burns after careful examination and she admitted her husband was into bondage as part of his new sexual foreplay much against her wishes.

This and other acts involving a riding crop had been the cause of her depression and stress. She was too frightened and embarrassed to tell anyone, but now of course I knew and I suggested she told her husband I had recognised the signs and see what happened.

Thankfully for her the practises stopped. He for his part blustered on and never mentioned my consultation with his wife.

Sadly, she died the following year but he is still a patient, and every time even years later, when he attends I remember his wife's rope burns.

After The Climb

As I ascended the tenement stairs, I again thought 'do all our patients live on the top floor?'

Slightly breathless, I paused and recalled that I had never done a house call to this particular patient, although he consulted very frequently at the surgery because of his osteoarthritis.

Normally this was well controlled with pain killers but recently he had seen one of our younger doctors who had prescribed a new anti-inflammatory drug because of increasing pain.

My patient had gone out for a couple of pints (perhaps more) and on return had taken his medication. A little while later he had developed severe abdominal pain and started vomiting and that was when I was called.

When I entered the flat I heard retching from the bathroom and found him, on the floor, clutching the w/c like a white telephone and vomiting copious amounts of pure fresh blood. He was as pale as the porcelain and had obviously lost a lot of blood.

However, after admission and transfusion of four pints of blood he returned home good as new. He vowed never to take his tablets with alcohol. (I did note he did not say he would never take alcohol!)

A Quiet Evening

The media do a wonderful job when they report the news accurately and fairly. However, sometimes the truth is not quite sufficiently newsworthy and a slightly different slant is put on the story.

Medical news is of course often a very good source of writeable material. Anything to do with health either good or bad is seized on by the 'hacks' and a good slant or spin is put on it.

Years ago before hospital security was heard of, Accident and Emergency Departments, being invariably busy and active, were a good stopping off point for journalists. They would pop in, late in the evening, hoping for news of accidents, attempted suicides, etc. They would bypass the junkies, drunks and hypochondriacs, looking for the juicy bits.

Late one particularly busy Saturday evening there was a lull and I took the opportunity to get a breath of fresh air. A journalist from the local rag, who was not popular with the medical staff due to some untrue remarks he had made about the A&E unit previously, approached and asked how my evening had been.

"Anything or anyone of interest?" he enquired.

"No, just a normal quiet evening," was my reply; forgetting that my white coat, (we did not wear surgical scrubs in those days) was covered in blood from a patient who had been in a particularly nasty road traffic accident.

There was no way I would admit to having treated one of Glasgow Rangers star players or even more significantly, a Socialist MP who had pulled rank, demanding to be seen immediately with what was a very mundane illness, which certainly could have waited till he saw his own GP.

"Do you know who I am!" and other such expressions, he thundered. He had been obnoxious in the extreme, both to nurses and doctors and it was extremely tempting to 'blow the whistle' and spill the beans.

The journalist would certainly have loved that one!

A Flight Too Far

Of course, it had to be one the highest tenement buildings in Aberdeen. Their flat was on the 6th floor and this was before the days of lifts.

He was a remarkably fit 70 year old, a retired shopkeeper who had married late in life and there were no children from the marriage. He had previously lived with his mother and elder sister and had been waited on hand and foot by firstly his mother and after she died by his sister. Eventually she passed away and he married the pleasant spinster next door.

She was several years younger than her new husband. He, perhaps typical of his generation did absolutely nothing in the home despite being retired. He spent his day, reading, watching TV and eating three cooked meals a day.

His wife for her part, cleaned, cooked, shopped and generally ran after him and progressively looked more and more tired and stressed. However, she struggled on and although she never admitted it to me, did hint to my Practice Nurse that she would have been better off staying single.

She found climbing the six flights of stairs more and more difficult and one day she almost collapsed on the final leg. He, typically complained that his lunch was not ready on time, and when she took herself off to bed, he demanded a house call for her.

He inferred when I visited her that there was nothing wrong with her and that she should get up and cook lunch and attend to his needs.

Examination revealed marked pallor and pitting oedema almost to the knees with severe breathlessness. I suggested hospital admission but she refused so I took off some blood for a variety of tests and instructed her to remain in bed, much to her husband's annoyance. After all, who would look after him?

When the tests returned from the lab. it transpired she had a haemoglobin of 19% of normal with a possible diagnosis of Pernicious Anaemia and hospital admission was advised.

She was duly investigated and treated and returned home after a few days looking better than she had for a long time. However, I took the opportunity to emphasise that she would not be so able to clean, cook etc., to the same degree and that he must take his share of looking after the home. I issued a veiled threat that I might have to admit her again if she became unwell and, thankfully, it seemed to succeed.

Even more sensibly, they moved into a newly built ground floor flat. Unfortunately, he only lived a very short time after the move and if truth be told, I think she was quite relieved.

And What Do You Do?

One of the standard questions asked by every doctor during a consultation is the patient's occupation. Obviously this may be very significant on certain occasions, such as asbestos workers having chest problems, fish workers with skin infections like Erysipelas, or cleaners using hydrofluoric acid when cleaning granite. Over many years the doctor learns to link certain jobs with specific illnesses.

Having met the rather overweight gentleman for the first time, suffering from a stress related disorder I asked him what his work was, in case it was contributing to his present medical condition.

He hesitated somewhat, which I found a little strange for what was surely a straightforward question. In my mind I wondered if perhaps he was unemployed, had been made redundant, had been sacked for some misdemeanor at work, or even worse been in court for some offence.

He told me he was a Work Style Transformation Project Manager!

I looked at him blankly not having the faintest idea exactly what that entailed, and asked him to elaborate.

Due to financial cutbacks he had been given this additional position to his normal job, but he was very vague exactly what this really entailed. He had been an office worker in the Local Authority Social Work Department, and had been advised by his Line Manager, (all these wonderful new terms) that he was being promoted to this new position. Part of his problem was that he did not know exactly what he was supposed to do and this was causing his stress. I immediately thought, poor training with extra workload and not coping, result – stress.

It appeared, however, that he was not alone. His closest friend, also on the Town Council staff was instructed to prepare an office prior to interviewing candidates for some newly advertised positions in his department.

These new positions included a Befriending Co-coordinator, a Multi-skilled Trade Operator, and most surprising of all a Waking Night Support Worker!

Suddenly I realized that Occupational Health was now a new specialty since my medical student days. Perhaps the most important first requisite was to understand what exactly these new titles actually meant. I secretly feel that they are well-known old established jobs in another guise.

A little I think like Hans Christian Andersen's tale *The Emperor's new clothes*.

Danger – Men At Work

At the height of the oil boom of the 1980s, I was MO to several oil companies. One of the main functions was routine medical examinations of the employees at regular intervals. One company proposed that instead of their workers coming in to my surgery in dribs and drabs I should take a trip offshore and examine the complete batch of their staff on board the oilrig. Thus, I found myself preparing for a new experience i.e. a ride in one of the helicopters, which were it seemed, always airborne above Aberdeen.

In those days, a casual visitor such as myself did not require an offshore survival certificate. It was only necessary to report to the heliport at the appointed time. So I found myself in a crowded room in the helicopter terminal with several oil workers of various ages but all regular travellers offshore.

I was issued with a survival suit which was awkward, uncomfortable and hot. We waddled a short distance to the 'copter and climbed aboard. Then lift off, nose down and away we went. My first impression was of the noise of the engines, and I was glad of the issued earplugs; there was also the regular strobe effect of the rotor blades making reading impossible. The space was cramped and I would not have liked to be tall.

The oilrig appeared 2 hours later as a dot in the ocean and I found it difficult to believe we could land there. But, land we did on the helipad and proceeded to fight our way in strong winds to the safety and sanctity of the accommodation rig. Through the mesh of the safety net on the edge of the pad was revealed the maelstrom of the sea 200 feet below, whilst rescue vessels circled the rig continuously.

Inside, the rig was remarkably spacious, warm and quiet. I was shown to my cabin with two bunk beds, a desk and chair and a tiny wardrobe. I was the only occupant so I stowed my gear and as requested presented myself to have my photograph taken and as Identification Card issued.

An orientation tour followed and I was shown the medical suite, which was well appointed. Then to the drilling platform where all the action took place and most of the accidents occurred. It was, quite honestly, a frightening place to the uninitiated; activity, lots of chains, pipes and machines in constant activity. The floor was slippery with 'mud' which is the chemical pumped down the borehole to facilitate the extraction of the crude oil.

30-foot pipes were manoeuvred into place as the drill penetrated deeper and deeper and chains assisted this being wrapped round the pipes and it seemed to me that the free end was in great danger of decapitating a worker.

It seemed absolute mayhem but of course everything was controlled and everyone knew their job and the operation was performed smoothly but at great pace. It was non-stop activity 24 hours per day and the squads changed regularly, 12 hours on and 12 hours off.

The squad coming off duty, showered, had a meal then as arranged, appeared at the surgery for examination. For the next 6 hours it was examination after examination coupled with masses of paperwork. I collapsed exhausted after dinner and had an excellent sleep.

My first appearance at breakfast was interesting; I was offered steak, chips, two or three fried eggs but when I demurred it was greeted with amazement. My request for one poached egg, toast and coffee produced remarks such as 'you will fade away' 'you must eat', etc.

The quality and quantity of the food was surprising; however, having observed the physical activity on the drilling platform, I could understand the need for adequate nourishment.

The next three days were taken up by repeated examinations, eating and watching TV or videos of doubtful sexual orientation. I tended to spend my little spare time reading or writing my diary or reports.

This operation I repeated on several occasions but the novelty of helicopter flights, life on an oilrig, dubious videos soon palled. However, it was an experience I am glad I had and I would be less than honest if I did not admit it was also financially attractive.

Come Home For A Holiday

Every doctor needs a holiday, to escape from the tedium of screaming kids, demanding patients, hypochondriacs, etc., who make up all GP's practice.

We enjoy cruising as a splendid way of relaxing and doing as little or as much as the spirit wishes. Lying on deck reading a book and watching the world go by (literally) is my pleasure, and getting away from my heartsink patients.

However, I thought my professional services would be required on one cruise. I appreciate there are medical staff on board, but I did not think these potential patients would make it to the Medical Suite.

Dawn was just breaking as they start the first of many laps of the deck – seven laps are a mile, but our worthy pair jog at least three miles.

Neither looks comfortable as they pound the planking, oblivious to other gentler walkers. Their vests are stained with their efforts, and the John McEnroe sweatband is working overtime. Still they continue, she is struggling to keep up so he forges ahead while she looks more and more likely to pass out at any moment.

They are of the strange opinion this is doing them good. Perhaps from their body shape, a little less of the good things in life might be more beneficial.

Circuits complete, the next stage is Pilates with Emma who stretches muscles they did not know they had, and have certainly not used for years.

Recovering from that experience, they emerge ready to face the rest of the day, knowing that lying before them is a fun filled day with bridge lessons, deck quoits, dance classes, shuffleboard, and needlecraft, line dancing and ending with the team trivia quiz. (They have persuaded their rather reluctant fellow table guests to join them.)

And this is only day one!

Who is with whom?

I went to the waiting room door as I always did to call my next patient.

Glancing as usual round the rest of the patients sitting reading or talking among themselves I could not believe my eyes.

Sitting very close together was a lady and her new partner. Nothing strange about that, except, her estranged husband was also sitting there with his latest girlfriend, the widow of a patient. Even more amazing was the presence of the wife of the male partner of the first couple who was sitting with her brother-in-law, who had left his wife for his sister-in-law.

Confused it is, coincidental it was, convoluted definitely, but true nonetheless.

At The Bus Stop

Dark haired petite and pretty she sat down and adjusted the sling supporting the plaster of Paris splint on her right arm.

I had known her since birth but she seldom attended and her medical records even for a fifteen year old were very sparse.

She was extremely reticent about how she had sustained the injury and the reason for her attendance was to request a certificate for her forthcoming examinations, as she could not write.

I was quite happy to provide this and she departed still not explaining the cause of her fracture. As luck would have it my very next patient was able to explain what had happened.

He had been standing at a bus stop when my patient and another girl had joined the queue. Some moments later, a group of 3 or 4 youths started molesting and jostling the girls. It was all in good fun initially but then it got out of hand and became quite violent.

At this, the girls squared up to the boys who were totally unaware and unprepared for what happened next. The girls went on the attack and my patient 'chopped' one of the boys and sustained the injury to her hand. The youths fled!

It transpired that both girls were competent and advanced members of a martial arts club.

The Worrier

It was 11pm (5pm US time) when the phone rang and a familiar voice announced he was very breathless. What should he do? Consultations 3000 miles apart are a little tricky and fraught with hazards.

I had supplied him, I thought, with sufficient medication during his ski holiday, for all and every eventuality, but obviously not! I gave him appropriate advice and asked him to phone back if there was no improvement after an hour or two.

The next call was from the Emergency Room of the local hospital (in USA). Yes, my patient was there but suffering no more than a panic attack and some tranquillisers were helping enormously.

This then was one of my classical hypochondriac patients. Every symptom he suffered, in his eyes, was indicative of the most serious life threatening illness, and required much time consuming psychotherapy to control.

He was, however, very well read and could not be fobbed off with glib explanations. He was also generous to a fault and many of his friends benefited from his largesse, even to the extent of Rolex watches and golf clubs.

Quite correctly, none of his doctors benefited in such a manner, but we still had to pick up and repair his psychological pieces.

However, as so often happens, he cried wolf once too often and was found to have a terminal illness. After the initial shock and disbelief at the diagnosis, he came to terms with it in a quiet and peaceful way.

Luckily a combination of good nursing, adequate pain control and supportive psychotherapy, allowed him to have a calm and dignified last few weeks.

Trust Me...

The cruise ship had been tossed all night by a force 10 gale and big seas in the Bay of Biscay.

Passengers dragged themselves down for breakfast but the sight and smell of food was too much for most. There were many pale wane faces.

We took breakfast in the Lido on the open deck and sipped orange juice, with poached eggs and smoked salmon and a cup of coffee, having previously taken Stugeron, an anti-seasickness tablet with good effect, while watching many unhappy passengers forgo breakfast for the safer fresh air.

One particularly sorry looking couple sat down opposite. "We just want to die," said the husband later identified as Colin. "This is our first and probably last cruise. How are you feeling?"

"Fine," I replied, "we took tablets which helped enormously."

"I don't believe anything can help," said his wife who had tried herbal tablets, anti-seasickness wristbands and even acupuncture, "so why should this treatment work?"

"Take one," I said, "I am sure they will help." But she still looked somewhat sceptical.

Looking her straight in the eye, smiling I gave her 'trust me I'm a doctor' the age-old medical adage.

Luckily for me, the treatment worked beautifully and for the rest of the excellent cruise whenever we met she smiled and said, "I'm so glad I listened when you said 'trust me, I'm a doctor."

Under His Pillow

"I cannot sleep," was the complaint from the smartly dressed middle-aged lady who sat before me. Certainly, she looked very tired and drawn.

I had treated her the previous year for a mild depressive illness, the cause of which I never discovered, but she apparently made a full recovery. I thought perhaps that she was again depressed and I questioned her further about other signs and symptoms.

She worked for the Health Board and her husband was a very dapper professional gentleman who walked everywhere and seldom used his Mercedes car, and only consulted when he required immunisations or malaria tablets for going on holiday.

Their home was always immaculate as they had no family or pets and they seemed a very happy contented couple.

Although she did not present any classical symptoms of depression she showed many signs of stress and anxiety. It appeared that she could not sleep because she was scared to fall asleep and she lay awake till her husband nodded off and even then she only slept fitfully.

"Why do you lie awake deliberately?" I asked.

"Because my husband has an axe below his pillow and he has threatened to cut my head off when I am asleep!"

I looked at her in amazement. Surely not the behaviour I would have expected from him.

"He has told me he does not love me anymore and the voices in the TV tell him that is what he must do!"

The thought of attending a decapitated body in the future was sufficient for me to arrange a visit with a Psychiatrist very promptly.

He was diagnosed as a schizophrenic and hospitalised immediately. After treatment he resumed a normal life so long as he took his medication and I still see him out walking, smartly dressed and dapper as ever, but with a rather more relaxed wife!

Where Is Your Heart?

'Haematopus ostralegus, the Latin name for the Oystercatcher, male and female similar, two to four eggs laid each year, feeds on cockles, mussels and limpets.'

Not quite paediatrics but the soon to be retiring Professor was a wealth of information about flora and fauna, which were often discussed during ward rounds. This explanation ensued after seeing a pair of those attractive birds on the lawn outside the ward.

'Now let us continue the ward round' and the large retinue proceeded to the next bed where lay 7 year old Henry.

I was one of the students in my final year of medical school attached to his ward where teaching and repeated examinations were part and parcel of the student's life.

"Now you, Mr Gray, (he was always very polite) please examine this boy's heart."

Nervously in front of everyone, I approached the bed. "Hello Henry, can I examine you?"

Henry was obviously used to being examined. He slipped off his pyjama top and lay back. Aware that everyone was watching me I did everything as I had been taught.

Inspection, I looked, looked again, nothing abnormal. Palpation, nothing abnormal. Percussion nothing abnormal, then auscultation, heart sounds very faint but appeared normal.

I stepped back and waited.

"Well?"

"Everything appears normal apart from very faint heart sounds."

"Where is the apex-beat?"

I admitted I could not find it.

"Look again."

Finally I found it, on the right side, i.e. the 'wrong' side of the chest.

So in front of my peers and teachers I had missed a dextrocardia – a rare condition where the heart is on the right side. I wanted the floor to swallow me up.

I only felt slightly better when the diagnosis was made of Kartagener's Syndrome, an incredibly rare cause of dextocardia.

The Guardian At The Gate

This may be one of the kinder descriptions of that person who is often the first point of contact of the patient, either personally or on the phone.

Some may label her a dragon, others a kindly helpful person who can only assist and answer their every need.

"Which doctor, what day, what time?"

"That is not suitable? How about...? I am sure the doctor will be able to see you then."

To others, however, she (and in most cases it is a she) is difficult, obstructive, protective (of the doctors) and just occasionally bordering on rudeness.

"An appointment when? No, that doctor could only see you a week on Wednesday."

"Is it an emergency?"

"No, the last appointment is 5.30pm."

"No, he is off that day. No, I do not think he is off playing golf!"

"He cannot possibly fit in another patient, even though you are a personal friend and he said you could phone him at any time!"

"There is no need to take that tone of voice with me," is not exactly the response you wished other patients to hear. Of course the job is difficult. Of course 1 in every 100 makes impossible demands, but there are ways of intimating that certain things just cannot happen.

"A house call? And it must be before 10am or after 12 noon, why, because you are going to the hairdresser!"

This type of contact can only cause frustration and this can certainly lead to some sharp exchanges. Coupled with the anxiety and worry that the patient feels, makes the ability to reach satisfactory outcomes very difficult.

In addition to this they have to cope with doctors not wanting more patients booked in, when they are already overloaded; nurses who complain about the extras, doctors are sending down; and being short handed whenever someone goes for her tea break.

Then there are the patients who turn up, on the wrong day, at the wrong time, or complain that they do not want to see Dr A and that it is Dr B who always sees them, and will always fit them in at short notice.

Still, these poor ladies at the desk have to smile to the sad, be helpful and bend over backwards to the difficult ones and do all this for the meagre salary that the NHS pays. A labour of love indeed.

The MP

A member of the Cabinet, tall, distinguished and instantly recognisable. A figure of absolute integrity, respected and respectable, in essence, someone to trust implicitly.

My Senior Partner had looked after the MP for many years but now it was my problem.

After introductions I was informed very politely, "I just require a repeat prescription."

I thought 'no problem' and I opened the medical records. I saw Dextramphetamine 10 mg and Phenobarbitone 100mg and these drugs had been being dispensed for many many months if not years.

Of concern also was the slow escalation in dosage of each over a period of months and obviously this had reached the addiction and habituation stage. What was to do I wondered?

"I require these to those to keep me awake and these to help me sleep. The Cabinet meetings may last 6-9 hours and as you know there are several very important issues pending at this time! I have to be at my best!!"

I thought 'be at your best under the influence of dextramphetamine or Phenobarb?'

Somehow, a lecture on the effects of drugs such as those would go down like a lead balloon and I did not fancy embarking on this at my first consultation with this particular patient!

Noting my slight reticence about providing the prescription I was then informed. "If you have any problem giving me these drugs, one of my MP colleagues who is a doctor will accommodate me. I only have to ask!"

I decided therefore to keep at least some control over the prescribing and quietly decided to embark on a reducing programme at future consultations, but I foresaw many difficult sessions in the months ahead.

The Minder

The walls of his dressing room were covered in black drapes, the windows also and a single spotlight revealed a chaise longue on which he reclined with his customary glass of champagne.

I had never met him before but had seen him on numerous occasions on TV and listened to his unmistakable voice on radio.

He was quite unwell and was due to perform the next evening in a solo concert, which was a complete sell-out. I examined him and found him to be remarkably fit despite his lifestyle, which was flamboyant to say the least. I treated him and he was extremely grateful for my visit and welcomed my decision to review him the next day.

I left him quaffing his chilled vintage Krug and wished perhaps that I had a similar lifestyle.

Next day, the day of the 'gig', as promised I visited him just prior to his appearance on stage.

I approached his 'dressing room' but his 'minder' barred my way; a gentleman about 6 feet 4 inches tall and weighing about 18 stones. He was dressed in an ankle length camel coat and seemed to fill the whole corridor. His face had a look of malice and truculence.

"And where do you think you are going?" he snarled as I attempted to pass him.

"To see my patient," I replied.

"Oh no you're not!" he said with his hairline almost touching his eyebrows.

"Oh yes I am," I stated and there followed an almost pantomime sequence of 'yes I am' and 'no you're not' as we argued whether I could proceed along the corridor or not.

My patience was running out and I finally suggested that he report the fact that the doctor was waiting to see my patient.

"Don't move!" I was warned as he knocked on the door of the dressing room. After a brief conversation I was allowed to pass. His face wore a scowl and if looks could have killed...?

"Thank you my man," I said and entered the dressing room.

The Phone Call

"Well I suppose you had better put him through."

This was my response to the receptionist who informed me that an MP was on the phone.

Perhaps I was a little biased as the MP in question was not of my political persuasion and I felt everything he did was for his glory and benefit, and seldom for the good of his constituents.

"I wish to discuss one of your patients," he stated and I was immediately on my guard.

"I believe you are unwilling to prescribe certain drugs for her illness."

"That is correct; they are unlicensed in this country."

"But they are available in Australia and USA," he said.

Then came the bombshell; "I will obtain these drugs and send them to you, and you can administer them to her, I believe by the intravenous route, similar to how she received them at the Alternative Medicine Clinic in England."

He really became quite upset when I declined to undertake this procedure.

"But why not, it is for the patient's benefit!"

"Well perhaps The General Medical Council, my Medical Defence Company and my own ethics would be a little upset if I did."

"Well, I shall speak to the Minister of Health and he will clear the way," he said in a forceful and commanding tone. "I am determined my constituent shall have this treatment."

He became even more upset when I informed him that the Minister himself could carry out the treatment, but that I certainly was not, and could not, be swayed by the threat of a Cabinet Minister. Perhaps the fact that this gentleman had done very little to endear himself to the medical profession by his bully boy tactics, his spin doctor manipulation of, the waiting lists, the claim for apparent huge increase in finance for the NHS which was completely false, and various other ploys he used to denigrate doctors.

Realising his tactics were not working; he then became charm himself and claimed he had heard such good things about our practice and myself in particular. He then mentioned other things like my involvement with Aberdeen Football Club, my membership of a local golf club, etc. I was fully expecting him to ask if I was a Freemason or had links with the local mafia.

When all this failed he slammed down the phone stating he 'would take things a step further, and that there would be action'!

Gosh, I thought, I do not think I will be available for any further phone calls from any MP. Well, maybe, someone from my Party!

The Sauna

Copenhagen is a vibrant and interesting city. However, at that certain drug conference (better known as a freebie) in that city I realised that I had seen little of the important sights such as the Little Mermaid, The Tivoli Gardens, etc.

We had arrived the previous day and had felt the need to slake our thirsts with a glass or two of the local brew, in this case Carlsberg. After dinner we again felt it necessary to help the Danish economy by supporting the local publicans!

Saturday was lecture day to be followed by a reception prior to the official dinner.

Having realised that this could be a long evening I decided to be quite virtuous and go for a swim and a sauna and miss the reception.

The pool was quiet and peaceful and after swimming about 20 lengths I made for the sauna. It was empty and, unable to read the instructions (in Danish) I lay back on the top bench.

Trying hard to convince myself that it must be doing me some good, and failing miserably, I was about to join my colleagues for a welcoming cool beer when the door opened and two beautiful young ladies entered.

They stood at the door and proceeded to peel off their swimsuits, chatting together in what I presumed to be Danish. They glanced at me and smiled and then stretched out on the benches close by.

So, here was I, with my swimming trunks on, and two most attractive young ladies, one blonde (real) and the other brunette with no clothes on!

It was an interesting exercise to 'keep eyes front' when presented with such a spectacle, but I managed (almost)!

(The instructions, written in Danish, said 'remove swimming costumes on entering sauna'.)

Repetition

"'Please state your full name, address and qualifications."

I answered the question as requested and waited.

"You are Doctor," and he stated my full name.

"Yes," I replied.

"And your address is?" Again I agreed.

"And your qualifications are?" And once again I agreed.

"'So you are," and again he asked my name, address and qualifications and seemed almost not to believe me.

Almost unbelievably he asked yet a third time and at this point I was very grateful for the advice of my daughter, a lawyer, with whom I had had coffee just prior to entering the courtroom.

"Do not get upset," she had said, "counsel will try to wind you up, even before you give your evidence. Count up to ten before answering the simplest question."

Taking her advice I mentally counted up to ten before even giving my name, etc., as requested.

But still he persisted. Thankfully the Judge intervened.

'Counsel' he stated 'even in my advanced years I think I now know who exactly we have in the witness box, please proceed.'

Thereafter, still being extremely careful and cautious in my replies, the rest of my evidence, which was strictly of a medical nature and on which I felt much more secure and confident was quite straightforward. Indeed the hour which I apparently spent in the witness box was not too unpleasant although I got the distinct impression that Defence Counsel would have loved to grill me mercilessly and exhibit his superior legal knowledge, but it was not to be.

Reversed Roles

He had joined the practice about 15 years previously but had seldom consulted as he was in excellent health for his age. When one of your previous head teachers asks to join your list it is difficult not to feel pleased that he has selected your practice.

As the years progressed, he began to consult me rather more, but only when he was discovered at a routine over-75 medical assessment to have hypertension did I see him on a regular basis.

He was a tall, very erect distinguished gentleman who exuded power and commanded respect. I always felt that I had to stand up straight and wait until I was spoken to, just like my school days, and was very tempted to call him 'Sir'.

Our relationship, however, was excellent and of course he called me by my first name from the onset.

Gradually he became a little more frail and developed an illness which prevented him being able to drive his car. This meant that he usually required a house call and he had a wonderful ability to 'suggest' that a follow up visit would be very welcome in a month or two. This, despite him being able to go out for lunch with former colleagues on a regular basis.

I felt I was losing some control, so one day when I visited I determined to seize the initiative. Taking a deep breath I said, "Good morning," and with a nervous hesitation called him by his first name.

There was a deafening silence and he looked at me with a little surprise. Then he smiled. "Yes," he said, "I suppose the roles are now reversed. You are now in charge."

Despite his advancing years, he is still very alert mentally and usually has the crossword completed before 9 o'clock. Our relationship is still very friendly and I always enjoy a visit to him, as he is delightfully entertaining and an absolute pleasure to meet.

Sit!

It was a Saturday evening at Accident and Emergency, Glasgow Rangers had been playing against Aberdeen, and the department was throbbing. There were drunks, drug addicts, patients with trivial illnesses, those who would not bother to make an appointment with their GP and lastly the genuinely injured patients who realised they had a long wait ahead of them.

The staff were working flat out, stitching, dressings, Plaster of Paris splints, checking X-rays and desperately trying to quell the aggression of the drunks and those high on drugs.

The noise level was escalating and everyone was just a little fraught with the pressures of those demanding patients who know their rights but not their responsibilities.

Suddenly peace reigned, silence descended and everything appeared calm. What had happened?

I and my other colleagues popped our heads out of the cubicles where we were treating the sad and sick.

There, sitting quietly but majestically in the middle of reception was a large German Shepherd police dog, doing absolutely nothing but simply by his presence reducing the behaviour of yobs and troublemakers to zero.

The sight of Brutus (his name) was enough to sober up the most difficult of patients.

If only we could have had him every night.

'Splish-Splash'

"Oh doctor, thank you, thank you so much." This was the greeting of a certain middle-aged gentleman in the ward.

I was a final year student doing a locum just before Christmas. I had been on the ward for only one day when it was our turn to be on call. From 9 a.m. the emergency patients poured in, abdominal pain, haematemesis (vomiting of blood), appendicitis, pancreatitis, etc., etc., etc.

By 7pm, I had clerked 15 patients. There was no time to eat, no time to drink and barely time to go to the loo. Filling forms, taking blood samples (no phlebotomists in those days), setting up intravenous drips, arranging X-rays, speaking to relatives, hardly having time to draw breath.

I had just sat down with a very welcome cup of coffee, when the phone rang again, yet another admission.

The tiny thin gentleman was in agony. He had been to a pre-Christmas office party, where he was the odd-job man, but had left after one or two 'ponsy' drinks and met his mates in his local pub.

Unfortunately he had several quick pints to catch up and then having drank steadily for an hour or two, he went to pass urine and couldn't.

When I examined him his abdomen was grossly distended, and I could hear the splish-splash of fluid in his bladder, and he was desperate to relieve himself.

I had only passed a catheter once before, but I decided to try as all the other medical staff were involved in theatre.

Trying desperately not to reveal my anxiety or nervousness I slipped the catheter into the urethra, and praying under my breath, pushed the tube higher and higher 'till I felt a slight obstruction, then, 'bingo' a flow started, and gosh did it flow.

Relief was almost instant and thus the profuse thanks every time I passed his bed.

Strange Voices in the Night

"I need some sleeping tablets," exclaimed the rather agitated patient perched on the edge of his seat.

"What is your problem?" I asked. "Have you any worries or concerns?"

My patient was however, rather reticent about his need for sedatives. Without good cause I was unwilling to hand out sleeping pills so I pressed him to explain his problem. Very very reluctantly he opened up.

"The pills are not for me but for my wife," he stated.

"Why is she not consulting me herself then?" I asked.

Again he clammed up but eventually he said, "While I was dreaming last night I woke her up by calling out a lady's name and I would rather she did not question me as this lady is a 'good friend'!!"

I felt this was an euphemistic explanation and perhaps she was more than a passing acquaintance.

I did wonder how he was going to persuade his wife to swallow sleeping tablets when she really had no problems with insomnia.

Ten Green Bottles O Shades Of Tony Hancock

For many years I was Medical Officer of the British Red Cross and gave lectures at the various courses run by the Society. One course was at the Aberdeen Town House for Council employees and about 30 attended.

The first morning progressed with talks, demonstrations and practical work and at 12.30 we stopped for lunch. We all crowded into the lifts to take us to the dining room and everyone appeared to have enjoyed the course so far.

The lift was full to capacity and we ascended towards the eighth floor. Suddenly halfway up there was a loud bang and the lift ground to a halt. There was some nervous laughter, then silence. What would happen next? we thought to ourselves.

"We will be on our way in a moment or two," it was suggested, but without real conviction, then everyone fell silent.

Part of my introductory lecture was about keeping calm in a crisis and not to panic. I sensed and felt everyone looking at me and expecting a lead in this situation. The car was full and after a few minutes the temperature began to rise. I prayed that no one, especially any of the ladies, would mention the need to go to the toilet as that I felt would make everyone feel they needed to go!

Visions of Tony Hancock's TV sketch floated before me. Would we start singing 'Ten green bottles' or a similar ditty or would someone take hysterics and really cause a panic.

Mentally taking a deep breath, I thought 'should I ask what do you think of the Common Fisheries Policy or how can you justify the level of rateable tax for the City?' But then I decided to relate some of my experiences as a doctor. I tried to tell humorous tales and even some rather risqué ones to divert attention.

Luckily, it seemed to work but we were marooned for 45 very long minutes and, if I am strictly honest, I had a trace of anxiety myself during our incarceration.

Not A Happy Boy!

"When I returned from the Job Centre I caught my partner kissing this man," was his opening line when I started the consultation.

"Well, it took my breath away, what could I do, it's shocked me, and I'll never be the same again! I'm so stressed I shall have to ask you for some valium for my nerves!"

This was a new patient with a very pronounced Yorkshire accent who had recently arrived from Leeds with his partner, intent on starting a new life north of the Border.

"Also I think I have picked up something from the Job Centre, I have this very itchy rash especially at night. There are some very funny people down there. I cannot sleep, I toss and turn and my partner is sleeping peacefully as a baby, without a care in the world. It's not fair, it's not right, why should it happen to me?"

I decided to end the anguished tirade and asked him to show me the rash. This revealed classical scabies with burrows and evidence of scratching.

Did I add to his problems by revealing my diagnosis, or did I prevaricate to save him further stress?

"It's from those men at the Centre, isn't it? I know it is, they are horrible and unpleasant, not refined like Pat and I!" waving his hands dismissively.

I decided to bite the bullet. "This rash is due to scabies, you only pick it up when you are in very close contact with another person. Does Pat have an itchy rash also?"

"I don't know, we haven't spoken since the kissing episode, and I go to bed by myself. I am not going to share my bed with someone who is unfaithful. What would you think?"

"Well you both require treatment or it will not be cured, so better make up and say you're sorry," I said getting a little fed up with his moaning.

"Never," he said, "Pat can get his own treatment, he's a big boy now!!"

Pictures On The Walls

The elderly grey haired gentleman sat down nervously opposite me and waited.

"How can I help you?" I asked, as he was new to the practice.

"I should like to become private patients and I should prefer you to call at our home rather than attend your surgery. We seldom leave the house and my wife is very nervous in company."

I ascertained that neither had major medical problems or were taking any medication and I informed him that I was happy to look after them. He requested that I call the following week to meet his wife.

On the appointed day I drove to a large detached granite house in the west-end of the city. It seemed a huge house for the two of them and the old-fashioned bell tolled in the distance when I pulled the metal chain.

After what seemed an age I heard footsteps on a wooden floor and the door opened to reveal my patient in a green velvet smoking jacket.

He ushered me in and I stood in a large hallway panelled with rather dark wood. We passed down a long corridor between many framed canvases of paintings stacked against the wall. It seemed that every available space on the walls was hung with works of art.

We entering the sitting room where his wife sat by the fire, a tiny grey haired, distinguished but nervous looking lady. I introduced myself and at her invitation sat down opposite her. She had been remarkably healthy so the medical part of our conversation ended quite quickly and for something to say I remarked about the vast number of paintings adorning the walls.

It transpired that her late father-in-law had visited London and Paris around the turn of the century and bought paintings from artists, little known at the time, but who have since become famous, to use in the calendars he produced every year.

These paintings he had acquired for a song but were now worth a lot of money. With some pride I was shown a Van Gogh, a Cézanne, a Matisse and an early (understandable to my eyes) Picasso!

These and many more wonderful paintings were hanging and few Aberdonians realised they were there, but it made each of my visits most enjoyable.

Please May I Have...

The elderly gentleman waited patiently in the queue at the reception desk. The practice was particularly busy that Tuesday afternoon as it was the day after a public holiday and all the doctors were consulting and the waiting room was packed.

He reached the front desk and said, "Please may I have..." and then clutched his chest and fell to the floor.

Luckily, one of our practice nurses was standing close by and she assessed the situation and after calling for help started cardio pulmonary resuscitation.

Within a very short time she was joined by two doctors, one pushing the crash trolley.

Resuscitation proceeded steadily until it became obvious that the patient required to be 'shocked' using a defibrillator.

Just as in the TV series, *ER*, his shirt was ripped open, jelly applied to his chest wall and the familiar 'stand back' call rang out.

"160 joules!" called my partner and shocked the patient. As always happens he levitated from the floor with the electric current.

During all this activity, which was in full view of the waiting room, patients were watching agog as another shock was applied and again the body lifted.

On this occasion, the treatment was successful and the heart returned to normal rhythm. However, the drama was not yet over as an intravenous drip was inserted and an oxygen mask place over the patient's nose and mouth.

At that time, the ambulance arrived and the paramedics rushed in with all their gear only to find that everything possible had been done.

He was transferred to hospital, but we were now required to treat several waiting room patients who had been affected by the drama, which had enfolded before them.

Several patients, however, left the surgery stating that their complaints were trivial and really did not need the attention of a doctor.

Gin And 'It'

A glass was thrust into my hand, "Thank you for coming so promptly, doctor."

I really had little option, as I was on call during the Christmas period, although my shift was almost over and one of my colleagues would take over. The reason for the call was a little vague but seemed sufficient to warrant a house visit and also, the patient's parents were private patients of my Senior Partner.

I visited and examined the patient, who thankfully was not seriously ill, prescribed the necessary medication, and came down from the bedroom to a roomful of happy party makers all obviously enjoying themselves despite the invalid upstairs.

It was at this point that the glass was produced and I was wished 'Happy Christmas'. I was a little reticent to accept as I had 10 minutes left on call and it would be typical, to have to go to another patient.

This I explained to the patient's father but he was insistent: "One small drink for Christmas will not harm you." I was still unhappy so I requested that I use his telephone (no mobile phones in those days!) to check with my wife (and phone minder as most GPs wives were in those days) that there was nothing outstanding for me to attend to.

I accepted the drink, returned his toast, and sipped the amber liquid. It was sweet and pleasant and very warming as it slipped down. I immediately was introduced to various members of the family and offered some rather delightful 'nibbles' and joined a circle of as it turned out later all patients in the practice who had obviously been imbibing for some time. My glass as soon as it was empty was immediately refilled and this worried me somewhat as I still had to drive home.

By this time the effect of the first drink was kicking in and I had a lovely warm glow so I carefully deposited my glass behind a pot plant and said my goodbyes.

The cold air hit me and I then realised that one drink was definitely sufficient. But what had I been drinking?

It transpired later that the favourite family drink was 'Gin and It' otherwise a large neat gin and Italian sweet vermouth. I shudder to think what would have happened if I had had the second drink.

I Just Want A Repeat Prescription

Weighing at least 20 stones, although she claimed she did not eat enough to keep a sparrow alive, she plonked herself down and deposited her M&S bags on the floor, bulging with food all of which seemed to be of the high fat, high carbohydrate variety.

I did not know the patient as she was relatively new to the practice.

"I won't keep you long," she said. "I just require my repeat prescriptions."

She then produced her complete printout from her last practice and handed over all three pages.

I scanned these in amazement and increasing horror. She had pills for almost every conceivable illness and many would obviously interact with each other. So it was.

"These cause nausea, so I take these to counteract them... these cause a little skin irritation so I take these... these cause thrush, so I..." and so it went on.

I counted her daily intake, 47 tablets, plus a scalp lotion, and a couple of creams for her skin.

'Wow' I thought, 'not much wonder the NHS is in difficulty'.

Trying to reduce the number and variety proved a challenge, as she was very resistant to dropping any medication. Just how much iatrogenic illness did she have?

Bravery Or Bravado

Dressed in a tee shirt with 'Victoria Falls' emblazoned across the chest, baseball cap with the logo of Chobe Game Reserve, and his right arm in a sling and hobbling on a single crutch he entered the consulting room.

I looked at him in amazement as he removed his cap revealing thinning hair brushed forward to disguise his receding hairline.

'All right what happened?" I asked 'Can I take it you have recently returned from Southern Africa?'

'Well yes,' he replied and told me the full story.

He had observed some youngsters bungee jumping off the Zambezi Bridge and decided much against his wife's wishes to have a go. He was duly prepared and the elastic cords were tied to his ankles and he stood on the tiny platform at the middle of the bridge. Counting backwards from 5, he was warned to 'go' on 1 but the controller of the jumps pushed him off at 3.

'I have never been so terrified in my life,' he admitted and was extremely glad when he was winched up and on terra firma again.

His wife berated him mercilessly and told the story to the other guests in their hotel – The Victoria Falls Safari Lodge. He was both embarrassed and greatly annoyed by her recounting his terror.

'So you will not be white water rafting with us tomorrow?' asked a guest.

Furious at what had happened he decided to join the party on the Zambezi River just below the bridge from which he had recently jumped.

'I shall be there to join you,' he said with some bravado.

The raft was large and eight men were attached by lifelines as sometimes a body was flung overboard in the maelstrom.

The first stretch was exhilarating and wonderful and he was delighted he had come. Unfortunately, the river was low at the time and the raft had to be carried along the riverbank to the next stretch of suitable water.

Coming down the bank to lower the raft into the water he slipped on the wet rocks. Result, one fractured arm and severely torn knee ligaments.

'Well,' I asked, 'was it wise to attempt these activities at your age?'

With a rather hurt expression he said, "Oh come on doc, I'm only 67, I'm not over the hill yet!"

Can You Confirm?

Any doctor who has worked in the Accident and Emergency Department of a large hospital has a fund of true stories to tell of the various events and episodes which occur almost daily. Most are run of the mill and quite mundane and one becomes used to the drunks, the druggies, the RTA's, the dog bites and the simple falls but occasionally there is something quite out of the usual which one remembers.

It was late afternoon and the department was relatively quiet when a police car with blue lights flashing sped into the car park. Everyone braced themselves for a nasty emergency although we were usually routinely warned if there was a serious problem or major incident.

The door was flung open and a red-faced police constable carrying a black plastic bag rushed into the waiting area. I approached him and enquired as to the problem as I led him into an empty cubicle.

"Doctor, doctor could you please examine this," and he thrust the plastic bag at me.

I peered into the bag and discovered pieces of flesh and bone totally unrecognisable as a human being. Tell me the story I requested.

"This man jumped in front of the Aberdeen-London express train about an hour ago and these are all the pieces we could find. Could you please confirm absence of life!!"

'En Passant'

Never has the demonstration of his intellect been better shown than by the instant diagnosis of a young boy in his ward.

James had been admitted with a vague history of tiredness and general malaise. Everyone in his consultant's team, resident, registrar, senior registrar and the consultant himself had examined, questioned patient and parents, ordered more and more exotic tests to try and make the diagnosis, but to no avail.

Inevitably, other consultants were involved but the question remained unanswered. Books were perused, discussions over coffee invariably turned to James and his illness and the inability to decide exactly what was wrong.

When the Professor returned from his summer vacation he immediately decided to have a grand ward round to familiarise himself with all his patients in the ward.

As was usual the other consultants joined him and the retinue set off with me as the junior doctor at the rear.

Patient after patient was seen, examined and discussed till we reached James.

Without breaking step the Professor glanced at the undiagnosed young man and exclaimed, "That's the first case I have seen since I was a young doctor, I presume you have asked the neurologist for his opinion, although today, the treatment is quite straightforward."

To say you could hear a pin drop in the assembled company would be an understatement. In the wink of an eye the diagnosis was made 'en passant' from the end of the bed. Remarkable indeed.

Foreign Creepy-crawlies (or Guests from Barbados)

Cold miserable February in Scotland, the tan should have warned me, the glow one gets from foreign travel in sunnier climes, this patient had been on holiday.

She was, however, a little concerned about a problem and had already consulted one of my partners but the condition had not cleared.

The offending area was the sole of her right foot. It was dreadfully itchy and there was an accompanying rash.

On examination, I was surprised to see the classical signs of Cutaneous Larva Migrans, a disease due to the penetration of hookworm larvae into the skin.

"You have been walking barefoot on a foreign beach, haven't you?" An inane statement if ever to make, as one usually walks barefoot on a beach.

"I must show this to one of my junior doctors, I am sure she will never have seen this before and perhaps will not see it again, it is quite rare, you are the first patient I have ever seen with it."

Now I had to explain to my patient that she had larvae crawling under her skin and the rash was due to their tracts. It took a little persuasion that they would not appear in other parts of the body. No, they would not come down the nose or flit across the eye, or bore holes in the liver or kidneys.

"Treatment is quite simple, although the chemist will have to order these specially," and I asked her to make an appointment for the following week.

These darned instruction leaflets in all packets of medication can sometimes cause a lot of worry. On reading the possible but thankfully rare side effects of the drug was enough to drive my patient to phone and seek reassurance before she swallowed the tablets.

"No," I reassured her, "you are unlikely to get liver or kidney failure, profuse vomiting and diarrhoea only occurs rarely."

Very reluctantly she agreed to take the medication and thankfully when I saw her a week later the condition had cleared and she was a rather happier lady.

There was, however, a sequence to this story. This patient was a journalist in a local paper and related her experiences to a rather wider audience about how she had 'beasties under her skin' and how the treatment had side effects almost worse than death. I must say her account was most humorous and thankfully did not identify me.

The Sun Worshipers
(or the Dermatologist's nightmare)

Mounds of flesh, acres of skin, rolling together like a Michelin man, gleaming with suntan lotion and overflowing the lounger. An altogether too common picture on board.

Determined to return home bronzed, but, at this stage red and peeling like a newly cooked lobster. But, still they continue, causing goodness knows what damage to their skin.

The ability to follow the sun from the most advantageous spots is an art in itself, and woe betide anyone who upsets their routine. Chairs turned in unison, lotion applied, sizzle back, sizzle front, avoid strap marks so clothing lowered to dangerous levels, when it might all spill out and that would definitely not be a pretty sight.

Lying nearby were examples of past participants of the same art. Skin like leather, hanging in loose folds, wizened and prematurely aged. Such was the penalty for a desirable suntan.

The Victorians were correct, pale is beautiful.

The Pipe Band

She was the widow of the ex-Senior Partner's chauffeur. When her husband was alive, he would often be seen lovingly polishing the Rolls Royce Silver Shadow, which was his pride and joy.

Unfortunately, she had been a widow for some years but coped fairly well and kept good health and was not a patient we saw too often. It was the first time I had seen her for some time when her daughter asked me to call and see her mother with very vague reasons for the visit.

I rang the bell and she answered the door and expressed surprise at my visit. "I am not ill," she claimed and she certainly looked the picture of health. Just to make sure I suggested I give her a quick check over and she readily agreed.

I had just wrapped the blood pressure cuff round her arm when she suddenly cried, "Step back Doctor they're coming through!"

"Who is coming through?" I asked mystified.

"The Pipe Band," and pushed me against the wall where we stood for about a minute.

"Alright now," she said, "they've passed by," and we resumed taking her blood pressure. I had just finished when in an agitated voice she cried, "They're coming back," and again pushed me up against the wall.

"Didn't you think they looked very smart in their kilts?" she asked and then I knew that it was time for my psychiatric colleagues to pay her a visit!

Sisters

I have never known two sisters who hated each other quite so much and I had the dubious pleasure of attending both.

Whenever either of them consulted me, it seemed inevitable that sooner or later a sarcastic reference would be made regarding her sibling.

I therefore found myself 'piggy in the middle' and despite requesting a blanket ban on mentioning their sister, it was unfortunately like trying to hold back a bolting horse by shouting 'whoa'.

I listened to nasty, vehement, sometimes slanderous expressions of hate so many times, that I visited each sister and threatened to discontinue attending them or even perhaps request their removal from our practice list. (A threat which could be carried out in those days.) Thankfully, this stopped the unpleasantness, although one was aware of simmering feelings below the surface.

Over a period of several years, they both deteriorated in health. It was the elder who had widowed for many years who suffered a prolonged and painful illness.

I thought that this might be sufficient catalyst for them to resolve their differences but no contact at all was made.

A few weeks prior to her death she presented me with a porcelain figure strictly on the understanding that on no account would I give or sell it to her sister or her sister's family. She was so insistent that I have the ornament in recognition of my assistance to her over the years that I agreed to her wishes.

When eventually she passed away, I anticipated that this would be the end of the animosity, but unfortunately this was not the case.

Some weeks after her death I received a letter from her nephew requesting that I pass the ornament to him, as it was one of a pair and rightfully was his. I responded politely saying this was impossible for personal reasons. To my amazement, I then received what can only be described as a threatening lawyer's letter demanding that I accede to his demands.

My response that I had made a solemn promise not to part with the gift was followed up with an offer to buy the said figure. The offer was quite derisory and I did a little research and discovered that the pair together was worth a considerable amount of money.

Eventually I requested my lawyer to respond; having checked my position with my Medical Defence Company, and nothing more was heard.

Truly a case of hatred being carried to the grave.

Shaking All Over

Sweating and tremulous, he perched on the edge of the chair. He had the fearful anxious look of someone just off an alcoholic binge.

His previous history did indeed reveal alcohol abuse, but he had been 'dry' for over a year. However, on previous occasions when he started drinking he could only stop with great difficulty when he would often drink a bottle of whisky a day.

On the last occasion he gave the classic story of seeing spiders on the ceiling, elephants on the walls and was so jittery he could not hold a cup or even sign his name.

This latest crisis was triggered by the discovery that his wife was having an affair with his neighbour and flaunting it in his face, his 15-year-old daughter was pregnant and intended keeping the baby. The alleged father being a 16-year-old with a major drug problem and unemployed.

I felt quite sympathetic to him and promised to help, although I could not but feel that his problems would not go away and in a fit of depression he would hit the bottle again. It was like sitting on an unexploded time bomb.

However, the baby went for adoption, his daughter stayed on at school, he found a new lady friend, so perhaps the future is not quite so bleak.

Red Or White Wine, Madam?

In the practice I was well known for being extremely anti-smoking and I 'persuaded' or occasionally 'leant' on patients to encourage them to give up the dirty habit. I personally was put off ever starting to smoke when I worked during the long summer vacations as a corporation bus conductor. Observing passengers on the early morning journeys light up a cigarette and then proceed to cough and splutter for the duration of their journey, put me off smoking for life.

However, I was not quite so strong in my views on alcohol, and, as long as it was in moderation (I know, less than your doctor, etc.) I saw no good reason for giving it up. This might explain the next tale.

We met them at dinner. They would be our meal companions for the next two weeks on board our cruise ship in the Mediterranean. They were an elderly couple with no family, who cruised several times each year.

He was a quiet gentle sort of man who said little but was very attentive to his wife who herself was a little more animated and belied her external appearance.

We usually ordered red wine and asked if they wished to share some with us but quite politely this was declined.

"My wife only drinks sweet white wine and, so, thank you, we will stick to that."

He then proceeded to order sweet Sauternes and this was repeated at dinner each evening. It transpired that she had never actually tasted red wine but had convinced herself that she would not like it. As a result her poor husband was forced to drink sweet white wine even with red meat such as steaks and venison.

He was, as I have mentioned above, a quiet individual who had been a carpenter and had built luxury one-off houses in the South of England and had made a lot of money in doing so. Cruising was their great pleasure and they had been all over the world with various cruise liners, and everywhere he had conscientiously drank sweet white wine to please his wife.

One evening we had ordered a particularly nice bottle of Merlot which was fruity and mellow and I offered him a glass. Very hesitantly he accepted, after first refusing, having glanced furtively at his wife.

The wine was drunk with obvious relish much, I may say, to the slight disapproval of his wife who stuck resolutely to her Sauternes.

The next evening was a watershed, what would he do now? Obviously he enjoyed the red more than the white, but he was in a dilemma. I attempted to help. Again having chosen a rather palatable (not cheap) red wine I persuaded his wife to at least try a small sip, just to see if she liked it. Well, surprise, surprise she enjoyed it enormously.

"I did not realise how pleasant it could be!" was her comment.

From then on she was converted; she would have red wine at dinner and discard the sweet white. The only slight drawback was that the red wine I had chosen was at the more expensive end of the wine list. However, he could afford it and was quite happy to pay for the pleasure of having a good wine with his meals.

In private he thanked us profusely and we felt that he would enjoy cruising in the future.

Newly Retired (Or life after General Practice)

Overnight from being a busy professional, to suddenly having time on his hands, insufficient to do and a wonderful ability to get under his wife's feet.

Her daily routine, which had evolved over many years, was suddenly upset. Her golf at the club, her day at the Charity Shop, coffee mornings with Sue, Penny and Ann. These have to take second place to his whims and wishes.

'Come, let us do this, that, t'other' and he expected immediate response as he had done with his members of staff who had previously jumped to his every wish and command.

But this was not the office, or the surgery, where he dispensed advice and expected it to be followed; this was home! Having previously spent more waking hours with his staff than with his wife, this was a major blow to both their systems.

His golf had previously been limited to his Saturday morning foursomes, but now he had to join the seniors and play with anybody and everybody for his prize of a ball in Texas scrambles, greensomes, stablefords and various strange competitions.

He now had to play with the Major, (retired), a self-centred, self-opinionated gin-drinking prat, who prized himself in knowing the obscure rules of the game and invoking them at every opportunity.

He had to play with that retired dentist who he detested, for he was a 'bandit' and always scored well in the stablefords. He was not unknown to pick up his ball to 'check that it was his' and replace it in a slightly more favourable lie. He also never spoke to his partners and was interested in no one but himself. Even worse, he never bought a round in the clubhouse, although he was quick to accept hospitality.

Home again, mealtimes were a nightmare. When he was working he always had plenty to tell about his day. Now however, he had nothing more to discuss than whom he met while collecting his morning paper, the story line in *Eastenders* which previously he had never even contemplated or deigned to watch.

Now he was on a cruise liner to celebrate his retirement. He was captive; he could not leave the ship. Now lying on the sundeck among semi-naked bodies, gleaming with oil, which would have been better covered up, was sheer hell to him.

He gave up the uneven struggle and ensconced himself in the bar and after a few gins, the world seemed a better place through rose tinted spectacles.

However, what of the future? One felt he would slowly decline and become a miserable, bitter man, older than his years.

He got no pleasure from his grandchildren whom he considered noisy, badly behaved and demanding. Leaving work had robbed him of all life's pleasures, but he was squeezed out against his will by a ruthless partner.

He viewed the future with dread and foreboding.

In The Dark

There was an audible 'pop' as the bulb of the angle-poise bedside lamp finally ended its limited life.

This was significant and important, when you are 3 days post-op, after a hip replacement, and only just managing, to go to the loo unaided.

This was the only light which was controlled from the handheld remote control. I could still select the channel and the volume of the radio station, also the emergency bell to summon help, but no other lighting for my room. The other ceiling lights were operated from a switch by the door.

To try to locate my zimmer frame and stagger to the toilet in the dark would be almost impossible, and frankly, stupid and dangerous. Thus, I reported the fault to the staff and was assured the matter would be passed on to the Maintenance Department, and an electrician would visit to replace the faulty bulb. No doubt, the forms had to be completed in triplicate; nothing is easy or straightforward in the NHS. I idly wondered how many men it would take, to change this particular bulb.

When the night staff discovered I had unsatisfactory lighting, I received strict instructions to call for help, and on no account to attempt to visit the toilet on my own.

Now, due to previous urological surgery, I suffer from nocturia i.e. frequency of micturition at night, so I make many visits to the toilet, and was quite embarrassed having to ring frequently for assistance. However, I was confident the problem would be resolved very quickly. After all, it was only a 30-second job, and something which all of us did frequently at home.

Surprise, surprise, surprise, nothing happened, and each evening, the night staff, repeated their advice that I had to call every time I went to the 'loo'.

After 4 days, one of the night staff expressed annoyance at the ridiculous delay, on finding my lamp had not been fixed. She stomped off and I thought nothing more of it.

Allegedly, about 2 minutes later, she reappeared, removed the useless bulb, and replaced it with another from her pocket.

I must have been asleep when all this happened, or else I was having a very vivid dream, as I am certain I was sworn to secrecy that such a thing could happen. I assumed that it must have been the dedicated maintenance people working late at night, for the benefit of the patients, who corrected the problem.

I was delighted to find a perfectly working bedside light when I awoke in the morning.

I Feel Quite Slim

My trousers are tighter, my shirt buttons are straining slightly, but I feel comparatively slim. The appetite and food consumption of some of our fellow passengers is astonishing. Course after course of rich, high calorie dishes are despatched effortlessly.

And, the results are there for all to see. Bulging abdomens, huge bottoms and rolls and rolls of fat in between, so reminiscent of Michelin men. Some men are enormous, and they wobble ungainly around the decks; they must be uncomfortable, and goodness knows what the pressure on their joints causes, but still they persist.

At set meal times they often have two starters, two main courses and a mountain of dessert with unmentionable number of calories. The waiters serve this without batting an eyelid but many must reflect on the starving millions when they observe this gluttony reminiscent of a Roman orgy.

Unfortunately, food is available almost 24 hours a day. One restaurant serves good food on demand, as well as burgers, corned beef hash, etc., which I must admit looks very tempting. At any time, day or night, there are our American cousins tucking into food swilled down with Coke (not diet) and 7-up.

Slim, lithe, svelte females are few and far apart. For once, the Brits look better than those from across 'the pond'. Our dress may be inferior to the French or Italians but the Stateside population cannot dress or eat correctly. It almost seems a proud statement to be big, obese, all-conquering American.

He Got His Own Back

As I parked my car outside the surgery, a taxi drew up and dropped off a passenger. I entered the building ahead of him and held open the door for him. Thinking nothing more about it I went to my consulting room ready to start afternoon surgery.

I called my first patient and who should appear but the man from the taxi. He explained he was now working in Aberdeen, and needed to consult a doctor to replenish his drugs.

He informed me, he suffered from anxiety for which he took diazepam, chronic back pain which required powerful pain killing drugs in the form of dihydrocodeine, and insomnia which was only helped by nitrazepam sleeping tablets. He was rather in a hurry he explained as he had another appointment, so would I just give him the prescriptions and he would be on his way.

He was deeply unhappy when I refused to give him a script, but I did explain that I would phone his last doctor to verify his story, as the drugs he wished were potentially addictive and should only be prescribed for a short period of time.

With this he became very abusive and called me all sorts of rather unflattering names. He then became frankly aggressive and leaned across my desk in a very threatening manner.

For the first time ever I pressed my panic alarm button under the desk. One of my young receptionists knocked timidly on the door and asked if I was alright. In a rather strangled voice I shouted 'no', and thankfully two of my male partners burst into the room.

We briefly discussed phoning the police, but decided rather, to escort the gentleman from the building, leaving it at that, having noted the name he had provided and taken a good description.

The whole episode left me feeling rather shaken, but worse was to follow. A patient who had left at the same time as my erstwhile patients, returned quickly to reception, and reported that this gentleman had drawn a nail or some such instrument along the length of my relatively new Saab car, and then run off.

Of course the police did not manage to catch him, and I was left with a deep score on my pride and also on the paintwork right down to the bare metal.

He really had made quite an effort to extract his revenge.

Do Not Bother Me!

Many years ago, my family were on holiday with a colleague's family. We were staying at a rather nice hotel and to this day I am surprised we were able to afford 5-star luxury, considering the rather meagre pay of young doctors. Those were the days, before European directives, when working a 70-80 hour, or indeed longer week, was considered the norm. Unfortunately our remuneration was not commensurate with the hours worked!

The children were all in the 8-12 age bracket and played very happily together in the swimming pool and other water amusements, whilst the adults soaked up the sun, read, snoozed or enjoyed cool refreshments.

One morning there appeared a very well-known TV personality at the poolside. He made no pretence of modesty, but flaunted his fame, prancing about simply soaking up the glances and smiles of recognition. It really was a case of 'look at me, I'm a celebrity'.

He spoke to no one but demanded instant attention from the staff. Fresh towels, cool drinks and his sunbed moved to a more advantageous position. Even worse, he insisted those sun loungers near to him be moved away so he could have privacy.

He very obviously became, and showed his annoyance, with the laughter and noise as children leapt in and out of the pool, shouting and splashing and having a good time. Unfortunately for him, there was no way of curbing this fun, which was upsetting him.

Things became a little quieter as lunchtime approached and families settled down with food from the poolside bar or made their way to the hotel for a more formal meal.

One little girl quite innocently approached the TV star and requested his autograph. Perhaps her parents should have advised against this, but no one was quite prepared for the stream of invective that the child was subjected to. You could hear a pin drop as four lettered words punctured the air. There was a feeling of tension, surprise and even anger in the gathered company.

Tearfully the little girl made her way back to her family to be consoled and the babble of voices grew as the incident was discussed. To say that he was ignored thereafter was a gross understatement.

And, the relevance to medicine in this story. The very next day a call went out for a doctor to treat this very gentleman (?) who had become ill.

Strangely not a single medical person, and we were not the only doctors in the hotel, was available, and he had to wait quite a long time, we were later told, for a local practitioner to visit.

Do I Need A 'Shot'?

When oil was discovered in the North Sea in the early 1970's, many Americans arrived in Aberdeen to lend their expertise in the new offshore oil fields. They obviously required medical attention and registering with a Practice was a new experience as at that time Family Doctors were not common in the US.

A charming American family consulted me one day and requested a referral to an Otolaryngologist (ENT specialist in UK), for their 7 year old son. He evidently had a sore throat and painful ears, and in the past while in Houston, mum had consulted with a specialist for this condition.

I explained that perhaps I might be able to treat this problem, but this suggestion met with some surprise and not a little disbelief.

Examination revealed a nasty infection of the tonsils and a middle ear infection, and I confirmed that treatment was straightforward and simple with some penicillin.

A look of horror appeared on the little boy's face. "Do I need a shot?"

When I announced that the treatment consisted of some syrup and no injection he immediately showed relief. Obviously in the past penicillin had been (painfully) administered intramuscularly.

Examination 5 days later revealed complete cure and I had made a friend for life, or at least during his stay in Aberdeen.

Called By The Cat

One learns in General Practice the wide variety of personalities present; some traits seem to run in families.

Two sisters, both widows, had the amazing ability to demand home visits when they really were able to come to the surgery. Perhaps in today's climate they would be persuaded otherwise, but in days of yore, GPs were far more liable to see patients at home. Of the two sisters mentioned above, I saw the elder while one of my female partners saw the other.

I had not been in the Practice when her husband was alive, but I guess he was a rather meek henpecked gentleman if the behaviour of his wife was anything to go by. She dominated everyone although she did it very skilfully and many were manipulated unknowingly.

I reluctantly have to admit for some time she persuaded me to undertake home visits quite unnecessarily. I was at the time quite a young doctor and probably more willing to visit than I needed to.

She did, however, suffer from quite severe asthma and recurrent bronchitis, possibly not helped by an allergy to her cat, which she steadfastly refused to get rid of. Also, the range of effective medication at that time was fairly limited.

However, she always seemed fit enough to undertake all her social activities and was often seen out and about at all the well-known tea rooms, the theatre and church functions.

I slowly became able to persuade her that the number of house calls she demanded was excessive and things became more manageable.

Over a period of years we gradually settled into a regime which I must admit was more comfortable for me than for her. Possibly this was helped by the emergence of newer and more effective drugs.

One day I received a demand from a neighbour to say that my patient's cat seemed very agitated and would I call immediately! I mean, a house call for an agitated cat! Most GPs will tell you a sixth sense often warns you there is something unusual and I did visit quite quickly.

Entry was impossible as both the front and back doors were locked, but with the help of the neighbour's key, I opened the back door. There, sitting quite peacefully in her armchair was my patient. Unfortunately, she had passed away but not all that long ago.

In this case, her cat had been quite correct in indicating the need for a house call!

Incidentally, my partner who attended her sister never managed to alter her behaviour and demands for attention. This only changed when retiral caused a change in her GP and he was definitely not one to be manipulated.

Always busy

It was 8.30 on a Monday morning and I was driving to the Maternity Hospital where I was a Registrar in the Newborn Baby Unit. It was a glorious sunny crisp morning as I drove on 'autopilot' listening with enjoyment to Terry Wogan on the radio.

Suddenly my reverie was shattered, a policemen in a luminous over-jacket, stepped out into the roadway and indicated I should stop. I opened my window and was told.

"You have been recorded doing 45 mph in a 30 mph area."

Hastily I replied, "I am Dr Gray and am on my way to the Maternity Hospital. If you have to charge me, could it be done later?"

"You work as a doctor there?" he asked. "You are going directly to the hospital?"

"Yes," I claimed, but I did not mention it was not an emergency call. He took the hospital phone number and allowed me to proceed.

I had just entered the front door when I was told that there was an emergency Caesarean Section and I was required in theatre right away.

Of course the police phoned while I was at the birth and sister explained that I was busy in theatre attending an operation so they rang off.

Approximately one hour later, I was busy carrying out an exchange transfusion for a jaundiced Rhesus affected baby when the police rang again.

"He is carrying out a delicate procedure on a newborn baby," Sister reported, so they rang off again.

Later, while on a ward round with the Professor of Child Health the police rang for a third time. Although the nurse was instructed to say I could not be disturbed, I requested that the phone number of the police office be obtained so I could return the call.

I did so a little later and was told by a very apologetic policeman. "I am sorry to disturb you as you are obviously very busy, but could you please try to keep to the speed limit in future and on this occasion no charges will be brought!"

A Shot To Be Remembered By

Rose was a particularly keen and good golfer and played with her usual partners at least twice a week, come rain or shine.

This particular Tuesday (Ladies day) it was raining cats and dogs, but she would have no truck with cancelling the game. "A spot of rain will do you no harm," she told her companions. So, waterproofs donned, umbrellas opened, they made their way to the first tee, where the opening hole was a challenging 198 yard par three.

As Rose teed up, the rain appeared to get heavier, and all one could hear as she addressed the ball was the hiss of torrential rain similar to the tropical storms she had experienced in her early married life when she and her husband lived in Malaysia where he was the manager of a rubber plantation.

Using her new graphite shafted 3-wood she swung her club with that slow and rhythmical arc, which has stood her in good stead in many competitions over the years especially last summer when she won the club championship.

Her partners followed the flight of the ball as it soared into the sky and the strangest thing happened. The rain stopped and in the distance a single shaft of sunlight shone down.

The ball towered upwards and landed on the front edge of the green and rolled towards the hole; could this be her first hole-in-one after all these years?

Rose was in no position to see her beautiful shot. She sank down gently without a sound and was dead before she hit the ground. At least she would have been delighted to end her golfing career with a magnificent shot in pouring rain with her closest friends there to witness the fact.

A Dysfunctional Family

I had known the family for many years and although I had no real problems with them, they did cause hassle. Inevitably they 'lost' their prescriptions, or someone stole their drugs, or the tablets ended up in the pocket of the jeans which were in the washing machine, or the dog/cat/parrot destroyed the script. Their excuses were endless and I only wished I had written them all down.

For once, the family dynamics had seemed relatively stable and everyone breathed more easily. Then, of course, a crisis arose. The daughter had started taking drugs quite out of the blue and became an addict. She was admitted, treated and discharged from drug detox. However, she was encouraged to explain why she started taking drugs in the first place and a horrendous story emerged.

Evidently, her mother had wanted a termination when she was pregnant with daughter and resented her after she was born. Younger brother came along and the sun and moon shone on him.

He, however, was a complete disaster and at quite a young age became hooked on 'soft' drugs initially but then progressed on to crack cocaine and heroin. During one of his really bad trips he had raped his sister and she became pregnant. The pregnancy, however, was blamed on a current boyfriend although it appears he was a convenient stooge in the proceedings.

Several years passed and the daughter's little boy grew up in a most unstable environment, sometimes being with his mother, sometimes with his implied father, occasionally with either set of grandparents and even in care under the social workers.

By this time her brother was serving a jail sentence and I was led to believe he had kicked his drug habit and was a reformed character.

The matter came to a crisis when his sister was asked by her mother to smuggle drugs into prison while visiting her brother. These were to be used both for himself and also sold to other prisoners. The story of being 'clean' was a total lie and one suspects that some of the 'lost' prescriptions or drugs actually found their way into jail.

A huge row had erupted when she had refused to carry in the drugs and she was threatened by both her parents. As a result, she had blown the whistle and revealed she had only started taking drugs after her rape. She had been forcibly told by her brother and his mates, that they would deal with her, if she revealed the true story.

What will eventually happen after he is released from prison I do not know, but I feel this scenario has not yet ended.

A Crowded Room

It was a Saturday, late in the evening, when the request or rather a demand for a house call came in. I was a very junior GP doing my Trainee year and I had heard about the family but had never met them. I believe they were well known to the police for their multifarious skirmishes with the law.

With a certain amount of trepidation I drove into the cul-de-sac in a less desirable area of town and parked beside a beat up Ford Cortina. The tenement corridor was dark and smelly as I made my way to the patient's flat. With some hesitation I knocked and a dog started barking. The door was flung open and I was told 'in there' pointing to a door. I entered a crowded room, where my patient, obviously the patriarch, sat at one side of a blazing fire and his wife opposite him. Six adults were standing around and three children were fighting for toys on the floor. A large Alsatian was padding around sniffing my bag and a cat sat on the back of the settee.

I surveyed the scene and felt a touch of apprehension. 'What do I do now' I thought. Taking a big breath and fully aware I might be making a huge mistake, I said as firmly as I could to the old man.

"Are you the patient?" He nodded but said nothing and appeared to be in some pain.

"Right, dog out, cat out, kids out, and the rest of you out."

There was silence, no one moved.

"Do you want me to treat you?" I asked, looking directly at the patient. He nodded slowly and miraculously the room cleared.

I examined him and found he had a kidney stone and was really quite unwell. I gave him an injection and issued some painkillers from my bag. I instructed him to go to bed, drink copious amounts of fluid and remain there till I saw him in the morning. I demanded that he keep a specimen of urine in a clean container for me to test.

The family, all crowded in the kitchen, watched in silence as I left, and I wondered if my car or I would leave intact. However, all was quiet as I drove away.

The next morning, promptly at 10am I arrived, and to my amazement the family scattered in front of me. I examined my patient and found to my relief that he had passed the stone and was feeling much better. It appeared he at least had faith in me.

I never had any further problems with that family; indeed, they specifically requested me for future consultations.

Rudeness Never Pays

My next patient had not arrived so I wandered down to the front desk, as I like to 'keep an eye' on what is happening.

One of the receptionists was having a difficult time with a patient on the phone who was obviously being quite rude and aggressive. She was becoming a little distressed so I motioned for her to hand the phone over to me.

I listened in amazement to the torrent of abuse pouring down the line, which continued unabated for about 30-40 seconds.

When he paused for breath I informed him whom he was now speaking to, and immediately he changed tack and became quite charming and effusive.

Deliberately raising my voice, so that the crowded waiting room could hear, I exclaimed, "I have listened to your foul and abusive invective, thinking you were still speaking to my receptionist. That behaviour is totally unacceptable in this practice. You and your family will henceforth find a new doctor as you are no longer welcome at this practice."

One observing receptionist was quite sure the patients in the waiting room exchanged knowing glances and even sat up straighter in their seats.

Stick To Medicine, Doc

The game between Gala and Hawick was tough and unrelenting, a typical hard Borders derby match, with no quarter given on either side.

With the score at 16 all, the game was finely poised and play was end to end. It had been a difficult game to referee with many personal feuds being settled, and especially up front where it was keenly contested and all the forwards were battling it out with every dirty trick in the book being used.

After a knock-on I ordered a scrum and with typical crunch the front rows packed down. The scrum-half fed the ball and suddenly the front rows collapsed.

The players disentangled and everyone except one prop forward stood up. He lay moaning and clutching his shoulder.

It was obvious he was in trouble and I quickly examined him and found he had dislocated his shoulder. Medical aid seemed to be taking an age, so I asked him if he wished my help. He agreed, and I attempted to reduce the dislocation, and thankfully, it popped back into place at the first attempt.

The surrounding players seemed very impressed by my medical intervention, but I somehow got the feeling they thought I was a better doctor than a referee!

What Are You Doing Here?

"Come in doctor, thank you for coming so promptly." I did think he looked remarkably fit having requested an urgent house call for chest pain. My patient was new to the practice and no notes were available.

He did not admit to any acute problem and looked rather mystified when I started questioning him about his problem.

"Doctor I'm only expecting the letter your colleague promised to pop in prior to my trip to the hospital."

At that point the doorbell rang and a GP colleague from another practice appeared.

"What are you doing here?" he asked.

I explained about my emergency call for chest pain and he inquired if I had the correct address. At that point I contacted the surgery and discovered I should have gone to Grove, not a Gardens in the area.

Unfortunately, my receptionist had noted down the incorrect address for the call. I hurriedly made my way to the correct address and found my patient had taken some Bicarbonate of Soda in water, burped violently and felt much better, thankfully!

Patients Are Everywhere

Even on holiday, it is impossible to escape from patients. We were in Rome with another couple and were visiting the Vatican.

Having viewed the magnificent Sistine Chapel and the various parts of the enormous St Peter's Basilica with its 60-foot marble altar, I was keen to climb to the top of the Cupola as it was reported that there were superb panoramic views over Rome.

It was a considerable climb to the top and a little scary if you were afraid of heights, and my wife and our friend's husband decided against it.

So, two of us proceeded up the stairway to the top of the dome. It was very dramatic seeing the Altar dwarfed and visitors looking like ants on the floor. We climbed higher and higher and the last part was up a very steep ladder with only room for two people to pass.

Halfway up, I heard a voice beside me. "How nice to see you Doctor, and this must be your wife!!"

Explanations seemed a little too complicated, but I did realise that despite the innocence of this meeting my patient might have viewed it in a different light and a completely erroneous interpretation put on the episode.

A Rare Condition

Although every day is different in General Practice there is inevitably a certain repetition of the same medical conditions. One of the best abilities is to spot the unusual at an early stage of the illness.

Every experienced GP will admit to running on 'auto-pilot' during some consultations and therein lies the danger of missing a potentially serious condition.

It is so tempting when Mr X or Mrs Y or a frequent child attendee appears to almost switch off. The story is almost always the same, whether it is a recurrent problem, a recurrent theme about a family member, or a mother fussing excessively over a minor childhood ailment. Mentally you think, 'yes, yes, yes,' I've heard it all before.

Thankfully there also seems to be that sixth sense which alerts you to something just that little unusual. The phrase, the tone, or the expression brings you back to earth very rapidly.

The patient sitting at the side of my desk came from a family of frequent attendees. Hardly a week went past without one or more members appearing in the surgery; and it was seldom any thing too serious. However, this member of the family was a fairly rare patient; he was a student and apparently doing quite well at University studying Electrical Engineering. He was in his final year and had already fixed up a job with an oil company in the city.

I listened with care as he rather embarrassingly told me he was probably wasting my time. Now, I thought, that's a first for this family, who thought nothing of wasting doctor's time any day. He was also a little reticent to elaborate what exactly was the problem.

Eventually he explained he thought he had a lump in his breast, but stated of course it was only females who got that. I agreed it usually was the ladies who suffered from that but that I had better have a look.

I confirmed he had a lump and mentally reviewed the common causes of this in men and realised there were not too many I could think of. He was not taking any medication, he was a little too old for hormonal causes, he did not have any testicular problems, so after that, I had to think of the unusual.

I referred him to one of my surgical colleagues who saw him fairly quickly. I was not however prepared for the diagnosis which was made. He had cancer of the breast and unfortunately it was a particularly aggressive type and the prognosis was uncertain.

He eventually underwent surgery followed by radiotherapy and then had a rather bad reaction to chemotherapy. Unfortunately all this did not prevent the relentless progression of the disease and he died about a year later. A very sad end to a very rare illness.

A Lesson To Us All

I have seldom heard anyone quite so vehemently anti-smoking as Dod. He preached this to every child with whom he came into contact.

He had very good reason to do so. From about the age of 10 he had smoked; initially as every schoolboy did, behind the bike sheds, or furtively in the local cinema.

When he left school he started work in a factory where smoking was de rigueur, and thence into the Army for National Service. There, of course, cigarettes were cheap and freely available. Soon, he was a 40-a-day man and this continued all his married life. Surprisingly, his wife did not smoke and interestingly none of his three sons ever started.

When I first met Dod he was still able to work, but had frequent absences for chest problems. Acute Bronchitis progressed on to Chronic Bronchitis and then to Emphysema, and his appearance at the surgery became more and more frequent. Time off work escalated as he became more and more breathless and disabled.

Finally, after much pressure from me and the Chest Physicians, he decided to quit smoking, but the damage was done and he slowly tipped into pulmonary failure. His ability to leave the house became more and more infrequent and each winter he resigned himself to four walls and the TV and the slightly unusual hobby of embroidery.

Seeing a man doing petit point still provokes a rather unreal vision, but he was very skilful and completed many complicated patterns. Many friends received elaborately stitched cushions or pictures at Christmas and I was the happy recipient of such as gift. His wife was a very keen knitter and she purchased a knitting machine and produced many scarves, jerseys and gloves while he patiently stitched away.

Inevitably he became completely house bound and could not walk across the living room without stopping at least once. He had to shave sitting down and even that took an age.

Oxygen therapy in those days meant the supply of large cylinders which had to be delivered weekly by the local pharmacy. This of course made his life just a little easier. I became quite used to carrying on a conversation through an oxygen mask.

However, the most surprising feature of Dod's illness was his failure to complain or moan about his medical problems. His response to any enquiry about his health was always positive. If, he was really ill, he might suggest that 'he was not worth a b*****', and that meant he was feeling really unwell.

Everyone who visited him received a warm welcome and because of his lack of lament at his (self-inflicted) ailments, he had a constant stream of visitors. It was a pleasure to pop in and neighbours children would carry out little tasks for him with pleasure. There was always a sweet or chocolate for them and kind words of thanks.

One November day when the sleety snow was at its most miserable, I received a request to visit. On this occasion he was really very ill; a visitor had brought in the flu, and he caught, not a fluey cold but true influenza. He was desperately ill and I wanted to admit him to hospital, but he flatly refused. He acknowledged his time was up and he preferred to die at home, surrounded by his friends and family.

Even to the very end, he never complained and thankfully he slipped away peacefully. A very sick man who it was a pleasure to know and treat.

In Control To The Bitter End

Domineering, forceful, aggressive, were some of the more acceptable adjectives used to describe the tall, thin faced, chronically unhappy lady. Some of the others were rather less polite.

In *her* eyes, she was of course, never wrong, and woe betide anyone who thought otherwise and dared to disagree. There was no point in discussing it, argument was futile.

She entered a room like a tempest and her loud penetrating voice, and her peremptory manner, could, and should have warned those in her vicinity that she would stand for no nonsense.

To have carried out any task in her home would have been a nightmare. Nothing would have been of an acceptable standard of workmanship or quality; something or someone would obviously not realise that her demands were not being met. Just how could one not see that the job was totally botched, or not completed within a realistic time?

She had one daughter who from all accounts had a miserable life. Her schoolwork was not of a high enough standard, her behaviour was certainly not what she expected and the poor girl was apparently not allowed any friends unless they had been vetted and passed acceptable in her extremely critical eyes.

At the first opportunity the poor girl, who until then was expected to be at home as a companion, or more truthfully a slave to her mother, somehow managed to meet a young man through the church. Of course it went without saying that he was not of the 'required breeding or social status' which she wanted for her daughter. Obviously the girl was marrying below her station; a titled gentleman would have perhaps been almost acceptable.

In today's terminology she would have been labelled a social climber, very similar to the TV personage of Mrs Bucket (Bouquet), and all this happened 65+ years ago.

Despite her mother putting every objection in her way, and criticising the young man for every perceived fault possible, they somehow got married and she escaped the hell-hole of the family home. Unfortunately, they lived not too far away, and mother continued her control freakery even from a distance. Gratuitous advice was constantly thrown in their direction and goodness only knows how the marriage survived.

But survive it did and her husband carved out a very successful and lucrative career and they brought up two lovely daughters. Still the voice from afar tried and sometimes succeeded in influencing her daughter, who it has to be said, had the patience of Job in dealing with the situation.

Eventually her father died, probably of complete exhaustion from living in that environment for so many years and being bullied and dominated non-stop. This of course placed even more pressure on the daughter as according to her mother she was totally unable to carry out even the smallest household task. Neighbours had by this time long deserted the irascible woman so no help was forthcoming from them.

Years passed and eventually she (mother) was admitted to a Retirement Home where, as expected, she caused problem after problem and general mayhem.

Finally, at the age of 102 she passed on, much to the relief of the family. But, there was one final sting in her tail. Her daughter suffered a heart attack at the funeral and had to be rushed to hospital in the middle of the ceremony!

Taken For A Ride

Wire-rimmed NHS spectacles similar to John Lennon's, but as remote from the iconic pop star, as a snowflake in the Sahara Desert.

His hair was permanently dishevelled and badly needing a shampoo and the attention of a good hairdresser; his nose seemed to be continually dripping and his skin pockmarked from juvenile acne and still spotty and red, at the age of 42.

He was a University Lecturer in Sociology and brilliant though he might be intellectually, personality wise he was a disaster. No spark, no charm, no charisma, nothing to make him attractive to his fellow human beings.

But, there he was, sitting in my consulting room, with the most attractive young lady at his side. Where he had none, she had sparkle and vivacity. Where he had a skin with scars and spots, hers was flawless. Her hair gleamed with that wonderful blue-black sheen, and she positively oozed good health and well-being.

Just what was the set-up? It appeared he had gone on holiday to Ski Lanka, met her in a hotel bar and lo and behold within two weeks they married and travelled back to Aberdeen.

It appeared that she was the patient needing to consult me, and she requested to see me alone. She was quite reticent and appeared slightly embarrassed. Eventually she admitted she was still a virgin and that the marriage had not been consummated in the few weeks since their marriage.

She then burst into tears and explained between sobs that she just could not bring herself to have sex with her new husband. Now I had a problem; what was the best advice I could offer?

She was absolutely adamant that she would not change her mind. However she was distressed and looking for help.

Obviously I could not order her to relent and consummate the marriage. I knew that no drug therapy would help and I suspected that psychotherapy would be worthless.

Then the obvious struck me. Had she used marriage simply as a means to enter the UK, and, shamefully she agreed that this had indeed been the case. I was a little unsure of the legal technicalities but I wondered if a non-consummated marriage could be annulled.

This would of course cause a further problem and on explaining this brought more floods of tears. I could foresee this consultation going on and on, so I promised to check the legal side and asked her to return and see me in a few days time.

This she did, and returned with what I can only describe as a determined look in her face. She claimed that sex had taken place, but, just how complete or satisfactory I could not be sure. She claimed that the legal requirements had been fulfilled, and, then the bombshell. She was leaving him and making a life for herself.

To this day, I have neither seen nor heard from her, although her 'husband' still attends another doctor in the practice. I do not think he wishes to consult me; perhaps he thinks I caused the break-up!

Surprise, Surprise

Mrs L. was a 'grump'. She seldom smiled and never ever seemed to have any visitors and her only companion was a ginger cat who appeared as miserable as her mistress.

I visited occasionally as required and always found her alert and 'on the ball'. She was inevitably sharp and quite brusque in her manner, and I was put in my place on more than one occasion. She had strong opinions on many things varying from the government of the day and especially the Prime Minister whom she absolutely detested. Thankfully, I agreed with her on that point.

The lack of manners and respect shown to those who deserved it also brought withering comments. She was of the slightly old-fashioned opinion that the doctor, dominie (schoolteacher) and Church minister should be so treated but only if they deserved that accolade.

Perhaps in her younger day those professionals had a higher standard of behaviour and morals, or more possibly there was not the media cover of today, to report on all the misdemeanours and indiscretions.

Despite not being the most amicable of persons, her neighbours did not have any real problems with her. She simply kept herself to herself and this seemed to be accepted. She seldom left the house apparently, but I discovered that she did her shopping late in the evening at her local corner shop, having met her there when I was buying some milk.

I was amazed to note that she had several greetings cards in her basket, which seemed surprising knowing how few visitors she had, but I thought no more about it.

In her neighbourhood there was a generous fairy godmother who distributed various little gifts and no-one knew who the benefactor was. Girls getting married, 21st birthdays and new baby arrivals all benefited from this largesse and it was widely thought that a well-to-do couple at the end of the street was the source. However, my patient never seemed to be a recipient, even on her 80th birthday, which was slightly surprising.

One day she requested a house call and on arrival I found her seriously ill with pneumonia and heart failure. She was experiencing a medical sensation known as 'a feeling of impending doom'. She realised she might not survive this illness and she asked (or rather demanded) that I post some letters for her. She was correct in her assumption as she died 5 days later.

As you may now have surmised, the secret benefactor was my grumpy patient. It was she who gave presents so generously to everyone. Indeed her last will and testament continued in this vein and many charities, friends and neighbours benefited from this kind lady.

Rags To Riches

She came to Aberdeen from Eastern Europe to escape the communist regime which was so alien to her upbringing.

Well-educated from a comfortable middle class family she had to learn English although she had a smattering from her schooldays. Her family were left behind, as she was the only one able to escape the clutches of the authorities who desperately and forcibly prevented anyone fleeing from the oppressive regime.

Using her considerable intelligence and courage, she arrived in Scotland albeit without a penny to her name, and with only the clothes she stood in. She had one contact in Aberdeen and he provided her with food and a bed when she arrived.

The only job available to her was as a shop assistant, where despite her limited English she managed to serve the general public. Her natural ability allowed her to learn English quickly and she worked incredibly long hours in the shop being willing to undertake any and every job, whether it was cleaning, stacking shelves, serving, opening and closing the store.

Her friend who had offered her the job suddenly found that she could turn her hand to anything. He asked if she could 'do the books' and not surprisingly she coped brilliantly. In doing so, she spotted ways to improve the sales by altering the type of products stocked. The net result was that within two years she was running the business, which was making more money than the owner could ever have believed possible.

Eventually the inevitable happened; her expertise had not gone unnoticed and she was approached by a business rival to join him. At this, her boss proposed marriage and was accepted.

They never had any family and she took great interest in my two daughters and neither birthday nor Christmas passed without a little present arriving. She greatly enjoyed getting their thank-you letters and admitted she looked forward to this simple act.

However, medically she developed some problems, one of which was a chronic condition for which there was no cure. Although it was not life threatening it was extremely debilitating and she became more and more depressed. Her wonderfully successful career was suddenly at risk. She tried all sorts of alternative medical cures but to no avail.

One morning she rose as usual at 6am and while making a cup of coffee she collapsed and died instantly.

A very sad end to a lady who had started with nothing and built up an incredibly successful business, in truth really a rags to riches story.

A Son To Be Proud Of

The joy of a newborn baby is wonderful for the parents, especially if there has been a long wait for it to happen.

Years ago, long before routine scans were available, there was always the worry of an undiagnosed congenital abnormality. Thankfully, of course, the majority of babies were completely normal, but occasionally not.

While working in the Special Baby Unit, a newly born little boy with Spina Bifida was admitted. The parents were naturally shocked, traumatised and disappointed at the outcome of what had been an apparently been a straightforward pregnancy.

The infant was operated on a within a day or two of birth, and the defect repaired. He was unfortunately paralysed from the waist down.

I saw him for review at the Paediatric follow up clinic and was pleasantly surprised how the parents were coping. In due course I entered General Practice and low and behold I discovered that this family were patients.

I observed the little boy growing up with his disability, and could only watch with admiration both the parent's stoicism and the little boy's resilience. He was encouraged to act like all the other children of his age and the parents never complained or expected special treatment.

However, there was one episode when he was due to go to school, which must have disappointed them. Some other parents wanted him excluded, claiming that the teachers would have to attend to him to the detriment of their own little darlings.

Unbelievably, the Education Authorities sided with these parents. The decision somewhat enraged me and I mustered as much support as I could from my medical colleagues.

The local MP, showing none of the attributes of his apparently caring for society party where privilege must be excluded, was of no assistance at all; he sat resolutely on the fence, obviously concerned that he would lose votes in the forthcoming General Election.

Luckily, I had a patient who was a journalist in the local press and I encouraged him to write a piece about the problem. And, to give him his due, he wrote a very emotive article and common sense (to a degree) prevailed. The Education Department, so as not to lose face, agreed to a trial period of attendance at the school. As can be expected, my little patient coped remarkably well and the grumbling parents could not complain.

Over the years I watched him develop; perform well with school work, become a proficient archer winning many prizes, learning to swim, and generally coping better than many of his peers. Because of his wonderful attitude, he was totally accepted by his friends. He went on holiday abroad with them and everywhere joined in most, although not all, of the activities.

Much to my delight, he got married and the last I heard of him was that he had a good job, a lovely wife, and a more fulfilling life than many of his contemporaries. Truly an inspiration of how to conquer adversity.

Good Advice

When I was a newly graduated doctor and doing my first 'House Officer' job, I received some advice from the Sister on the ward.

I happened to pick up the phone and it was a relative enquiring the well-being of a patient in the ward. I being new and very green, spoke at length about the progress our patient was making and of the prognosis we expected.

Sister collared me thereafter and admonished me (in a pleasant manner) to never be quite so expansive in my dealings with relatives.

Was I sure the patient would wish that particular relation to be told such details? Was that relative entitled to know such details? Could these details be sufficiently sensitive to cause family problems?

In today's climate, of course the ethics of non-disclosure are more rigidly applied, but this was not so strictly observed in those days.

Correctly she warned; if you said the patient was doing very well, and there was a sudden deterioration you would look very foolish. Likewise, if you painted a very black picture, and the patient was sitting up in bed having his tea when the relatives rushed up to see their dying relative, you also would look very foolish. What if a son / daughter flew halfway round the world to be at the bedside, and it turned out to be a red herring!

Your response she advised should be: 'as well as can be expected'.

This she explained covered a wide range of health issues. The patient could be one breath away from full recovery. Likewise, the patient might be one breath away from taking his last on Earth.

Wise advice indeed.

Young And Foolish

When we graduated from Medical School as young doctors we really thought we were something special. I know it is said that when you qualify you apparently know more medical facts then you will ever know again. But really, we knew nothing! We knew the theory, but had very little practical knowledge.

But, there we were, suddenly thrown into the big bad medical world, where patients expected us to diagnose, investigate, treat and discharge them back into the community hale and healthy. Fat chance!!

Symptoms not found between the covers of any published medical textbook were presented to us.

"Pain below the left ear when you pass urine?" Really?

"A powerful sexual urge when you eat oranges?" In this last example it was tempting to advise eating oranges every day, but not perhaps to an unmarried fifty year old female Religious Education teacher! But then perhaps, yes?

Exposed in the wards to a wide variety of the sick and not so sick proved how ignorant and innocent we were in sorting out the wheat from the chaff. Instead of referring each and every patient for a myriad of blood tests and x-rays (thank goodness there were no scans in those days or everyone would have had an MRI), we had to, in today's parlance prioritise (the word had not been invented then). And, who was the best person to advise? Yes, the nursing staff.

In those days there seemed to be a far closer (professional, as well as other) relationship between the medical and nursing staffs. Perhaps because there were more full time nurses led by the ward sister, and junior medical staff who did not work 'office hours', but were available day and night on call.

I very quickly realised the most important friendly liaison to set up was with Sister and her Senior Staff Nurse. I found by swallowing my intellectual pride and asking advice, paid handsome dividends.

This also helped in those cases where for some reason other an investigation had not been arranged or had been forgotten, and the consultant on his ward round had enquired as to the result. Our helpful nursing colleagues would cover up and explain that for some reason the test was delayed. I am sure the chief knew exactly what was going on, but I suspect he had done exactly the same in his day.

Another advantage was that respectful query 'are you sure that is the dose you wish to prescribe?' meant politely 'check it, you have got it wrong'! It was a very foolish doctor who ignored this advice.

Somehow, it seemed that the wards ran more smoothly, the patients benefited and the long hours we worked were that bit more enjoyable. It was not quite like the 'Carry on, Doctor' films but there was an element of truth in that particular romp.

Embarrassing

The expression 'cobbler's kids' is well known. It can however be sometimes a little embarrassing.

My elder daughter complained one Monday morning at breakfast that she had a sore ear. As usual, I was anxious to get to the surgery, having first to drop off the girls as school, and I promised to examine her in the evening when I arrived home after work.

Needless to say, I was late home having done two house calls after evening surgery.

On Tuesday, there was almost an identical scenario and I was home after she was in bed. In those days we certainly did not work 'office hours' and would often pop in to check on patients who were causing concern.

I did not take my daughters to school on the Wednesday morning as I had left early to visit a terminally ill patient.

However, when I arrived home in the evening there was a letter waiting for me. This was from her Form Teacher requesting that I, or another doctor, (that was rather pointed!) please examine her as she really appeared quite unwell.

Suitably chastised, I checked my daughter's ear and found (of course) a grossly inflamed and bulging eardrum. She did in fact have severe otitis media and required fairly urgent treatment. If she had consulted me in my surgery I would have been quite concerned.

But, as all doctors know, as far as family are concerned everything is played down. I did of course treat her and allowed her *one* day off school; after all, it was only a sore ear!

However, my family played me at my own game many years later, when I was given a fairly unpleasant diagnosis.

'Just get on with it Dad, nothing to worry about' I was advised! I really had no justification to complain.

A Costly Rejection

I suppose it is a not uncommon occurrence for a GP to be blamed by the family after bereavement.

Like many doctors, I have experienced the harsh words said after a death. This is always worse when you have visited regularly, often out of hours, altered drug regimes to combat nasty symptoms experienced in terminal illness, and generally done absolutely everything possible to alleviate the patient's suffering in their last days.

Conversely, patients and their relatives with whom you have only had minimal contact in the end stages of serious illness, were often very grateful for your care and attention, and sometimes wrote charming letters of thanks for making the patient's last few days so peaceful.

One lady, who had been retired from teaching for many years and seemed to lead a rather lonely and Spartan life with her two cats, developed a serious and life threatening illness. She required nursing care at home, but none of her family could possibly spare the time to help. Admittedly, her house was not too comfortable and was seldom warm enough for an elderly person. Also, her personal care was not as exacting as it had once been.

The excuses provided by the family were weird and wonderful as to why they could not, or would not assist their aunt/great aunt.

She gently requested her relatives in general to visit occasionally and help with those little tasks she was now unable to perform, but to no avail. I was visiting her fairly frequently and my District Nurses were of great support.

She admitted to me one day that she was greatly saddened by the actions, or inactions, of the family, to many of whom she had regularly sent birthdays and Christmas presents. She did in fact become quite distressed and weepy and admitted she felt lonely and abandoned.

I felt quite annoyed with the family as she only required a little assistance to improve her quality of life, and I expressed my feelings to one such member when she consulted me with her own problems. For my pains I got a 'flea in my ear' and told it was none of my business! Just you do your job properly I was informed!

One day my patient requested that my nurse and I visit at the same time. This we did and were very surprised when she produced a carefully hand written will, folded over for privacy, and wished us to witness her signature. This was of course slightly unusual but we did what she asked and observed her seal the envelope and place it in her bureau.

She appeared to have been quite perceptive as she slipped away a day or two later and then the fun and games started.

I received a very abusive phone call from the patient whom I had recently treated, accusing me of pressurising and influencing the old lady into changing her will. She complained that my District Nurse and I had acted to cut out the family from any financial benefits; I was going to be in trouble!

I rapidly explained that I had no idea what was in the will and I certainly had not even discussed any details with her. Thankfully, in her medical records I had noted that she was fully compos mentis in every way. There could not be any chance that she was incapable of executing her last will and testament.

It appeared that, unknown to her family, a distant cousin had left her a considerable amount of property on his death, and that she was an extremely wealthy lady. She left all her money to charity including medical and nursing ones, and not a single penny to the family. They got nothing!

My first impression on hearing this was, 'it serves you right' but, on reflection, her last days could have been so much more pleasant with her family round her.

The Photograph

The well-known comedian, renowned for his wry and accurate observation of life and his ability to translate this into highly entertaining humour, was a guest in the club Board Room.

As usual, pleasantries were being exchanged with well-known faces from the opposition visitors and there was constant movement between the groups prior to the game while enjoying the hospitality provided.

I happened to be in the company of the aforementioned gentleman, when somehow the conversation turned to photography. One subject mentioned was the difficulty in persuading everyone in a group picture to smile, or, at least look cheerful.

The old chestnut of asking the participants to say 'cheese' was of course mentioned, but also the inability to achieve the desired effect.

I happened to mention that in medical circles, a favourite and usually successful 'word' to get everyone smiling, was vagina.

As always happens, virtually every person in the circle smiled, (believe me, try it on your friends). Our comedian delighted me by saying, "If you don't mind, Doc, I'm going to remember that."

Perhaps one day on TV, he might incorporate 'the word' into his stage routine.

Never Marry A Medic

In years gone by a bridegroom always held his stag party the night before his wedding. I am sure many men, and ladies, could relate tales of incidents which occurred during these drunken evenings. Two such events, which involved my group of medical students, spring to mind.

One such gentleman, who had had a very long term relationship with a fellow student, but had broken off the engagement and promptly proposed marriage to another young lady, suffered almost a revenge fate.

Having consumed a considerable amount of alcohol – even more than the usual medical student / doctor intake, he was in no fit state to prevent what happened.

Gentian violet solution, which was commonly used as an antiseptic on minor wounds, was produced. One of his 'friends' (?), who was less drunk than the others, wrote in neat writing across his abdomen.

'I will always love Susan' (the name of his previous long-term girlfriend).

Now, gentian violet does not fade for about 4-6 weeks, so, the first night of the honeymoon would have been interesting.

Another episode was again as the result of excess of Macewans ale or perhaps Carlsberg Special Brew (remember that one?).

At some point our main player had fallen down and someone decided to take him to A&E, or Casualty as it was called in those days. He had a full length leg plaster applied quite professionally.

The next morning, his wedding day, he was advised he had broken his leg, so he was forced to walk up the aisle and attend the reception with crutches and his plastered leg.

It was only as he was leaving the wedding reception to go on his honeymoon, that it was revealed he had no injury and the splint was removed.

The bride was not a happy lady! (nor were her parents!).

Your Time Is Up...

I suppose I knew it was bound to happen sometime; I was past retirement age and living on borrowed time.

The metaphorical tap on the shoulder came, however, quite suddenly.

"Can you come and see me this morning after surgery?" I suspect I was a little naïve and not prepared for what was to come.

"We think that you should 'go out on a high' at the end of the month." No discussion, no softening of the blow.

I staggered out of his room, dazed and numb, feeling almost detached.

I sat at my desk and contemplated the situation. In my heart I knew it had to happen, but the shock was how it had happened.

I suppose I had wanted to be in control as I had been for all these years, but my plan was stymied and perhaps that is what really hurt. He, who had 'tapped me on the shoulder', had stolen a match on me, and truthfully that was what irked me.

Until then, my life professionally had been wonderful. I really looked forward to my working days each week. My knowledge and relationships with the patients meant I knew them and their families, and, even better, they knew me. I was able to use my experience to occasionally make a diagnosis which had been missed, and I knew the partners did not have to double check my work as might be necessary with an unknown and untried locum.

Now that the fateful date of my 'hanging up my stethoscope' has passed, I feel a hollow emptiness. It is as if my professional right hand has been cut off.

As I spend my 'working' mornings reading the newspapers or doing the crossword, I feel I am being idle, indolent and lazy. I should be doing something positive, something of value, and something to help others, just as I have done for the last 38 years.

Alas, however, the die is set, the decision irreversible, the matter a 'fait accompli'. I should reflect instead on my super professional career, and thank my lucky stars. Many a person would have given their right arm to have been as fortunate as myself.